THE WAVE MASTER

Good and Evil: Battle of the Minds

Mark Ingle

ISBN: 979-8-218-85705-9

Original Manuscript titled "Mental Pleasures"
Library of Congress Control Number: Txu000759673
Revised Manuscript titled "Mental Pleasures"
Library of Congress Control Number: Tx002403676

INTRODUCTION

The Wave Master addresses the subject of ESP (Extrasensory Perception) and how, if used to its fullest capacity, it could change the world. However, to understand ESP, one must also analyze the human brain—the complex organ that controls thoughts, memory, and every process that regulates our body. Physics could play a role in the development of ESP.

Because the human mind needs to access the atoms in the air for ESP to reach its full potential, if people can harness their brains to this degree, they can be tempted to shape our future. Thus, evil ideas could be formulated against the people's will.

The book addresses these kinds of psychics—psychics with special abilities beyond what one would find in an average psychic. Depending on their state of mind, these unusual psychics can use their special skills to create havoc on the world stage.

New concepts and terms are introduced to explain the configuration of ESP and how it can change the paradigm in our lives. The concepts and terms used throughout the book guide how ESP can affect our behavior and history. A more detailed explanation of these concepts and terms can be found in the section "The Definitions" at the end of the chapters.

PROLOGUE

Our world is made up of many aspects of life. Many particles and substances create our planet. They are called atoms. Most of the atoms that make up the Earth and its inhabitants were present in their current form in the nebula that collapsed out of a molecular cloud to form the Solar System.

Within this array of cosmic elements came many types of energy in the form of waves. Waves, as we know, are the travel of energy through time and space. But there are many different types of waves. We have grown accustomed to waves providing critical everyday uses, such as music, heating, lighting, and the Internet.

In the air, many forms of waves travel all around. Every day and every night, waves provide planet Earth with the essence of life. The waves are usually invisible and can pass through us, and we will never know it.

When you are in your vehicle, the radio waves hit your vehicle's antenna, allowing us to hear your favorite music to enjoy. Waves go into our mobile phones as we talk to someone. Anyone? Can you see the microwaves heating your favorite dish? Oh, about that wave that allows you to see your movies on the satellite disk. And one of your favorite waves that will enable us to access our wireless Internet. Oh, how I love my waves! And I am sure you love your waves too. "Come on, wireless wave. Do your magic so I can watch the mud wrestling brawl on my TV screen."

Waves mean energy, and they are everywhere. And without waves, we would be helpless as a civilized society. However, waves also mean power. And if one person. Just one! Could control all forms of wave energy. That person would surely be influential indeed. However, no such person exists. At least that we know of.

There is one wave we humans know little about. It hardly crosses our lips in idle conversations, which is generated from our heads. Wait! Are we talking about telepathy here? This wave can penetrate our minds and our thoughts. Can this wave control us and destroy us if it is powerful enough to do so? A wave that could enter our nervous system and wreak havoc on our physiology. A wave that can paralyze an electrical grid. Shut down a car battery and provide a brain hemorrhage if the situation were just right.

What if a person had access to this wave? A wave

that is, in fact, inside the individual's head. And the person can wheel this wave any way they feel fit. This person could grab various thoughts and energy levels from many people simultaneously. This access to energy could produce adrenaline, which would allow the person to never sleep. If it did exist, such a person would be unusual—different from all other human beings.

Chapter 1 - BEGINNING

Before all living creatures existed, only Supernatural Powers existed—the Powers of Right and Wrong. Like today, they struggled against each other. But there were no intermediaries or agents during those times. The Powers would fight each other directly—clashing!

When they fought in the sky, the fireworks were spectacular. Boom-boom-boom: Like a Fourth of July. But with much more flair. The sky would turn to ten different shades of colors as if flames spouted from many 16-inch guns. But with more intensity...so very much more. Their full armament. Lethal weapons they were, and still are. They were never stopping and never yielding.

There were no half-time shows or time to sleep. The Powers never restrained, never tired, and never slept. They were Powers on a mission—a mission of total control. Total control was essential. It was absolute. What good were their lethal weapons if they could not control them? Control who? Control the other side. The opposition. The enemy. And the Great Struggle went on, year after year... But the Right would turn back the Wrong, and the Wrong would continue.

Then, living creatures in the form of intermediaries and agents came upon the earth. Now, both sides have found a new way to conduct warfare. Both Right and Wrong would utilize humankind in the Great Struggle—the Great Struggle of Control. Humans are the intermediaries and the agents. Their reward was satisfying the Powers. Because satisfaction would mean happiness for them. And when humans die, they would transfer to the Powers chosen. The Bible called it Heaven and Hell. Many, of course, don't believe in such things. Others would say they all descend to the same place. That is to say, a young little child will co-exist with someone like... Like Hitler. Hard to believe. But some do.

Most go through life mindlessly, unaware of what might lie ahead after death. Why? Society is preoccupied with surviving the turbulent economy and the tide of crime. Most crimes are undoubtedly caused by the destitute economy. The pressure of surviving causes most crises—just plain surviving. So, the goal is to survive. And most do. And when individuals do, it is time to relax. But for others, it became the time to die.

Along came a fellow named Robert Yellowstone. He was a twenty-three-year-old just trying to survive. He just wanted a little piece of the big cheese. After all, there is plenty for most, if not all. His dream world was significant, however. Some days, he would fantasize that he was a star. Always in the limelight. He was half Comanche, and his physical appearance denoted it. He was a little on the short size with an average-looking face. However, his desires were like those of most young men growing up. He had wanderlust and lust for sex in his mind. But he only wandered a little. And he was no ladies' man. On the contrary, he was shy, melancholy, and unspiritual. If you think about it, he was just a tiny grain of sand on the beach. A big beach. No. A huge beach. Like the Pacific beach. Stateside. He was just a plain ordinary fellow with dreams of grandeur.

If it weren't for the events that unfolded in Dallas in 1999, Robert Yellowstone's life would be bland. But destiny has a way of changing people's lives. The changes can be pretty small. Not much to tell the grandkids. Not much to say to friends. But Robert's destiny took a 180-degree turn. It changed his life all right. But it did so much more. His outlook on life changed forever.

He began to understand the Powers of Right and Wrong: no school book, no college text. Nothing could prepare him for 1999. The funny thing was, he could tell no one. He kept it a secret for many years. It wasn't because Robert was not interested in the limelight. His dreams would say to you differently. It was because no one would believe him. No one dared believe him. Believe what? Robert met an intermediary with immense power. And this intermediary took sides. And he would bring terror. But especially for those on the other side. An awful kind of terror. And he was the Wrong's brightest star.

Chapter 2 - NOW IT BEGINS

Driving down IH-35, Robert could see the skyline of Dallas, with its tall, modern glass buildings displaying a variety of colors. At night, the skyline appeared like the Emerald City of "The Wizard of Oz." For Robert was now in Dallas, the Big D, the land of opportunity.

Robert settled in the Chaparral apartments. Robert made prior arrangements to rent a one-bedroom flat. Robert's apartment was small and unfurnished. Yet the carpet was new, and the area was clean. In the morning, one could see the fresh paint on the exterior and the new greenery of small bushes and trees. One was under the impression that management was preparing for the arrival of Robert himself.

Later in the day, Robert managed to buy a folding chair and a used twin-size mattress. He also gathered a large empty box from the apartment's trash dumpster, which served as a table. Otherwise, his apartment was bare of any other types of furnishing.

For the first week, Robert sat on his tiny chair and studied the classified ads from the "Dallas Morning Herald." The rest of the paper would lay in the box for later reading. Several trips were made to a job counseling office. The job counselor promised a position for Robert. A career Robert desired. An entry-level accounting position with a respectable company. After all, his newly earned degree was in accounting. He worked hard for that degree. Unfortunately, those positions were not easy to come by. When Robert came across an available position, employers were requesting experience. And Robert did not want to go back to live with his parents.

His mother did not relish the idea of her son moving. After all, he was only home for several months after graduating from university. However, Robert soon grew bored with Oklahoma City (OKC), and the only employer that would offer him a job was the massive Ford Air Force Base (AFB) in OKC. However, Robert wasn't interested in working for the government for the rest of his life. Although his parents worked there. Robert was educated all right—the first Yellowstone to graduate from college. However, semester after semester, the professors would drill into Robert's head the follies of working for the government. "Capitalism is in the private sector. If you want socialism, go work for the government. The government is not profit-motivated. With the government, it's always spend, spend, and spend. No real challenges there." So, Robert turned down Ford AFB and broke his mother's heart.

With several weeks now passing by, Robert's determination and money were slowly evaporating. He purchased a small couch and coffee table from a pawn dealer. He remembered what his job counselor had told him about the importance of having faith. "This is Big D. Something is bound to happen". So, there was Robert, taking it all in. He felt he was being tested. A test of his determination to find a respectable job in Dallas. But since he was in Big D, he might as well view its surroundings. After all, there was more to Dallas than just his apartment, the local store, and his trips to the employment counselor's office. So, Robert decided to go on an excursion. A Dallas excursion.

Climbing up Reunion Tower via the glass elevator on a beautiful sunny day, he saw how majestic the city looked. Although everything below appeared small, the panoramic view was broad in scope. As Robert observed the sweeping view below him, he thought it was better to be down than up.

Robert then strolled through a city park. Here, Robert saw an older man walking his dog. A young man and a woman were kissing on a bench. Children learn how to fly their kites. Dogs skillfully catching frisbees in flight. Dallas was also, and still is, the city of entertainment. Where one could observe music concerts, trade shows, the city ballet, or a seasonal opera. Robert also examined an authenticated copy of the Declaration of Independence at City Hall. He then toured the John Neely Bryan Cabin. (John is still considered the founding father of Dallas.) Robert was in luck because the Texas State Fair was commencing. Dallas always hosted the fair every October, where Big Tex (a 60-foot cowboy portable statue) greeted everyone with a big Texas smile. Robert saw the livestock exhibit, where a big Brahman from Beeville won first place as grand steer. Robert also saw the elegant fashion models stroll down the catwalk, showing the latest women's wear. And there was the Midway, packed with various carnival rides and games.

Dark was approaching, so Robert decided to take in some of the nightlife. Cruising down Lovers and Mockingbird Lane in his car, Robert could not help but see plenty of University of Texas (UT) and University of Oklahoma (OU) fans cavalcading on the walk strips. Robert then remembered that the UT-OU football game had been played earlier in the day. UT fans sporting their "hook'em horns" sign with their index and forefinger. Some OU fans painted their faces with the school colors of maroon and white. Robert regretted not attending the football game. But that was then, and this is now.

Robert went into one of the night spots. The club was packed with people from wall to wall. With a drink in hand, Robert tried to circulate among the crowd. But that wasn't easy. Suddenly, a surge of celebrating people knocked Robert's drink from his hand. His glass fell to the floor and was lost in shuffling feet. Having had enough, Robert decided to leave for another club with calmer surroundings. From the skyline, brilliant fireworks from the Texas State Fair can be seen. But Robert was by now half intoxicated to appreciate the beauty of anything so illuminating.

Robert then finally entered his apartment, bringing an end to the day-long excursion. There were unpacked boxes everywhere. He walked his half-intoxicated self to the small bedroom. Robert struggled to pull off his shoes when he clumsily fell onto the used mattress. Robert decided to sleep, not bothering to take anything else off.

The following day, Robert appeared relaxed on the couch with "Purple Haze" over his speakers. In front of him was his coffee table. On top was a small silver tray with a neat line of white powder, accompanied by a razor blade nearby. With a snuff bullet in his hand, he bent over and took another hit. A grin came over him as he lay back on the couch.

He recalled a time he had with his high school buddy, Mike. It was sunny, and Robert and Mike were driving in Mike's red Spitfire convertible. The song "Purple Haze" continued from his car speakers. Both were seniors in high school. They portray a sense of coolness with their shades. Mike pulled up on a street corner. A Dealer in his late 30s gave Mike a small brown bag. He handed it to Robert. Robert opened it. He saw a clear plastic bag of coke. He opened the bag and tasted it with his finger. He then gave Mike the thumbs up. Mike reached over and gave the Dealer a small roll of bills. The Dealer quickly leafed through it and walked away. Mike drove off. A grin appeared on his face. "We aren't popular with the chicks. But when it comes to the snow. We'll be in a different league."

Mike and Robert laughed as they gave each other a high five. His recollection ended with a smile printed on his face as he lay on the couch with the song filling his ears.

Robert always had a habit of blending his fantasies with his music. Just like a pipe tobacco smoker blending his tobacco. And what were his fantasies? Fame. Because fame would bring attractive women. What kind of fame? A Rock star, a sports star, or a business star. But as lustful as Robert was, he was still a virgin. Yes, the lustful Rock and Roller from Oklahoma City was still a virgin. Why? Pride.

Of course, there are different levels of pride. There's the pride that commended a reasonable or justifiable amount of self-respect. Then there's pride, which is deemed an excessive amount of self-esteem. Generally, individuals with the ladder type of pride tend to exhibit a sense of conceit about themselves. In other words, they were experiencing vanity. Either way, when one's pride was hurt, they would feel scorn or a sense of disrespect. In Robert's case, however, vanity made him appear arrogant. Afraid of rejection by women who did not fancy his company. He feared his image would be tarnished if he were rejected by women he admired or organizations that would not accept him. He would be so hurt by rejection or nonacceptance that Robert would avoid the circumstances that caused the hurt for long periods. When a woman rejected Robert, it took a long time before he committed to asking another woman for a date. There was nothing wrong with being a virgin. After all, the Bible preaches chastity. But Robert did not desire to maintain his virginity. He was not a churchgoer, and he was horny as hell. So, being a virgin was the last thing on his mind.

This average-looking person had vanity, all right. His pride would explain why he also had an enormous amount of determination. Robert's goals were big. Not as big as his fantasies. But big enough. Some of his goals were obtainable, while others were not. However, it wasn't for lack of intelligence. After all, most careers only require an average amount of intelligence. What Robert lacked was a willingness to be outgoing. Personable. A player. A talker. Sociable. Robert was none of those. He was shy and withdrawn. Add this to his physical features: he was in trouble, heading for a downward spiral, and always aiming for the most attractive woman. Like women, he would crave in magazines. Who knows, maybe he could have been lucky. But because of his shy, timid manner, somewhat caused by his vanity, he never found out like a captain anchored to a ship. A very slow boat, he was lost at sea—the constant fear of being rejected. Being rejected was part of life. However, Robert's stubborn pride wanted no part of it. Women and love can come and go.

The following morning, Robert sat on a folding chair, studying classified ads on a makeshift table. There was a small stack of porn magazines nearby. His phone rang. Robert stumbled off his chair and picked it up. A surprised look came to his face.

"Hello, Hillary."

Smiled. "A job where?"

He rubbed his head." Maverick Oil? Are you sure?"

He waited for a response. "I have a college degree in accounting."

He shook his head. "Is there a problem?"

Listened for her reply. "I'll be there tomorrow."

Robert hung up the phone, pumped his fist, and collapsed into his chair.

Maverick Oil was a major player in the exploration, production, and retailing of petroleum products. The company's headquarters had a fantastic view of Dallas. It occupied a 45-story glass building in the heart of downtown. The glass structure was erected in 1986, replacing the old brick building constructed during World War II. The Maverick parking garage occupied the space where the old parking lot was. The lobby was of polished marble, with snack bars and company restaurants scattered throughout the building.

Robert was on the 25th floor, sitting across the desk of his new supervisor, Bill Simpson. Robert was wearing a respectable shirt and tie. He admired the view as he waited. Bill Simpson, a round man in his mid-fifties who dyed his hair, leaned back in his chair and flipped through his resume.

"You're certainly qualified. You have an accounting degree."

Robert responded with a warm smile.

Bill nodded his head. "I think you'll manage."

Robert reinsured like an eager scout. "I'm a fast learner!"

Bill smirking, "I'm sure you are. Well… Welcome to

the team. Let me show you around."

"Great." Robert enthusiastically replied.

Bill reached across his desk. Robert shook his hand.

They both stood and proceeded to leave the office. Robert and Bill walked down the main hallway, better known as management row. Several general accounting supervisors, besides Bill Simpson and Tom Walker's (Bill's supervisor) offices, were there. Several other management offices were also there. Suddenly, two attractive female employees left a nearby office and walked toward Robert and Bill. The women acknowledge a hello to Bill as they walk past them. Bill, in kind, answered with a cordial greeting. Robert, not one to forgo a visual sight of attractive women, turned to have another look. A few moments later, Robert and Bill approached the Accounts Payable office. Bill playfully knocked on the open door.

They entered the office as Wayne Smith, thirty-five, and Jim Benston, twenty-five, were busy working away on their computers. They immediately stopped their work as Bill and Robert entered. Wayne was the same height as Robert and always kept an immaculate appearance, wearing pleasant suits to work every day. He was easy to labor with and wasn't annoyed by constant Accounts Payable questions posed to him. Wayne was the lead clerk for several years. He was expected to take on the pressures assigned to the job. Jim was black and, like Wayne, was single. Jim kept the professional attire in place by wearing a tie to work. But Jim was reasonably new to Maverick, only working with them for several months. He would make Robert look positively homeless. Seriously, this guy could be an underwear model. Like Wayne, he was easygoing and several inches taller.

Bill moved over to them. "I hope I wasn't disturbing anything important?" Bill announced.

"Not unless you call closing out this month's payables important," Wayne said with a laugh. Bill and Jim join in the laughter.

"Well, we won't dwell on important close-out matters," Bill said. "However, I would like to introduce Robert Yellowstone as our newest member to the Accounts Payable team."

Wayne and Jim both stood and walked over to Robert. They shook Robert's hand and introduced themselves.

Bill said with a smile, "Robert is from Oklahoma City."

"So, how long have you been in Dallas?" Jim asked with a grin.

"About a month," Robert replied.

Wayne asked seriously, "What is your accounting background?"

"None. I just graduated with my accounting degree in the spring. But I did graduate from OSU," Robert said with a certain amount of pride.

"I heard Oklahoma State University is a fine school," as if Bill was assuring Wayne that Robert was qualified for the accounting position.

"No experience?" Jim said.

Robert was about to reply when Wayne interjected.

"Oh, you'll do fine. Besides, Jim's degree was in the performing arts," Wayne responded. They all laugh.

Jim, feeling apologetic, said, "I was just kidding, man. Besides, you'll like working here."

"We like it so much; we've both been seeing a shrink

to find out why?" Wayne beam.

Everyone laughed except for Robert, who shyly smiled.

"Well, I would like to chit-chat, but I have to attend a staff meeting," Bill said. "And those meetings can be pretty nasty."

"Hear you," Jim replied.

"I will leave Robert in your care."

"Don't worry," Wayne said. 'We'll make good use of Robert. Right, Jim."

"That's right."

Bill smiled as he started to leave. But as he approached the doorway, he turned toward Robert. "By the way, Wayne is your team lead. So, get with him if you have any questions about your workload, but beware. He tends to let his position get to his head." Bill turned and left. Wayne and Jim laugh. Robert managed a smile.

It was a cloudy day in suburban Dallas. The subdivision, Spring Meadows, was an upper-middle-class area. Kids played in their spacious, green carpet lawns. A few old folks sat on their porches, watching the light traffic go by.

The Honeys' house was a lovely stone/brick one-story home. The living room had a formal dining table. There was an expensive crystal in the adjacent cabinet, above which hung a picture of a young woman with long blonde hair. Her name, Linda, was engraved on the frame. In the den, a small couch was against the wall next to a plaid wing chair, in which Muriel Honey, in her fifties, sat knitting. She was precise in her actions and deliberate in her style. Nothing was out of place, not even a hair. She had the air of someone who never fully relaxed and liked it that way. Henry Honey, Muriel's husband, who was also in his fifties, sat nearby in an expensive recliner, sitting in front of her. His hands were folded on his lap. Like Muriel, he was articulate and undeniably prude. Their beautiful white Turkish Angora cat, Gigi, entered. Henry gestured to Gigi, and the cat hopped on his lap. Henry patted the animal gently.

"You've been a good girl today, Gigi. Why can't all employees at Maverick be like you?"

Muriel looked at Henry and spoke telepathically. *"Anything new at work?"*

He was answering telepathically. *"He's taking the filly for a ride again. Promising her bogus overtime."*

They continue with their telepathic conversation. *"That's the IT manager. ... Ah...Torrez?"*

Henry nodded. *"Bill did pick up an accounting clerk today... a Native boy..."*

"That's interesting," as Muriel looked up from her sewing.

Henry patted the animal gently as if addressing Gigi. *"He'd better be a good boy. Oh yes. He's better!"*

Gigi purrs. Suddenly, a ray of sunlight pierces through the window and hits Henry's face. He looked like a modern-day Boris Karloff. He smiled at Gigi.

Linda Honey, in her early twenties, entered the room. Like in her photo, she was tall and slender with long blonde hair. She had matured into a beautiful young woman. She gave both of her parents a kiss on the cheek and took a seat.

"You know I don't like these mental conversations when I am at home."

Muriel complied as she responded with her voice. "All

right, dear."

"So, what were you discussing?"

"We were about to discuss this new fella.", Muriel said with a smile.

"He's an employee at Maverick," Henry replied.

This piqued Linda's interest. "What's he like?"

Henry said eagerly. "He's from OKC."

Linda smiled, "Oklahoma City. Our neck of the woods."

Henry replied, "His father is Comanche from the Lawton area."

"Sounds interesting."

Linda went to a nearby table to retrieve the car keys. "Well. I am off." She left.

Muriel, sounding like the caring mother, said, "Be careful, darling."

Linda replied, her voice carried from the living room as she approached the front door. "Don't worry, I will."

After a few more moments, the front door opened and closed. Muriel responded mentally, *"We could have involved her in our mental conversations."*

Henry responded in kind, *"It's not like her anymore."*

Muriel was not pleased. *"When she was a child, she loved it."*

"She is an adult now. She wants to feel normal. In sync with her friends." Henry then gazed at the window. *"Yes. Her world is changing."*

Chapter 3 - BAD HABITS CAN CAUSE WEIRD IDEAS

It was another rush hour morning, and early traffic grumbled by on the Dallas highways. Robert hurriedly walked to the Maverick Oil building, sporting his dress slacks, white shirt, and tie. He eagerly looked up at the skyscraper with a smile on his face. He entered the building.

Robert sat at his new desk at the Accounts Payable office. He typed away on his assigned computer, intently focused on his work, scared to mess this up. Standing nearby him was Jim, who filed payable vouchers in a cabinet. Robert stared at his ledger.

"So, uh, do you know when Wayne will return from the doctor? I haven't had the chance to talk to him this morning."

"Around noon," Jim answered.

"Was it anything serious?"

Sara, a red-haired beauty in a miniskirt, entered the office. She was in her twenties and walked toward Jim. Jim replied with a killer smile, which she returned.

Robert, oblivious to the situation, continued with his conversation. "Jim, was it serious?"

However, Jim ignored Robert as he and Sara began to flirt with their expressions. Robert turned around to confront Jim, but instead found himself staring at Sara's firm behind, the hint of a thong peeking out.

Sara, with a come-on smile to Jim, "Are the Sterling Pipe vouchers for last month here?"

Jim grinned, "You bet. But, first things first. What's your name?"

"Sara Franklin."

"I've never seen…" Gave her a quick look over.

"…You here before?"

"I am sure you have."

"Believe me. You're not someone I'd likely forget."

Robert half listened to the interaction. Unable to pull his eyes away from Sara.

Sara flashed a smile. "I guess I should take that as a compliment...?"

"Jim. Jim Benston."

"My name is Robert!

Sara and Jim turned to Robert, looking at him with a "what's wrong with you" expression. Then, Jim and Sara walked over to the file cabinets.

Robert whispered. "I have never been much of a hit with the ladies." Robert decided to hit the restroom down the hall. He entered and noticed it was empty. He decided to step into the last stall. He pulled out a small mirror from his pants pocket, a small snuff bullet, and a plastic straw. He formed a line of powder from the bullet on the small mirror board. He snorted it using the straw. He closed his eyes, feeling the rush.

As Robert took a hit, the conference room on another floor at Maverick was active, with a management meeting in full swing. Henry was in attendance. Unexpectedly, his eyes went out of focus as he became distracted. His face then turned to a sense of irritation.

Meanwhile, Robert scrubbed his hands under the sink, shaking his head. He checked his eyes and noticed the redness. He pulled out some eye drops. After applying a few drops, he was good to go. Staring at the mirror, he said, "Control yourself."

The door opened. An employee entered the

restroom. He gave Robert a weird look. Robert decided to leave.

Meanwhile, in the management meeting, various managers sat around a large conference table as a speaker gave a lecture. Sitting next to Henry was Tom Walker, in his early 40s. He had a square jaw and a business-like manner. He tapped his pen on a notepad. Henry leaned over, whispered something into Tom's ear, and excused himself from the meeting.

Robert was back at this desk, and Jim strolled in. He walked over to Robert with a beam in his eyes.

"So, what do you think?"

"Huh?"

"Sara! The hottest babe at Maverick, and she happens to walk in here."

Robert appeared to be unimpressed." Oh yeah. She's okay, I guess."

"Okay? Are you blind?"

Meanwhile, Henry sat behind his desk. Henry's office fitted the criteria one would expect from a person in his position. His desk was made of splendidly finished wood, and all his furniture pieces were made of impeccably finished wood. Oil paintings hung on the walls, and an antique grandfather clock stood by a wall in the right corner, telling him the time. Henry's clothes were made of custom, fine-made material and always starched well. His shoes were expensive, which one would only find in the exclusive gentlemen's shops.

However, Henry was also reading something that wasn't in any newspaper. He was able to read other people's minds. Because he had the unusual ability to perform more than one mental function simultaneously, he could mentally monitor more than one person at a time. This remarkable ability was rare, even among psychics. How Henry could do this was unknown, and Henry himself did not accurately explain it. But it existed. It's like explaining love at first sight. It exists, but no one can scientifically explain why it exists. But it does.

The door opened. Kyle Lucas and Margaret Lucchese, both in their 30s, entered. They were both impeccably dressed in smart suits and reported to Mr. Honey.

Henry firmly said, "Take a seat."

They did. Their eyes fixed on Henry's every word.

"You both know that Maverick Oil is a reputable company with certain standards to uphold."

Kyle and Margaret answer in sync. "Yes, Mr. Honey."

He leaned forward. His eyes were fixed on them. "Well, we have a bit of a... situation, if you will."

Henry looked deep into their eyes. For a brief moment, their eyes went blank. They snapped out of it and looked up at Henry, disgusted.

Margaret was appalled. "That's just..."

Heney cuts in before she can finish. "I agree." Henry leaned back in his chair. He smirked. "He needs to be taught a lesson."

Chapter 4 - TROUBLE BREWING

Robert's apartment was now furnished. It was nothing fancy, but it was functional. Robert sat alone at a small dining table, reading a book. He closed the book in frustration and laid it on the table. The book's title was "HOW TO FIND THE PERFECT WOMAN." He took a hit of coke from the small tray up his nostrils. His face lit up. Satisfied, he leaned on his chair, lost in thought.

In the rat race of any major city, people come and go rather quickly. Be it by foot, car, bus, or any other mode of transportation, everyone must be at their appointed destination before the whistle blew. Maverick Oil was no exception. And Robert was no exception either. Robert usually drove thirty minutes through horrid morning traffic to his destination—the Maverick Oil parking garage.

Robert entered to find the office empty. He took his seat. A folder on his desk stared at him. He opened it. Inside was a message written in red ink: "COKE ADDICT." Horrified, Robert slammed the folder shut and looked around. He breathes heavily. He decided to reach for his office phone. He placed a call to Sally. She was Bill's administrative go-to person.

"Sally! This is Robert."
Sally picked up the phone at her desk. "Robert, who?"
"Robert Yellowstone."
Sally looked confused. "Robert, who?"
"Robert Yellowstone."
"Okay."
"Have you seen Wayne or Jim? They haven't been in this morning."

"They're attending a leadership class."

"Leadership class? Here? Who's teaching it?"

Sally yawned. "…Your supervisor, I assume."

"Bill?"

"If he's your supervisor?"

Sounding upset. "But I wasn't informed… Shouldn't I be there too?"

"Ask him tomorrow."

"Tomorrow?" Robert continued with his whining.

"I can't say. Now, if you don't mind, I have work to do."

She hung up the phone, and Robert heard a click. The line went dead. Furious, Robert tore up the folder. He rammed the pieces into a waste basket by his desk. His face flushed as he took a deep breath. He bolted from his desk.

Robert went to the restroom. An employee was washing his hands. He saw Robert and snickered at him. Mortified, Robert decided to go into the stall where he took his coke hit. Robert stood in the stall and waited for the employee to leave. He did as he heard the door close. Robert then studied the stall for any clues of a camera. But he found nothing. Out of frustration, Robert pounded the stall door.

Robert went back to his desk. He saw no one. After pondering for a moment, he reached for the phone and called Sally again.

"This is Robert again."

Robert…?

"Yellowstone! Come on!"

"Oh, you again. What now?"

"I think I am coming down with the flu. So, I need to take the rest of the day off. Since Bill is not here…"

Sally cuts him off. "Whatever." She hung up the phone.

Robert again heard the click. The line went dead.

Robert was alone in his bed, hopelessly staring at the ceiling. He did not understand how anyone knew of his ordeal at the restroom, so he self-analyzed his weird predicament.

"I don't understand... How did they find out?" Thought for a moment. *I was alone in there, and there were no cameras.* Reflected. *It's illegal to have them in restrooms. Right?* He started to yawn. His eyes began to close. He fell asleep.

Usually, Robert greeted several employees at Maverick— not acquaintances, just employees working for the same company—and always received a friendly reply. But this morning, he did not. This morning would be different.

Robert entered an elevator at Maverick Oil. Several employees were chatting pleasantly, so Robert decided to put his best foot forward.

"Good morning. How is everyone?"

There was nothing but silence. They all turned and looked the other way, not wanting to make eye contact. Robert became increasingly uncomfortable as the elevator climbed. With the elevator climbing up, Robert wondered what had happened. Did he miss a news flash on the car radio, predicting doom this fine morning?

Later that day, various employees sat around the breakroom at Maverick. The place was on the 19th floor and a favorite area among the Maverick employees in the accounting division. Various snacks and soft drink vending machines line the walls. Employees were very talkative and laughed freely, as they had been in previous days. Some employees were engaging in their usual gossip, while others were playing cards or dominoes. Robert entered, and the area became silent. The gossip stopped, and the card and dominoes players played in silence. But no one noticed Robert as he proceeded to buy a soft drink from a vending machine. Mortified at this point, Robert's face grew bright red as he shuffled over to the vending machine. The machine rattled as his drink fell. Robert quickly took it and left. When he's out the door, Robert can hear everyone talking and laughing again. It is as if each employee were a mechanical toy being pushed by an emotional button.

Robert, still flushed, entered the Accounts Payable office and sat behind his desk. He didn't touch his drink.

Wayne stood over Jim, who was working nearby. He gave Jim a solid pat on the shoulder and left. Robert tried his luck again.

"How is it going, Wayne?" However, Wayne did not respond as he exited.

Robert turned to Jim. "What's his problem?"

Jim ignored him.

"Jim?"

Jim snapped back. "C'mon man, I have work to do."

Robert stood and approached Jim. He's a bit relieved that someone has finally acknowledged him.

"Man, today's been sort of weird." Softly to Jim. "So…What's up with Wayne?"

"I don't know. Think he fought with his boyfriend."

Robert looked confused. "Boyfriend?"

Jim stopped working and faced Robert critically. "Wayne is gay. Does that bother you?"

"No. Why would that bother me? One of my friends growing up was gay and…"

Jim interrupted. "Let's just get back to work, okay?"

Jim turned back to his desk.

The following day, Robert, Wayne, and Jim were busy at their desks. Robert looked up and stared at the doorway. He caught Margaret staring at him from the outer entry. She sarcastically grinned at him and left. Robert turned toward Wayne and Jim, but both were busy working. Robert grabbed a pay voucher and peeked out in the hallway. It was empty. He looked worried.

Later in the day, Wayne left the Accounts Payable office to deliver several checks from vendors to the treasurer's office. The checks were payable to Maverick Oil and represented the purchase of salvage equipment from Maverick. Jim was not in the mood to converse with Robert, but Robert needed someone to talk to, so Jim was the unwilling partner.

"Have you noticed how many minorities are working in accounting?"

"Minorities!" Jim said sharply. "Why?"

"I would say about 30% of the employees are minorities. And yet, only one accounting supervisor is a minority. Don't you think that's a little strange?"

"Are you insinuating that whites don't have the right to be supervisors?"

"No. But how many minority supervisors do you know at Maverick?"

"Wayne has been here for a while, and he's no supervisor."

"Maybe he's been blackballed by management."

Jim, sporting a serious look. "Because he's gay."

Robert ran his hands through his hair. "Like I said. He being gay doesn't bother me, none."

With a no-nonsense face, Jim remarked, "Good. Now let's get back to work."

Unaware by Robert and Jim, material auditor Chase Matters, age fifty, stood at the doorway. Chase, an overweight, overbearing fellow, was a starched Maverick employee. His fat cheeks always turned red when he had something exciting to say. He always had a habit of listening to someone else's conversation.

"But still," Robert continued. "Don't you think this is something EEO should know about?"

"Don't look at me, man."

Chase now became visibly upset. He decided to approach Robert. Robert and Jim turn toward Chase. Robert stood to greet Chase. "Hi Chase, how's it going?"

Chase's face was built with rage. "What kind of trash are you talking about now?"

Sounding apologetic, "What do you mean, Chase?"

"Talking about this EEO crap! Who in the hell do you think you are?"

"What's your problem?" Robert's voice rose in excitement.

Chase's cheeks turn red. "You heard me, asshole!"

"Look," Robert said. "When people with a different ethnicity from yours can get equal treatment. Then you won't be hearing this!"

"Look here, you addict piece of shit," Chase said vehemently. "You'd better keep your mouth shut and your ass clean. Because your big mouth is going to get your ass out of here faster than you can say EEO."

"You son-of-a-bitch!" Robert inches closer to Chase as if to strike him. However, Jim quickly jumped from his desk and moved to restrain Robert. Wayne entered the office.

"Settle down, Robert," Jim said.

"What is going on here?" A baffled Wayne remarked.

An unexpected calm flowed over Chase's face. "I just came to find an invoice." Chase's eyes then fell on top of a nearby file cabinet. "Oh, there it is." Chase nonchalantly proceeded to pick up the invoice on top of a file cabinet. He flashed a smile. "See yaw'll later."

Chase walked out of the office as Wayne nodded disapprovingly at the situation. A subdued Robert slowly walked over and sat at his desk while Jim took a sigh of relief. Robert turned toward Wayne and Jim. "Why did he call me an addict?"

"Just trying to get under your skin," Wayne coolly said.

A smiling Jim added, "You know how Chase is."

Chapter 5 - SOMETHING SEEMS FISHY

A month had come and gone, and Robert was desperate to find a solution to his dilemma. Because of the increased hostilities Robert was experiencing at Maverick Oil, he needed answers. The worriedness was taking a toll on him. It appeared he hadn't slept much as he slumped into his car in the parking garage at Maverick Oil after another day of work. He started the car to drive to his apartment. He turned on the radio. A News Reporter made an announcement. Robert was about to change it to a CD when he paused...

Radio Broadcaster announced, "... John Daricek is at it again! He claims to solve crimes and forecast people's futures with the power of ESP. Can you believe it? ESP! He has written multiple books and..."

A serious look registered on Robert's face.

A week later, Robert's car roared down a Houston freeway, heading away from the city and toward a suburban area.

Robert's car stopped in front of a beautiful house. He stepped out of the vehicle and approached the front door, wearing a suit that didn't quite fit. Lilly Daricek, in her mid-40s, opened the front door. Robert greeted her with a smile. Lilly returned it and shook his hand.

"You must be Robert Yellowstone, from Dallas?"

"Yes, I am."

"Well, welcome to Houston. We've been expecting you."

"Thank you."

Robert followed Mrs. Daricek as they came to the

nearby hallway. Robert could not help but notice the many photos of John Daricek with celebrities were hanging on the walls—movie and television entertainers, politicians, sports heroes—that sort of thing. John had a very distinguished clientele. At the end of the hallway, Mrs. Daricek took a sharp right and entered the study room with Robert close behind.

There was dark hair John Daricek, as he appeared in the photos. He was forty years old and fifty pounds overweight. He also sported a mustache and a receding hairline. He wore a light pullover sweater and casual slacks. He sat comfortably on a recliner chair and read a letter when Mrs. Daricek and Robert entered the study.

"John. You have a visitor," Mrs. Daricek announced.

"Good." John then folded and inserted the letter into a pouch on the side of the chair.

He stood and shook Robert's hand. "Hello, Robert."

"So, you'll John Daricek?"

"That's right," John said with a smile.

John motioned for Robert to sit as Mrs. Daricek exited. Both seated, Robert quickly scanned to find various newspaper clippings of John pinned to the wall about John Daricek's abilities to solve homicides through his ESP. John wrote something on his notepad in his lap. His eyes glazed over Robert.

"Now, let me begin by telling you I'm a psychic registered with the Psychic Institute of Texas. It is a non-profit organization supported by psychics throughout Texas, promoting the safe and reliable profession of psychics. So, I'm not here to steal your money. But I will tell you, I'm 85% accurate in my forecast. No psychic is 100% error-free. I have been on radio and television shows. And have aided the police in solving murders and kidnapping cases. You might have seen me on "Hard to Solve Mysteries" several months ago.

Robert shook his head. "No, Mr. Daricek. I heard about you on the radio and felt... well, I really hoped you could help."

"You can call me John."

"Sure."

"So, you're having job issues? Tension with people at work?"

"Yes."

"Now, people in my profession have different ways of determining one's forecast. I prefer to use colors and numbers. So, I want you to tell me your three favorite colors and numbers."

"Sure. Blue, green, and... brown."

John wrote his response.

"Now, your numbers?"

"Three, seven, and ten."

John wrote down the numbers.

"What is your date of birth?"

"August seventh, 1976."

John wrote this down and reached over to Robert.

"Now, I want to look at your palms."

"My palms?"

"Yes, Robert."

Robert showed his palms. After a short examination, John moved back in his seat.

"Just give me a brief moment."

He wrote down his findings.

Robert looked around the room as he waited. He noticed several books on a glass table. One of the books about telepathy interested him. The book's title is "HOW TO HARNESS YOUR TELEPATHIC ABILITIES."

John finished, looking up at Robert with a somber look. "First, let's start with your job." John took a breath. "I don't see you losing your position at Maverick Oil. But I do see a transfer of some sort. Does your employer have some business connection in Tulsa?"

Robert thought for a moment. "They do have a central division office there."

"I see you're transferring there."

"When?"

"I can't say."

Robert could not accept it: "Tulsa, Oklahoma?"

"Do you have any relatives? Or acquaintances who live there, Robert?"

"My family lives in Oklahoma."

"May I ask your nationality?"

"I am Native American from my father's side and Mexican from my mom's."

John looked down at his pad and wrote something quickly. He turned his gaze back to Robert.

"What do your parents do? May I ask?"

"My father is a disposal specialist, while my mom works as an item manager at Ford AFB."

"You'll grandparents?"

"They are not around anymore." Robert brushed back his hair. "And I didn't know too much about them. But my grandfather on my mother's side earned a living as a fortune teller. Able to pick up on things." Shrugs. "Sort of a psychic, I suppose."

"Don't believe?"

"Not really."

"But you'll here."

"Ya... I know." Paused in thought. "I thought I give it a swirl. Being how bad things are at work."

"Do you get along with your co-workers?"

Robert shrugged. "I thought I did. But lately, I feel I don't belong there."

"Do you feel isolated? Alone?" Smiled. "Not part of the team?"

"Kind of."

"I don't see you as a troublemaker... Tell me, are minority employees fairly represented at Maverick?"

Robert shrugged, "Not really."

John wrote for a moment. "Maybe a lack of cultural diversity could be a problem. But this is just an initial observation. Follow-up visits will give me a better picture."

John briefly wrote. "Robert, I'm also picking up something else. And I believe it to be more important than your job. And that's your social being. Do you find it difficult to communicate with people?"

"What? "Uhh... No. Not really. Well… I don't do well with women."

"It's nothing to be ashamed about. I've met other men who have the same sort of problem." He winked and smiled. "Women are a different breed, are they not?"

A dejected Robert offered a slight smile, but he was embarrassed. He glanced at the floor.

"Robert, you need not feel sorry for yourself. Remember, despite what you think, women are just people. Just like you and me. Just ask my wife." Paused. "Do you drink?"

Robert felt reluctant to answer as he cleared his throat. "Occasionally."

John felt Robert was holding back. "Anything else?"

Robert gave him a deer-in-the-headlights look. He replied with a smirk.

"Okay… I dabble in coke."

John's eyes widen. "Dabble?"

"Oh... I would say several times a week. When I can afford it."

"Don't let it be a cure for resolving your social being. I sense the main goal is to share your life with someone special. And this misguided habit is not a substitute for finding this love you seek."

"Yeah... I know."

The phone rang from an adjoining room. Lilly appeared and motioned to John.

"I'll be right back." He stood with his notepad and followed Lilly as they exited. Robert turned his attention back to the telepathy book on the glass table. He picked it up and began to read it.

John returned. "Robert. Something came up, and I have to leave." He smiled. "I see you're interested in my latest book. I am not a professional mind reader, per se. But I thoroughly researched the topic, and it should be an interesting read."

Robert placed the book back on the table. "I was just glancing at it. Besides, I don't believe in telepathy."

Gestured to Robert. "You might change your mind. Keep it as my gift for cutting the session short. Who knows? It might come in handy someday. How would you like to pay for your session? We take personal checks, credit cards, and, of course, cash."

"Cash," Robert said.

Robert handed him the money. "I'll let you know when I can see you again."

John smiled back at him. "No worries."

A week had passed, and a picture of Cara Wakelin, the Playmate pin-up model for November, graced Robert's apartment wall. Below the porno calendar, Robert sat at his small dining table. He was engaged in his studies. Around him were several Maverick training manuals. Robert rubbed his head, frustrated. He looked up. His gaze fell on Cara. After a moment, Robert pulled the calendar off the wall and headed into his bedroom.

Later that evening at the Honey house, Muriel did her usual knitting. The TV, muted, was turned to the news. Henry watched the screen from his recliner. Muriel looked up from her knitting. They speak telepathically.

"Our society has become increasingly violent, Henry. Murders are up 5 percent. Rapes another 6 percent. When will it end?"

"I agree. The world is a pretty dreadful place. Especially with all this perversion running around."

"Yes. Like that Yellowstone employee with his coke. I'd say he fits into that cat..."

"Hush," as he put his index finger to his lips... *"She's coming."*

Moments later, Linda entered. She gave both of her parents a kiss and took a seat.

"So, what's new at Maverick?"

"We were about to discuss this new fella at Maverick. We mentioned him to you before, dear."

"I remember. His family is from our neck of the woods." Pause." So, what's he like?"

A dread look came over Muriel. "You don't want to know."

"Oh?"

Henry shined in. "He's a loner. Fantasizes about women all the time. He even took cocaine in the men's restroom at work. He can't help himself. Disgusting."

Sounding interested. "Married?"

"No! I don't believe the women he lusts over would want him," Muriel replied.

"Why?"

Henry smirked. "Let's just say he has a pizza face with caviar taste."

Muriel laughed.

"Let me take a look."

Muriel looked at Linda with dismay. "No, Linda... not this time."

"You brought it up. I'm curious to see... What's his name?"

"Robert Yellowstone."

"What does he look like?"

"Linda, he's not your type."

"Mom. I didn't say I wanted to hook up with the guy. I just want to know what he looks like, okay?"

Suddenly, Linda's eyes went blank and widened as she picked up something. Linda mentally witnessed Robert on his couch, watching TV. Or, more accurately, watching attractive women on his TV.

Linda looked at her parents, a small smile on her face. "That's him?"

Muriel was also curious. "What's he doing?"

"He's watching some program on TV. Oh, wait... Now, he's getting up and walking somewhere."

Henry guided his daughter. "He's headed for the bathroom."

"Henry!"

"Now, wait, Muriel."

Linda now observed Robert standing in his bathroom, facing the mirror. He took off his shirt, and his eyes were glazed.

Linda turned to her father and gave him a stern look. "You made him do that?"

"I just want you to see how unattractive he is."

Linda shrugged, not seeing what her father desperately wanted her to see.

"He has a decent body. I don't know. He's not movie star hot, but he's not bad." She gave a look of disappointment. "Sorry, Daddy. I don't see him the way you do."

"Linda. He's Native American!" Muriel scolded.

Henry added. "His mother is Mexican."

"He's leaving. And now his image is gone."

"Father decided you've seen enough."

"He's still a virgin," Henry said.

"Really? Interesting. I want to know more about him."

Muriel shook her head in dissatisfaction. "Was that necessary, Henry?" Turning to Linda. "Why would you be interested in this fella? He takes coke at work! You could easily find men who would want you."

Linda stood and sternly looked at her mother. "You're right, Mother. I could find lots of men. But I don't want to. Besides, he's interesting... in a curious way."

"Curious?"

"He's a virgin, Mom. Imagine the things we could teach each other!"

Henry allowed himself a chuckle.

"Besides, some people are social coke users. I am sure Daddy can testify to that. Of course, the men's restroom is a bit of a stretch... "

Henry interrupted. "Linda. The world is what it is. But at Maverick, I run a tight ship. Or they accept the consequences."

"I see."

For a moment, his eyes appear to glow. "Let's hope he does not pull off a stunt like that at work again."

Linda was undeterred. "You could have easily had him arrested."

"Margaret and Kyle found out about him, and word got out. So, I decided..."

"Wait! You told them?"

Henry replied with a cool stare.

Linda gave off a whatever look and walked away. "Keep me posted." She left.

Henry and Muriel heard the door open and close. They both communicated mentally: *"What are you going to do?"*

Henry revealed a devilish smile. *"Don't you worry."*

The following morning, Robert exited the Accounts Payable office and headed to the coffee room, cup in hand, carefully avoiding unnecessary interactions with anyone.

He entered the coffee room and was about to pour himself a cup, but the coffee pot was empty and dirty. He sighed and retrieved the dirty pot.

Robert walked down a small hallway with the empty pot. He entered the restroom and cleaned the pot at a nearby sink. Suddenly, Tom entered. This surprised Robert because Tom did not typically arrive early to work. Tom was part of a vanpool, and Maverick employees riding on the various van pools always arrived on time but hardly early. Especially early enough to witness Robert clean the coffee pot. Without saying a word, Tom walked past Robert. Robert suddenly felt tense, knowing Tom was in the restroom with him. After all, he was Robert's accounting manager and Bill's boss. Tom stood at the other end of the sink counter in front of the wall-length mirror. He began to comb his thin brown hair. Kyle entered, walked over, and stood between Robert and Tom when he started to comb his hair.

Tom turned to Kyle. "How's it going, Kyle?"

"Great, Tom. Planning to play golf this weekend?"

"I reckon so. And you?"

"Visiting my in-laws."

Tom smiled, "I know the feeling."

They both chuckle. Kyle went over to a urinal.

Tom went over to wash his hands and then dried them. Fuming, Robert continued to scrub the dirty pot. Robert thought, *"That self-centered, pompous idiot wouldn't give me the time of day. And yet he parades himself as some sanctified church-goer. Yeah, right."*

Unexpectedly, Tom stopped. He turned to Robert and glared at him with a "watch it" look. He then stormed out of the restroom.

Robert remained frozen in confusion. Kyle went over to wash his hands. His eyes were on the mirror. "You ought to keep your thoughts quiet."

"Huh?"

Kyle flashed a sarcastic smile in the mirror and went to dry his hands. He gave Robert a smirk and left.

Robert was stunned. Water overflowed from the pot, spilling into the sink. He composed himself, turned off the faucet, and left.

Robert hurriedly walked down the hallway with the pot. His face appeared to be perplexed. He thought, *"Keeping your thoughts quiet. How do you keep your thoughts quiet?"* Robert then entered another hallway leading to the coffee area. Robert felt a rush of heat all over his body. Maybe it was anxiety that brought it on. Thinking about what Kyle said earlier, Robert wondered, *"What was his meaning?"*

Robert entered the coffee room and quickly dried off the outer glass of the pot. He threw the used paper towels in a waste basket. Robert then began to prepare the coffee. He laid the pot full of water on the coffee burner. All along, continuously thought about Kyle's message, *"Keep your thoughts quiet".* And the way Tom stormed out of the restroom. Robert retrieved the coffee package and paper filter from a nearby supply shelf. He placed the paper filter and the coffee grounds into the plastic holding filter underneath the funnel. Robert then reached for the pot and poured the water into the top drain opening of the coffee maker. *"Why did Tom do that? He gave me a furious look. It looked like he wanted to bite my head off."* He placed the empty pot on the burner, and the hot brewing coffee began pouring down the funnel into the transparent glass pot. Satisfied with the coffee, he poured a cup and walked out.

Robert entered the Accounts Payable office with a cup of coffee and noticed Wayne at his desk. Robert was flustered. He examined some invoices and then turned to Wayne.

"Wayne? Uh, do you know a person named Kyle?"

"What's his last name?

"I don't know. But he's friends with Tom Walker. Our Accounting Manager."

"That would be Kyle Lucas. He and Margaret Lucchese are managers at Projects Management."

"Projects Management?"

"Yeah. Projects Management came from Tulsa after the big merger with Jones Oil. They provide recommendations and solutions to Maverick. You might say they unofficially run this place."

"Who runs Projects Management?"
"Oh. That would be Mr. Henry Honey."
"I see. And..."
"Enough chat, Robert. I've got work to do."
Robert turned back to his desk.

Robert left the office later that day to turn in the monthly payable vouchers to the Treasury office. So, he entered the main hallway towards management row. Robert took just several steps, and to his surprise, he saw Margaret Lucchese. She was chatting with a fellow employee in the middle of the hallway. Unexpectedly, the mental image of Margaret's sarcastic grin flashed in his mind. She was in the outer entry of the Accounts Payable office the previous month. The image left him. Robert immediately stopped walking. He did not want Margaret to notice him. Not here. Margaret already knew where Robert worked. So, what did it matter? Margaret did not know Robert was observing her, however. She ended her conversation and walked in the opposite direction. Robert then noticed Ralph, in his twenties, leaving a nearby office. Robert stopped him as Ralph walked toward him.

"Hey Ralph, do you know her?"

Ralph turned in the direction of Robert's stare. "That's Margaret Lucchese. She works with Henry Honey. He runs Projects Management. Or should I say, he is Projects Management. Henry, Margaret, and some of the other management folks came from Tulsa after the big shake-up of Jones Oil. But I heard Projects Management unofficially runs this place."

"Oh really?"

Robert studied Margaret, approaching Henry's office at the end of the long hallway. She knocked on his door. Henry quickly opened the door and let her in. He then produced a devilish smile at Robert as both Robert's and Henry's eyes locked. Henry then closed his office door. Meanwhile, Ralph, on the other hand, continued talking about his latest adventure.

"By the way. Did I tell you I met this fantastic chick last weekend at this strip club? She says she attends law school. So, she dances to supplement her tuition. Isn't that something or what!"

Robert did not respond; his eyes were fixed on Henry Honey's closed office door.

"Hey. Robert. Are you listening?"

Robert turned to Ralph and answered nonchalantly, "Oh, yeah. Sure."

Chapter 6 - ATTITUDES

Muriel had been Henry's only wife. She was born and raised in Kansas. Lawrence, Kansas, to be exact. Her views on life were conservative. Very conservative. Even though Muriel gave birth to Linda, her only child, Muriel was not fond of performing sex. Her view concerning her physical and sexual demeanor was simple. *"Sex for me was only good for one thing, and one thing only: to create life. After that, all my sexual desires will be bottled up and put away on a dusty shelf."* Sometimes, Muriel would watch restricted-rated films on the networks. Some of the romantic scenes could be pretty frisky. But Muriel did not mind. Because, like her husband, she liked to watch other people. Other people do it, that is. But Muriel's sex life was all bottled up. And that's the way her husband liked it.

Being from Kansas, Muriel had to adjust to her husband's way of life in Oklahoma. When Henry relocated to Dallas, Muriel had to adapt to another state again—the Lone Star State. But Muriel didn't mind, as long as she was close to her husband. Muriel had strong moral values. Being a Presbyterian by birth, Muriel was not an atheist. Although her husband was, she did side with him on the most critical issues. But Muriel held fast in worshipping the One Supreme God based on her Christian beliefs. However, as time passed with Henry, he made her an agnostic. She halted her Presbyterian ways. Religious organizations did not interest her anymore. And that's the way her husband liked it. Muriel was racist, but up to a point. Like her mother, she did not care for prejudices towards African Americans. She firmly believed African Americans should have the same rights as White Amtericans. However, she had a different view towards Native and Hispanic Americans. Her logic was simple. Native and Hispanic Americans did little to forge America's government. In history, they played a minor role in deciding America's destiny. They should not be treated equally with the White and African Americans.

After all, the bloody Civil War was caused by slavery. As far as Muriel was concerned, the Native Americans were in their tepees smoking their pipes, and the Mexican Americans were too busy preparing tortillas to be involved in the American Civil War. Granted, the War between the States was primarily a White American affair involving the slavery of African Americans. However, if Muriel were a true student of American history, she would have realized that Native Americans, as well as Hispanic Americans, fought in the Civil War. Some for the North and some for the South. After all, history would say the Civil War was America's War. Joshua Chamberlain once said to his federal troops the day before the battle of Gettysburg. "It's the ideal we all have value. You and me. What we'll fighting for, in the end. We'll fighting for each other."

Before Texas became independent in 1836, the Lone Star State was in Spanish hands for centuries. Many Texas towns and cities were named after Spanish missions. The creation of the cowboy by White American settlers in Texas was primarily influenced by the Mexican cowboy, known as the "vaqueros." Mexican Americans played a paramount role in shaping Texas history. Muriel did know about the Alamo. The Hollywood version, that is. However, her views of Mexican American history aligned with Henry's. And that's the way her husband liked it.

Every year, thousands of Oklahomans celebrate the Cherokee Run. The Run involved the arrival of the first White settlers, who claimed tracts of land in the Oklahoma Territory. The White settlers were better known as Sooners.

These large tracts of land were once Native-American land. However, the Native Americans signed a treaty with the federal government that created the Cherokee Run. Native-American played a predominant role in shaping Oklahoma's destiny. Many cities and towns in Oklahoma were named after Native-American tribes. But Muriel usually turned away from any historical contributions made by the Native Americans in Oklahoma.

Sitting in his recliner chair was Henry Honey. His eyes were physically focused on the TV screen. He was watching the daily CNN news broadcast. His face appeared to show no emotion. Not a care in the world. His dark shark eyes beamed at the television screen. But in his brain, a whole other world existed. The images in his mind were not fantasy. He was not daydreaming. The images in his brain were sharp, clear, and real. Images of other people doing real things. Because Henry's brain was not that of a normal human being.

Henry did not fancy statements labeling the mind and brain as two different entities—statements like the mind within the brain, the mind commanding orders to the brain, and the mind acting differently from the brain. To Henry, there was no mind—only the brain—the protoplasm with its electrochemical network within the skull. The brain was the mind, and the mind was the brain. The brain and mind were one.

If individuals could place themselves in the interior of Henry's brain, they would think of being in the television store. An array of different television sets, each broadcasting something different in different locations and time zones. Each screen simultaneously and independently displayed a different scenario of people Henry was monitoring, such as individuals dining in restaurants, driving in their cars, or watching television. Therefore, Henry was not just a mere Telepathic who occasionally monitored an individual's thoughts. He was a multi-channeler. One of Henry's mental images was someone reading a textbook. That individual was Robert, as he momentarily glanced at a nearby mirror in his apartment. Another image has Robert's parents arguing in their kitchen. Another image showed Bill Simpson in the produce section at a grocery store. Henry was also monitoring through the eyes of a nearby shopper. Bill then looked at the customer and smiled. Through Bill's eyes, the nearby shopper was an attractive female with a grocery shopping cart. Another image revealed the President of the United States. The President was sitting behind his desk in the Oval Office, and a young secretary was listening and took dictation. Now, through the eyes of the President, an image of a young female secretary was seen. Still, in another mental image, a woman stood in front of a full-length mirror in her bathroom. She then slowly peeled off her clothes, revealing only her bra and matching thong. From her point of view, Henry could mentally see her walk over to the bathtub. She turned on the water faucet. Putting her hand on the water, as the temperature suited her. She then peeled off her bra and thong and laid them on the floor. She stepped into the bathtub as the water splashed all over her body.

All these images were going through Henry's head. Every day, image after image covered his brain. All sorts of images. Violence, sex, greed, lust, love, hate, murder, and spiritual worship. Whatever humanity had to offer, Henry was there. During his lifetime, Henry monitored the beginnings and endings of Wars, assassinations of World

Leaders, and the explosion of atomic bombs. He could have altered some of these worldly events, but chose not to.

So, Henry consumed all of these images. Every last image his brain could handle. And his brain could handle plenty. But physically, he just sat there in his recliner. His shark eyes were glued to the television screen. Looking at him, one would never suspect his hidden talents. His ESP talent. His telepathy talent. He was gifted, and there is no doubt about it. But he was like a chameleon, very difficult to detect.

He was always looking for something to crave. Something new to digest. And once he found something that interested him. He would not let it go like a skilled fisherman reeling in a new prize catch, constantly searching and always looking and seeing all things around him. His brain pulsing to the beat of something new. To feel the rhythm of the music on the dance floor and the flow of the blood rushing to the brain. To touch the nerves of the human body. To know every thought of the human mind, or, shall we say, the brain can produce. To see the lust of the human soul. To know the lie from the truth. And to create the lie from the truth. To snicker at the all-powerful and to sometimes help the unworthy. To be all-in-one and yet to be none at all. To observe the helpless and do nothing. And watch the sinners participate in their follies. To bring entire systems and laws down and create new ones. All around him, his waves entered—all things around the world. The brain waves pierce all living matter.

From the rich to the poor and from the famous to the common. He craved it all. All the sex, all the greed, all the lust. From the powerful to the very weak. To know all things and pretend to know nothing. To mentally see and not to be seen. To feel all and not to be felt. To cause, and not to cause. To understand and not to understand. To see the very wise and the very foolish. To see pain, misery, and sorrow. And to inflict the very same. To make decisions and not to make none at all. To see the world for what it is and to crave all things thereof—yes, always looking for something new. For it was Henry's world, and the world was his. Humans had nothing on him. At least not here on planet Earth. Because the blue planet was Henry's turf. His home ground. He had the home-field advantage over all of them. And he knew it!

In the broad scheme of things, Henry was also a judger. A judger of people. A judger of society. And with this, he had an obsessive habit of comparing people with people, usually within a given category. He would compare people with people living in the same apartment complex. Compare people with people living in the same subdivision. Compare people with people working for the same employer. His brain would do the comparison and decide the fate of people he was interested in within their given category. And the judgment on people he was interested in was based solely on the Henry Honey standard.

A family could pay their bills with the Henry Honey seal of approval. Keep their jobs. Find promotions. Their prayers would be answered. Non-approval meant financial chaos for those Henry was obsessed with. Hope and dreams were destroyed. Families torn apart. Yes. Henry was the judge, and Muriel sometimes chimed in. Henry fancied himself playing the role. He was proud to play the judge with no interference from the law. Henry felt he had a heavy burden to perform. Weeding out what he considered the bad from the good. It was as if he was given this ESP for this sole purpose. And Muriel liked it too. She wanted her husband to play the town judge. The untouchable. The ruler of fate.

After Henry placed judgment on a household, the sentence was final. There was no turning back. No second chance. At least not from Henry. He would watch people pray and seek advice from social counselors, their pastors, their religious ministers, and half-baked psychics. Henry observed them and took it all in. Laughing at those who believe in the All-Mighty God would hear their prayers and come to their rescue. And Muriel would laugh with him. Laugh at those who were deemed undesirables. The All-Mighty God would not help an undesirable. Not God. That was impossible. Unthinkable. Not acceptable. Besides, Henry did not believe in God. So, Henry and Muriel would enjoy watching the undesirables struggle day after day for their very existence. Henry would ensure their prayers were not answered and observed them crook on their watery tears. Watch them die. And if, by chance, a prayer was answered for an undesirable. Henry would say they got lucky.

Chapter 7 - PART OF GROWING UP

The Immaculate School for Girls was an elite private institution where only the selected could enroll. Graduates from the institution typically pursued higher education. The curriculum was challenging, and the discipline was rigid. But that is what parents expected from the school. Morals were a high value to instill in the girls. The girls were required to wear uniforms with the Immaculate emblem embroidered on their blouses. One of the shining stars in the 5th-grade class was Linda Honey. Blonde and with blue eyes, she always had the highest marks of any student in her class. Quick with the answers and early to class. Her middle-aged teacher, Mrs. Brown, posed a question for the class one day.

"Class. What is the strongest bone in the human body?"
Linda quickly raised her hand. "Yes, Linda."
"That would be the femur."
"That is correct."
"What part of the human body is responsible for getting rid of harmful toxins?
Again, Linda raised her hand. Mrs. Brown nodded to Linda.
"That would be the liver".
"Yes, that is correct again."
"What elements on the periodic table, when combined, will make the ingredient we call table salt?"
Like magic, Linda raised her hand again. "Now, surely, is there anyone besides Linda who can answer this?"
One student managed to volunteer. "Yes, Sara."
"That would be carbon, hydrogen, and oxygen."
"No, Sara. You are describing carbohydrates."
"Anyone else?"
No one raised their hand. But there was Linda with a bright smile coming over her.

"Okay, Linda."
"That would be sodium ions and chloride ions.
"That is correct."

On a warm afternoon at Immaculate the following week, twenty or so girls were preparing to play volleyball. Two captains were selected for the game: Linda and Rachel. The physical education coach, Ms. Barnes, set up the game. "Okay, girls. Who wants to play on Rachel's team?" Only a few girls raised their hands.

"How about Linda?" One of the girls shouted. Others also wanted to be on her team.

"This is not going to work. I guess I will decide who plays. Okay, Susan, you will be on Rachel's team."

"But I want to be on Linda's team."

"You'll be with Rachel.

"Oh. Sorry, Linda," said Susan.

And all it went: the girls complained. Linda was not only the smartest but also the most popular, the Miss Congeniality of her school. This pattern continued during her school years at Immaculate.

Her parents expected the best from her. And she would deliver. She did her very best to make her parents proud. It was Henry who initiated the idea of informing their darling daughter about his ESP. Muriel did not like the idea. But maybe it's best that she knew. Informing her could keep her from doing prohibited activities she might have done otherwise. In order words, keep Linda on a leash. A mental leash. That could extend for miles. Muriel thought about it and agreed. But it was decided to tell her when she was young. This way, she could accept it more easily, as kids do for Santa Claus or the Tooth Fairy. Except that Henry was real. Therefore, bringing her up in Henry's ESP world early would have less impact on her teenage years. So, she was introduced to this strange concept by the time she was old enough to talk. They would play mind games with her to slowly establish an understanding and comfort with this knowledge.

Henry and Linda were sitting at the dining table. *"Darling, do you want to play 21"?* Henry would mentally tell her.

The four-year-old Linda would respond with a lovely smile. "Sure, Daddy."

Henry injected his message into her brain. *"No, Linda. You're supposed to respond mentally."*

"Oh, Daddy. I forgot." She looked into his eyes and said mentally, *"Yes, Daddy. I would love to play 21 with you."*

Henry smiled as he nodded his head to her. Linda went to the dining cabinet and retrieved a deck of cards. She sat back down across from her father.

Mentally to Linda, *"You would want me to deal?"*

Linda mentally said, "Dad, *I think I can do this."* She began to shuffle the deck, but the cards fell on the table.

"Honey. Let me do this."

"Oh. Right, Daddy."

Henry gathered the cards and began to shuffle them. They both smiled at each other. And this was how it went: slowly introducing Linda to Henry's ESP. However, Linda was also told to keep this secret to herself. No one was to know about this. It was their little secret. Besides, if she did reveal this information to any of her friends, Henry and Muriel would deny it. Linda understood, and life went on during her younger years.

The years passed, and Linda blossomed into a lovely teenage girl. Of course, no one knew this better than Henry. After all, nothing was kept from him. Muriel initially felt uncomfortable about her husband being able to monitor Linda while she took a shower or undressed. But Henry assured her everything was safe, and he usually avoided monitoring her in those situations anyway.

In her high school years at Immaculate, all her friends were fellow female students. They had their social gatherings, slumber parties, and so on. But a few of the girls already had serious boyfriends. And some asked Linda, " Why don't you have a boyfriend?" Linda smiled and said she was not ready for that kind of relationship. But at 17, Linda was becoming very attractive. She was becoming tall, and her breasts were developing. Her mom always had a weight issue. However, Linda was slender like her dad; her waist was small, and her hips were narrow. Her face was becoming increasingly beautiful, and her high cheekbones and bright blue eyes were a legacy from her mother. Her profile demanded attention.

For example, when they went shopping together, Muriel noticed men glancing at her daughter. She let her daughter stand by the exit door while Muriel was in the checkout line. Sometimes, men would stop and flirt with Linda.

This happened on a typical Saturday evening at Walmart. A man briefly conversed with her while Muriel checked out.

A short time later, Muriel and Linda headed to the car with their items. They conversed.

"Honey. What was the guy talking to you about?"

"Oh, Mom. It's nothing. Guys talk to me all the time?"

"About what?"

"You know."

"No. I don't know, darling."

"Dad doesn't tell you?

"No."

"What's my name? Do I have a boyfriend? My phone number?"

"You don't give them your number?"

"Of course not."

"That guy in there talking to you must be at least thirty."

"Oh, that's nothing. I have even older men talking to me."

They finally approach the car. They loaded the items in the back seat and drove off. Muriel was visibly upset. But not at Linda. Linda could not help that men found her desirable. No. It was someone else as they entered the driveway. Linda went to her bedroom to play some of her music on her earphones as she finalized a school project due the following Monday. Muriel marched to the den to confront Henry, sitting comfortably in his recliner and staring at the TV. His mind was usually somewhere else. Monitoring various individuals, primarily employees at Maverick. She closed the door and approached him. Without looking at her, Henry addressed Muriel mentally.

"I know."

"Then why don't you tell me these things?"

"This is part of life, Muriel. Linda, as we both know, is becoming a young woman—a beautiful one. So naturally, men are going to hit on her." He turned to her. *"There is not much we can do about it. Unless we lock her in the basement like Cinderella."*

Muriel took a seat next to Henry. *"But I worry about*

our darling. Suppose a stranger…"

"You have nothing to worry about. You forgot. I am monitoring her. I know when things get out of hand. Besides, Linda handles these encounters well enough. This is all part of growing up."

Muriel paused, and she gathered Henry's remarks. *"I wonder what will happen once she wants to leave us. Go her way. Fall in love with the wrong man."*

"We just have to worry about it when we reach that bridge."

They reflected on this as their eyes stared at an old rerun of a "Gunsmoke" episode. Henry felt that Linda's knowledge of his ESP might influence her sexual activities. After all, who would feel comfortable engaging in an intimate sexual relationship knowing your father is watching you? But this was all theoretical. There was no way of knowing for sure. After all, it was all part of growing up.

Linda immediately attracted attention in her first year at a local university. However, Linda selected female students as her companions. She did talk to a few guys. But none of them interests her. However, Linda felt trapped living with her parents. After heated discussions with her parents, she convinced them to let her stay at a school dorm in her sophomore year. Muriel was reluctant at first. But Henry assured her it would be fine. He would be monitoring her anyway. After all, it was all part of growing up.

At the dorm, Linda met Carlos. He was a year older than her and was an exchange student from Argentina. His accent and good looks attracted Linda to him. They would have lunch together and casually see a movie. However, the sexual intimacy was not there. Linda was not ready for that, and Carlos did not want to pursue it if Linda was not prepared. But Linda was ready. She had sexual thoughts of engaging in coitus with him. But what to do about her father? She was aware he was monitoring her. However, he did not indicate that he was. She longed to feel Carlos next to her in bed. Making love and exchanging their passion for each other. However, mentally blocking her father was always a challenging task to achieve. So, friends they remained. One day, Carlos informed her that he was returning to Argentina. There were personal problems back home, and he was urgently needed. This broke Linda's heart. Because she was beginning to fall in love with him. However, Carlos's leaving was no coincidence. Henry worked behind the scenes and used his ESP to cause problems in Argentina. Linda was not aware that her father had a hand in this. However, Henry knew what her relationship would lead to and, pressured by Muriel, arranged for Carlos's swift exit from the university.

In Linda's junior year, she went about her business with her studies. She was majoring in marine biology and hoped to start a career studying life in the oceans. This was something she was always interested in. But her mind would wander off to Carlos. She still had strong feelings for him. He never bothered to contact her again after his abrupt departure. Henry would observe her daughter's feelings and emotional pain and sometimes felt guilty about his actions with Carlos. But he believed it was the right decision. Henry thought she was not ready to have a serious relationship with a man. And besides, Carlos was not the right guy for her. After all, in Henry's eyes, he was a foreigner.

Linda's senior year saw a change in her. She was no longer interested in just "college guys." She saw most of them as being immature. Not fully developed in the ways she felt a man should be. However, she also became interested in men from different cultures. Exotic men who had a different take on life seemed to fascinate her. She knew her parents would prefer that she date men of her racial background. After all, this was the norm. But Linda wanted to be different. Not the usual Ken and Barbie relationship she was used to seeing.

In her last semester, she had a Spanish class. It was a required course, but she waited until this semester to take it. The associate professor was Juan Gonzalez, who was in his mid-thirties.

"Okay, class. Next time, we will go over adjectives and adverbs in Spanish. Until then. Adios."

The class adjourned, and everyone left except for Linda. She sat at her desk as Juan erased the chalkboard. He turned and found her sitting there and smiling at him.

"Oh, Linda. I did not know you were still here."

She gave him a seductive smile. "I hope I did not upset you?"

"Of course not. How can I help you?"

"You mentioned you've been to Spain."

"Why. Yes."

"Well...I plan to take a trip there this coming summer after graduating. Sort of my graduation gift."

"How nice."

"Well... I wanted to find out which cities you

recommend."

"There are many places to visit in Spain. It depends on what you are looking for." Juan approached her. "Do you like to see history? The arts? The beach?" He stood near her. "How about romance? Spain has about everything."

Linda blushed. Their eyes lock. They smile.

"I imagine Linda, you, and your boyfriend will have no problem finding things to do."

She shook her head, "I don't have a boyfriend."

"Really!"

"How about you?"

"I am not married."

"Really!"

They both laugh.

Juan glanced at his watch. "I plan to go for a bite."

"You mind if I join you? Or are professors not allowed to socialize with their students?"

Juan smiled. "I won't say anything unless you do."

Linda smiled in return.

Linda and Juan were sitting in a booth, eating at a Mexican restaurant. The restaurant was not busy—it was as if they had the place all to themselves. They seemed to have a good time, talking and laughing while enjoying their margaritas.

"So, how long have you been a professor?"

"Well… I am an associate professor."

"How long until your tenure ends?"

"Oh…Three to five years. It all depends."

"Depend on what?"

"My achievements in teaching, research, that sort of thing."

A waiter came. "Anything else?"

Linda gave the waiter her now-empty glass.

Juan moved closer to her. "You want another margarita?"

"Sure. Why not?"

"Make it two."

The waiter nodded, and he removed the empty dishes.

"It's hard to believe you do not have any…"

"Boyfriends?"

"Yes. No male admires."

Sounding a little tippy, "Oh no. I have many of those. Just no boyfriends."

"No one interests you?"

"Not until now."

Their eyes lock. Juan reached over and kissed her. Linda decided to back away.

"I'm sorry."

"Don't be Juan." She looked into his eyes. "It's okay if I call you by your first name."

"Sure. Senorita."

This time, Linda moved over and kissed him. They kiss with more passion. They smiled at each other as the waiter came back with their drinks.

Linda drove back to her dorm. She entered her room and laid her purse on the nightstand. She opened it and took out a napkin with Juan's phone number and address on it. She smiled at the note and laid it next to her purse. She decided to take off her clothes and go to bed.

The following week, she looked forward to her next class with Juan. She wanted to call him. But she decided to wait until she saw him in class. She was the first one in the classroom. She usually sat near the back row. But today, she was sitting front and center, waiting for her Spanish love to arrive. Others started to file into class. But no, Juan. Finally, a professor arrived. But it wasn't Juan. Instead, the professor was female. She wrote her name on the chalkboard. "MRS. JUANITA JOHNSON". She was a black woman in her forties.

"Hello, everyone. My name is Juanita Johnson, as you can see on the board. I will be your new Spanish educator for the rest of the semester."

Quickly, Linda raised her hand.

"Yes, Ah…"

"Linda."

"Okay. Linda"

"What happened to Professor Juan Gonzalez?"

"You meant Associate Professor Juan Gonzalez. He is no longer with the university."

"He quit?"

"That would be something you would have to ask the front office. Now, if I have it right. The class left off on Spanish adjectives and adverbs. So, in your book, please turn to page …"

Linda's mind was lost as Mrs. Johnson continued to raffle off her lecture. *"What happened to Juan? Why would he quit? He did not indicate to me that he was unhappy. Something does not add up."*

Class ended, and Linda drove to the address Juan gave her. It was a lovely one-story ranch-style contemporary house. She rang the doorbell, but no answer. She did not notice any vehicles parked on the driveway, and none of the lights were on. She rang the bell a few more times. But still no answer. She returned to the car and called the number he had given her. The phone rang, but there was no answer. She left a message. "Juan, this is Linda. I am trying to find you. I heard you are no longer employed with the university. What happen? I drove to the address you gave me. But you don't come to the door. What gives? Please get in touch with me. You have my number." She was about to end the call. "Oh…For what it's worth? I miss you. And I want to see you again. Bye." She put the phone down. She lay her head back on the seat parked in front of the house. She stayed there for a few more minutes. She looked at her watch and left.

As she drove, her mind was on her romantic missteps. *"I can't believe this. First Carlos. And now Juan. Is my luck that bad?"* She drove a few more blocks, and something hit her like lightning. *"Dad!"* She slammed her hands on the steering wheel. She started to communicate with him mentally. *"Dad, did you do this? Dad! I know you are listening to me. Don't play dumb. I know you're listening." Damn it!"* Unexpectedly, she made a U-turn in the middle of the street and headed in the other direction, almost hitting a vehicle approaching the other way. She began to accelerate her speed. Linda did not possess Henry's ESP. But she knew enough about her father to figure he had something to do with her failures with Carlos and Juan.

She entered her parents' house and headed straight to the den as Henry and Muriel waited for her. They were calm, with smiles written on their faces. *"Come in, dear,"* Muriel mentally says. *"We've been expecting you."*

"Yes, dear. Please sit." Henry injected.

"No. I would rather stand. I will communicate with you with my voice, like normal people do."

Henry spoke, "Oh. She now lives with her college friends and wants to be like them."

"Did you have something to do with Carlos and Juan's sudden disappearance?"

"Now, darling," Muriel spoke with a calm voice. "It was for your good. Those men were not right for you."

"How dare you determine who I can and cannot date!."

"They are not the kind of guys…"

Linda interrupted. "Because they're foreign! Different from the type you would rather see me with. You have been monitoring them, Daddy. So, you tell me. Do they have a police record? Are they escape cons? What illegal activities are they engaged in?"

Henry smirked. "Carlos occasionally smokes weed."

"You've got to do better than that, Daddy!"

"Why aren't you interested in your kind?"

"Mom. I know you are into the Ken and Barbie thing. But that does not necessarily mean all women are into that."

"So dear. You speak for women everywhere?"

"No, Dad. I speak for myself. And as the old saying. Different strokes for different folks. Besides…" Linda gestured quotation marks with her hands…"The type of man I should be after…" Puts her hands down. "… Are men who should have my knowledge of ESP? So, tell me, Daddy. How many men have this unusual knowledge? I will give you the answer. No one. This means any guy I choose to be with will not have a clue about issues you are causing. Because if they did, they would freak out and leave me in the dust. So, when you think about it, I don't have much in common with men. I will always have to live a double life. One is trying to be normal with the man I love, and the other is dealing with you. This is something I will also have to live with. So, the Ken and Barbie world is fiction."

Henry and Muriel do not say anything as they digest Linda's piercing words.

Linda went on. "Now, here's the deal. I will choose the life I want. And if either of you stand in the way. I will go to the authority about this ESP shit!"

Henry grinned. "You have no proof."

Muriel injected. "They will institutionalize you."

"Now you choose. Let me live the life I want. Or see your darling daughter in a mental hospital for the rest of her life."

Linda turned and stormed out of the house. Henry and Muriel heard her slam the front door as she left. They were lost for words. Muriel finally turned to Henry and communicated mentally.

"What now?"

"We will see," Henry responded.

The following Saturday, Linda was alone in her dorm room, moping. The loss of Juan devastated her. Linda then heard a knock on her door. She went over to find Susan and Kelly.

"Hey Linda, let's go?"

"Susan, I am not in the mood. "

"Come on. It's us ladies", Kelly said with a beam on her face.

"Ya. Liz and Esther will be tagging along. Besides, you've been pretty down lately. So, we thought going out might cheer you up. Who knows..." With a grin. "You might meet someone interesting."

Linda took a deep breath and said, "Alright."

The girls arrived at a men's strip club. Several men were stripping on the stage. Linda was sitting alone at a table and did not feel comfortable. However, Liz and Esther gave dollar bills to a male dancer onstage. He squatted down so the young ladies could reach over and slip their bills into his thong. Meanwhile, Susan and Kelly came back from the restroom and approached their table. Susan looked around. "Where are our drinks?"

"You notice there are a lot of guys here," Kelly injected.

"Ya." Susan shrugs. "Maybe it's gay night?"

"No. There is something else happening here tonight, Sue."

"How many times have you girls been here?" Linda replied.

Kelly smiled. "Well… Actually. This is our first time."

"Oh…Great," Linda said sarcastically.

Finally, the waitress approached with the drinks. Kelly turned and let out a loud whistle in Liz and Esther's direction. Like trained dogs, they instantly turn toward Kelly. Kelly pointed to the waitress as she brought the drinks. Liz and Esther smiled back at their favorite male dancer. Liz grins at him, "We'll be back." They left as the male dancer turned and danced toward another group of women.

The waitress said, "Okay, I have the cosmopolitan."

"That would be Liz's." Susan pointed to the vacant seat next to Linda.

The waitress placed the drink there. "I have two martinis.

Kelly smiled. "That would be Esther's and mine."

The waitress handed Kelly her drink and placed the other drink in the vacant seat next to Kelly's. "Here's the mojito."

Susan, "That would be mine."

Kelly's eyes latch onto the drink, "That looks mummy."

"And finally, the margarita." She handed the drink to Linda.

Liz and Esther took their seats and drinks.

The waitress was about to leave. Susan stopped her. "What with all the guys?"

"Oh. It's ladies' dance night."

The women look at the waitress like confused little children.

"The ladies tonight will have a chance to dance on stage."

A surprised look ran over Susan, "Really?"

Kelly injected, "So, what do they wear?"

"Whatever they want."

Susan said, "Nude?"

The waitress beamed, "Well…This is a strip club. But only topless."

Esther took a drink. "Wow!"

Kelly sounded interested." Are there prizes?"

"Of course. The winner takes "$3,000."

Susan and Liz's eyes widened, "$3,000!"

"Yup." We do have costumes, in case any of y'all are interested." She threw them a wink and left.

Liz took a drink. "That's not bad for one number."

Esther finished her drink. "I'll do it."

Kelly is taken by surprise, "Esther?"

"Why not?"

The girls argued about who would dance. Meanwhile, Linda sat and drank her margarita.

A short time later, the waitress approached the table. "Any of you ladies need another drink?" They requested another shot. "I'll be back." The waitress left.

As the girls talked, Susan nudged Linda. "You have been quiet. Anything you want to discuss?"

Linda frowned. "Just thinking about my future."

"You plan to graduate next month?"

"That's just it. I don't know what I am going to do." She took a deep breath. "Should I stay? Should I go? I don't know."

"Your degree is in marine biology?"

Linda nodded.

"Travel. You can get a job almost anywhere."

"I need to stay to get my graduate's. And I don't want to move back with my parents."

"Go to another school?"

"I can't afford it. Besides, the school has already accepted me for their graduate program, and my parents will pay for it."

"All of it?"

"Yep. But with one stipulation. I move back to live with them."

"It can't be that bad."

"You don't know my parents, Susan."

"No. I guess I don't."

The waitress came back with the drinks and left.

The girls continued drinking as their spirits ran high. Esther and Liz returned to the stage area to admire their favorite male dancer and place more money in his thong. Linda drank her margarita and gazed at it. She then recalled Juan and her at the Mexican restaurant. They talked and drank. Juan moved over and kissed her. Linda decided to back away.

"I am sorry if I did that."

"Don't be Juan. It's okay if I call you by your first name."

"Sure. Senorita."

This time, Linda moved over and kissed him. They kiss with more passion. They smile at each other. The DJ spoke over the sound system, and Linda's flashback quickly ended.

"Okay, ladies and gentlemen. It's time for the ladies' dance off. Which one of the beautiful ladies is willing to show their dancing skills and walk away with $3,000 tonight?" The DJ looked around and saw no volunteers as the male dancers left the stage. Meanwhile, Esther and Liz walked back to their table. "Come on. Surely. A few of you would want to take the chance to show off your beautiful body and dancing skills to win the prize?"

A lady in the audience raised her hand. "I will." Then another raised her hand.

The DJ looked around." Who else?"

Everyone at Linda's table just looked at each other. Esther yelled out. "I'll do it."

Susan and Kelly, "Esther!"

Esther beamed with excitement, "Hell, ha!"

Two other young ladies said they would join in. Linda stared at her empty drink as the DJ sought other willing partners. Sadness filled her eyes as images of Carlos and Juan filled her mind.

Liz nudged Kelly, "You should enter. You have a nice bod. I think you can win."

"I don't think so."

"If anyone has a chance. It's you."

Kelly raised her hand to the cheer of everyone on the table except for Linda, who was lost in thought. Her attention turned toward her parents and how they kept her from Carlos and Juan. Suddenly, her sadness turned into frustration. DJ announced, "Okay, last chance. Anyone else? Going once. Going twice."

Linda raised her hand. "Am in."

Everyone at the table was speechless.

"Great. Now, if all of the sexy volunteers follow Emma." Emma raised her hand. "She will escort you all to the dressing room for your number. And good luck."

Kelly reached for Esther and Linda's hands. "Well. It's the three of us."

All three smiled. Linda turned and looked away. She grinned sarcastically, whispering, "For Dad and Mom. "

One by one, the women emerged with their costumes on stage. Some dance to the pole, while others move up and down the stage. While others did both. A few dancers, like Kelly, who had very fit bodies, threw in some gymnastics moves. Kelly was dressed as Princess Leia, wearing the metal bikini slave outfit. She did some leg waves and back kicks, ending with a lunge on the floor and her heels clacking to the beat of a remix. Esther came out as a Prisoner Convict Girl to the audience's delight. She danced to the beat of the music. Doing several back hook spins, yogini, standing, and hanging positions on the pole. Unlike Kelly, she removed her top, revealing her ample breasts to the delight of the audience, as she continued with her pole moves. The last dancer to appear on stage was Linda. The song began with a jazzy rock beat. Linda finally emerged as the singing started, wearing a sexy Heon Purple Lace Halter Dancer Mini Dress. Her dress was tight around her body. Her long-legged look and gorgeous face stood above everyone else. She slowly moved to the center of the stage and began to dance some jazz steps. Her moves blend well with the song. The audience was mesmerized by her on stage. She used the stage to the best of her skills. Every step appeared choreographed, as she danced with the skill of a professional. Her moves and looks had everyone's eyes wide with her presence. As the song went into an instrumental, Linda danced and gasped at the pole. The pole and she were one. She spun around the pole and did flashy floorwork, allegra, and ballerina spin moves to name a few. The singing continued, and she released herself from the pole. She did flashy jazz steps with some pirouette moves around the stage. The song ended, and she moved to the center of the stage. She yanked off her mini dress with one hand behind her back, revealing only her matching purple thong. Her nipples were covered with tiny purple boobie tassels. She ended with a slut dropping move. Her number was finished. The crowd went bananas.

Henry was monitoring the event in the den in his favorite recliner and was not pleased. Muriel was not watching her daughter's performance, as she was fast asleep in her recliner. He mentally injected, *"I could not let her see this."*

A short time later, all the contestants reentered the stage bearing their costumes. The DJ asked everyone to applaud their favorite dancer. It was no contest. Linda won, hands down.

Cinderella was back in her dorm room after the dance ball at the popular gentlemen's club. Linda was Cinderella, alright, as she dazzled everyone. Men lined up to give her their phone numbers. Others begged for hers. Even the owner wanted her to dance at the club. But she would have none of that. Instead, she managed to drive back to the dorm. Even though she was lit up with all the margaritas she had consumed, she sat in a chair. In front of her was a full-length mirror. She removed all her clothes except for the thong and matching bra. She slurred her words as she addressed her father. "Since I can-n-o-t f-u-c-k who I want… I g-u-e-s-s I will have to p-l-a-y with my-s-e-l-f. She started to place her hand inside her thong and reached for her crotch. Her other hand pulled off her matching bra. She began to play with her breasts. "Oh…, I… h-o-p-e you like this, D-a-d-d-y. Because I am going to e-n-j-o-y it." She started pleasuring herself and began to moan. Without warning, she started to become drowsy. Her eyes began to close, and she fell fast asleep on the chair. It was as if someone had turned off a switch inside her head.

Meanwhile, Henry sat in his recliner, continuing to monitor his daughter. He had had enough and jammed her neurotransmitter activity, causing her to sleep. Living apart from her parents started to embolden Linda's attempts to satisfy her sexual curiosities, even though she knew her father was monitoring her.

The following day, Linda received a call from her mom inviting her to dinner. She reluctantly accepted. She saw a shiny new sedan in the driveway when she arrived at the house. Henry and Muriel informed Linda that the car was for her graduation. They made up during dinner, and Linda decided to move back in with her parents after completing her undergraduate program. However, she would move back on the condition that she was free to choose who she wanted to date. Her parents agreed. Henry also proposed that she work at Maverick. He could set her up with a managerial intern position. Linda declined. She was devoted to her field of interest. However, she indicated that she wanted to take time off before beginning her graduate studies. She needed time to digest her decision to stay with them. Henry and Linda smiled in agreement. Henry and Muriel also agreed to speak to her only verbally.

Henry smiled, "Honey. Your mom baked a delicious cherry pie."

Returning his smile, "I can hardly wait."

Moments later, Muriel brought out her cherry pie from the kitchen. She began to slice it with a knife. Henry made sure Linda received the first slice. Linda took a bite.

"Wow, Mom. It is delicious. You will have to tell me your secret."

"Sure, Honey."

Everyone smiled.

Chapter 8 - DISCOVERING A NEW ZONE

After work, Robert was at his apartment sitting by the dining table. He was reading the telepathy book by John Daricek. *"Telepathy is an integral part of everyone's life. The possibility of direct mind-to-mind communication can draw people closer together and add to their individual security, comfort, and power."* He marked the page with a bookmark. He pondered what he read.

The following morning, Robert, Wayne, and Jim were busy at their desks. Robert looked up and stared at the doorway. He decided to grab a pay voucher from his desk and left the office. Robert walked cautiously down the hallway. Paranoid. He checked his surroundings frequently. He walked down another hallway. Robert continued to walk when he noticed a door was slightly open. A sign upon it read: "HENRY HONEY - HEAD OF PROJECTS MANAGEMENT." Robert stopped to study the name. The door opened, nearly knocking Robert over. Kyle and Margaret left the office.

Kyle turned to Margaret. "Hey, let's get some lunch." Robert hurried off. Kyle and Margaret turned and noticed Robert. They burst into loud laughter. Robert picked up the pace.

A short time later, Linda entered Henry's office and closed the door. She looked at her father. Henry nodded. She took a seat across from him.

"Now, I am rather busy, and we could have waited later for this."

"Does he deserve..."

"Yes."

"I see. Well... I want to get more involved. You know?"

Henry leaned back in his chair, crossing his legs. "You could have discussed this at home."

"I don't want Mom to know."

"She will find out anyway."

She threw him a warm smile. "I prefer we discuss this first. Alone."

Henry studied her for a moment as he picked up her thoughts.

"You want to live near him?"

"I'm curious. I want to see if he's as bad as you say."

Henry chuckled and stood, walking toward a window. He looked outside. "Despite all my abilities, love is one subject that always seemed to puzzle me."

"Love?"

Henry turned toward her. "You are falling for him, and you know it. And you both haven't even met. Suppose he rejects you. I can't create love. And I won't even if I could."

"I just want to know more about him."

"If you are that desperate, I could introduce you to someone here."

"Will you help?"

Henry frowned at her.

A week passed, and Linda walked toward her apartment on the first floor. She glanced up at Robert's apartment above hers. She opened the door. She entered, and the movers followed with her belongings.

Later that day, Robert entered his apartment. Linda opened the curtains. She looked up at him from her apartment. She smiled and closed the curtains. Linda reached for the phone.

"He's here, Dad."

She listened.

"Okay. Bye." Linda hung up the phone and stared at the ceiling as if observing Robert.

The following day, Robert entered his apartment after another day at work. He dropped his keys on the dining table and entered the kitchen. He poured himself a glass of water. He drank. The telepathy book from John Daricek on the kitchen counter caught his eye. He set the empty glass on the counter and reached for the book. Thinking to himself, *"I don't know. I'm not convinced, John. Telepathy is pretty weird."* Unexpectedly, Robert heard several sharp noises from the ceiling below. Robert paused and listened. Silence. He shrugged it off and set the book down. Thinking out loud, "But if it is real, it sucks." Again, several sharp noises from below. "What the hell is going on?" He went over to his bedroom. He opened his dresser, pulling out a small tray. However, the tray was empty. *"No coke."* He shook his head in frustration. He took a porn magazine off the dresser and went to the adjoining bathroom. He closed the door.

The following morning, Robert was asleep, wearing only a pair of shorts with a Playboy issue next to him. He awoke and walked to the window. He raised the blinds and saw Linda. She was sunbathing in a thong bikini by the pool. She's a beauty. Linda decided to stand and walk over for a swim. She was about to dive, but turned directly toward Robert. A sensual smile came over her. Robert dropped the blinds. "Oh shit!" He heard a splash. He peeped through the blinds and saw Linda swimming. He could not believe how attractive she was. And all alone. Suddenly, he had an urge to go to the bathroom to relieve himself, so he went and closed the door.

A short time later, he came out and washed his hands. He quickly went to the bedroom and checked the blinds. However, Linda was nowhere to be found. A frantic Robert pulled the blinds up and stuck his head outside the window. But again, no luck. He closed the window and pulled down the shades. He walked over to the bed and lay. Disappointment ran over his face.

Later that day, Robert walked toward the stairway to his apartment with a sack of groceries. He caught Linda wearing Daisy Dukes sweeping the front porch and grinned at her. With her back to him, she entered her apartment.

Robert opened his front door. He looked at Linda's apartment again before closing his door. "She's one hot number." He placed his keys and groceries on the table and turned toward the telepathy book on the counter. Robert then had a flashback to when he was in the restroom with Tom and Kyle. Tom turned to Robert and glared at him with a "watch it" look. He stormed out of the restroom. Robert remained frozen in confusion. Kyle walked up to the sink with a smile. He washed his hands. His eyes were on the mirror. "You ought to keep your thoughts quiet." His recollection of Tom and Kyle ended. Curiosity then came over him. He picked up the telepathy book.

A loud noise came from Linda's apartment below. Robert looked at the floor for a moment. He turned toward the book and walked to the couch. He pondered. *"John Daricek did say I was supposed to move to Tulsa. And that's where the Projects Management team transferred from."* Robert slumped down on the couch. *"If someone with telepathic abilities exists, they would have to come from Projects Management because of Kyle and Margaret.*" He thought momentarily, "*...Someone above them who has a major influence over the company.*" Robert stared at the book and said the following out loud. "Henry Honey...? It must be him."

Another loud sound from Linda's apartment below. He stood and stared down at the floor as if addressing Linda. "Telepathy." Again, the same deafening sound from Linda's apartment. He thought to himself. "*Is she connected to this?*" He closed his eyes. He went to a dream. He was in Linda's apartment. He walked over to her living/dining area. He was holding a large knife. He walked into the kitchen area. He spotted Linda as she prepared dinner. Her back was facing him. Robert slowly walked toward her. He began to raise the knife. The dream quickly ended. Robert expected a reaction from Linda below. But nothing happened. There was complete silence. Robert had another idea. He ran to the kitchen and retrieved a large knife from one of the cabinet drawers. Suddenly, Linda's front door slammed. Robert quickly went to the bedroom window. He saw Linda hurry to her car. She drove off in a panic. The sound of tires burning rubber as the vehicle roared off. Robert had a stunned look on his face as he dropped the knife to the floor. He walked over to the edge of the bed and sat. He was lost in thought.

The following morning, he went to the bedroom window and searched for Linda's car in the parking lot. But the vehicle could not be found. He walked down the stairs. He saw Linda's apartment. He wanted to approach her apartment. However, he thought otherwise and decided to visit the apartment office instead.

He entered, and two employees, Ruth and Ann, sat behind their desks. Ruth appeared to be in her 50s, and Ann in her 20s. Robert greeted them. "Good morning. I just wanted to know the name of my new neighbor downstairs."

Without giving much thought, Ann said, "Linda Honey."

Ruth was upset. "Ann!"

Ann caught herself and apologized, "Oh, I'm sorry. We can't provide that information for the protection of our tenants."

"You said, Linda Honey?"

Ruth snapped at him, "No, she did not."

Robert looked into Ann's eyes, seeking confirmation. Instead, she turned to Ruth.

Robert addressed her again. "Ann. Is that what you said?"

Ann looked back at Robert with a customer service smile. "You must have misheard me."

Ruth wanted to end this. "Besides, the apartment is empty. The tenant moved out early this morning."

The phone rang beside Ann. She answered. "Hello, this is Ann from Chaparral Apartments. How may I assist you?"

Ann continued to chat on the phone. Robert was downcast and left.

It was nightfall, and Robert was wearing his clothes on his bed. He stared at the ceiling. Moonlight was basking on his face. He appeared frozen, lifeless, and utterly defeated. He pondered. *"My mind became totally void. Numb from the shock that someone could be reading my thoughts, and I was powerless to stop it. And the police would not believe such a person exists."*

Chapter 9 - EVERYTHING SEEMS SO STRANGE

It was the following morning, and Robert had awoken
from his bed. He had not bothered to change his
clothes or shower. He appeared comatose. He was
afraid to move from his bed, except to the bathroom to
deposit his waste. But the question came to him. Like a
calling from an unknown force. What is telepathy?
Robert needed answers, but he would not find them
lying in bed. He finally left his bed and went over to
the dresser mirror. He stared at himself. His
mummified face expressed no rhythm. No emotion.
And yet the question came back again. What really is
telepathy? Or better still, what is ESP?

Sitting on his couch the following day, Robert
anxiously called someone who might help. Someone
who had the knowledge that could help him with his
ESP dilemma. He called John Daricek.
    Lilly picked up the phone in the hallway. She heard
Robert at the other end of the line.
    "Hello, Mrs. Daricek? This is Robert Yellowstone. I
saw your husband not too long ago. I need to speak to
him. It's very important.
    "Oh...I'm sorry. He passed away."
    "What? When?"
    "The day after he saw you."
    "What happened? If you don't mind me asking."
     "A heart attack."
    "But... he looked fine when I saw him!"
    "I know." Her voice cracked. "I miss him so... He was
everything to me. And now he's gone. Just like that."
She rubbed her hand over her forehead. Sadness filled
her eyes. She took a deep breath. "Oh...well. Unexpected

tragedies do occur."

Robert was lost in thought at Lilly's words.

"Robert?"

"Yes."

"Is there something I can do for you?"

"No... I don't think there is anything you can do now."

"You take care of yourself."

"Wait! Did you experience any psychic episodes, John would have?"

"No, my dear. Only John had that special gift."

"I see. Well... I am deeply sorry. John will be missed."

"Thank you, Robert. Goodbye."

Robert heard the click. He leaned back and closed his eyes.

Later, Robert was in the shower. He thought, *"Got to keep my mind off of him."*

That night, Robert lay on the bed, staring at the ceiling, and became upset. He pondered, *"Of all the lonely losers in this crazy world, I was chosen. But for what? To be a witness to this shit?"* He decided to pull a small stack of porno magazines from under his bed. He decided on an issue and sat up. He flipped through the pages. His eyes widened as he touched his right ear in pain. He closed the magazine, and the pain subsided. He opened the magazine again, and the pain intensified. Robert stumbled to his feet and dropped the issue. The pain was gone. Robert was utterly baffled. Dread filled his face. He picked up the magazine and opened it again. The pain intensified, and Robert screamed. He threw the magazine onto the floor. The pain lessened. He walked over and exited.

Robert went and sat on the couch. He reached below to pull a small mirror tray with enough coke for one good hit. He picked up a straw and took the hit. He lay and closed his eyes. He coughed violently. He quickly went to the kitchen. He opened the fridge and grabbed a glass of water. He drank and held his throat. He took another drink. He put the glass down and decided to go back to sleep.

The following morning, his lifeless eyes began to show some determination. He touched his unshaven face and realized he had a mission. A mission to find out what telepathy was all about. Researching this ESP phenomenon could give insight into what he was dealing with. Answer questions that he could not answer. Robert believed the Dallas Library had a limited selection of books concerning ESP. So, he decided to find out. Now, a small smile came over his face. A smile that hadn't appeared for a while. Like rain falling on the dry, dusty plains. Rain, which hadn't appeared for a while. Now, it was time for him to take a shower.

Hardly anyone was on the fourth floor of the library that weekend. This suited Robert since many people might have distracted him from his research. So, Robert was sitting on an old oak table, reading about telepathy. Beside him was another book on the subject matter. The books themselves were pretty dusty. It was as if the books hadn't been touched in a long while and were waiting for him. Robert didn't think he would be able to function this quickly. But there he was, reading in the library several days after discovering a new dimension—the dimension of Henry's ESP. A group of college students decided to enter and gather around Robert. They began to giggle and horse around. Robert then decided to collect what books he could find and left.

In his apartment, Robert sat at the dining table. He pulled out two books about ESP from his briefcase. The books were marked with Dallas library stamps. The books were "TELEPATHY AND THE PHYSICAL CONNECTION" and "ESP WAVELINK." He opened the second book and began to read. *"In the world of telepathy, for brain waves to function telepathically, an individual has to undergo changes in the level of consciousness in the neocortex. These changes must also alter the brain's electrochemical activity, i.e., the firing of neurons..."* Robert continued to read with interest.

As he read, Henry was watching the news on TV. Gigi was sleeping on his lap. Muriel was knitting. Robert continued, *"...But the mind must also produce factors other than just relaxation to achieve this effect..."* Suddenly, everything appeared to change into a black-and-white ambience. A brain wave had already exited Henry's head. It traveled through the room and out of his house. Robert read, unaware or unable to see that the wave had already entered his apartment through a nearby wall. He continued, *"... Or altered states of consciousness will be limited..."* Henry's brain wave was already in Robert's head.

Inside Robert's head, the hair-thin laser wave lit up a neuron, creating an electrical signal beginning at the dendrites. The signal went through the axon, and an action potential developed. The signal reached the microtubules and shot out from the axon terminals. A neurotransmitter synapse occurred. However, Henry's brain wave began to jam it and other firing of neurons in Robert's brain, causing his brain wave frequency to decrease. As a result, the electrical information moved slowly over his network of neurons to his visual cortex.

Robert's eyes started to shut as he became sleepy. He slumped down on the couch and fell asleep with the book in his hands.

A dream was initiated in Robert's mind. He was lying in bed, fully awake. The bed floated in the night sky, with the moon as the only source of light. Robert was shaken as he realized the bed was a thousand feet off the ground. He looked at the bright, silvery moon in total dismay. Robert was only wearing his underbriefs and wristwatch.

Unexpectedly, the bed took off like a rocket as it raced along the night sky. Robert held on for dear life. It was as if the bed were Robert's magic carpet ride. But a ride in which Robert did not know the destination. The bed then climbed faster and faster up the Earth's atmosphere. Robert was heading to space, with the bed now serving as his makeshift spacecraft.

In space, Robert saw a million stars dotting the vastness. Robert realized how small the Earth was. Even the sun was only one of many stars in the known universe. Robert then witnessed an enormous prism passing in front of the bright sun. Each side of the three-sided ends of the transparent glass prism was approximately 100 miles long. A bright white light of the sun passed through the prism on one side, and an array of different color light waves streaked across space, shot out from the other side. The solid light energy of the sun had bent into different color waves.

Robert's bed flew right through the color waves, but the assortment of colors did not harm Robert. However, other waves were being produced. These were the ultraviolet and infrared waves. Robert could not see these waves, but his skin became sunburned. His whole body looked like it was reddening with first-degree burns. Robert uttered an earsplitting yell as the ultraviolet rays hit his skin.

In pain, Robert's bed continued alone on its journey into space. Robert was both amazed and confused at the trip he was taking, and did not understand his voyage through space. Unexpectedly, his bed was coming upon a whirlpool of sorts. Robert was heading into a black hole. A monster whirlpool was sucking everything near its path. The powerful gravitational pull brought everything into it, including light. Robert's face turned a ghostly white. He wanted the magic flying to turn around. But it did not matter. He was too close to the black hole. Redirecting the bed would not have benefited him.

Nearing the powerful sucking force, his body began to pull, as his bed flew away from him. Hovering in space, Robert felt he was being stretched as he approached the vast whirlpool of the gravitational force, with its event horizon coming ever so close. Robert's physical form began to compress on its sides in response to the direction of the gravitational force. His watch also stopped working. It was as if time was suspended.

Robert now found himself on his bed in a remote

desert. The bed was on the sand as Robert lay on it. It was dawn, and no living creature seemed to be in sight. Robert was again only wearing his briefs and wristwatch as he awoke to his startling surprise. His skin no longer had the look of a burn casualty. Looking over the desert, everything seemed so peaceful. So serene. A cool breeze was blowing against Robert's confused face. Without warning, a nuclear explosion ignited the sky. The blast was about fifty miles away. But Robert could observe the vast mushroom-shaped cloud of radioactive material the blast generated. Robert was stunned by the sight. He shielded his eyes with his arms. To protect his eyes from the fireball of dust and scorching gases. Robert then looked up at the sky above. He was worried about the fallout the blast would generate. However, Robert did not observe any particles coming down on him.

Robert was now walking down Main Street in a small town in the USA. It was a gorgeous Sunday afternoon. People were milling about, all dressed in their Sunday best. Robert himself, however, was nude. To say the least, Robert was quite embarrassed at his strange new predicament. However, no one seemed to notice him. They walked right past him as if Robert were nonexistent. Robert could touch them as they walked. But they could not feel his touch. He then yelled at the crowd. He was crying for help and trying desperately to be noticed. But his cries went unanswered. It appeared no one cared. It was as if Robert were invisible.

Robert was now in a doctor's examination room. He was wearing only his briefs as he sat on a tall stool. His feet were dangling above the ground, giving him the appearance of a little boy. Physicians in white coats gathered around him. He pleaded with them.

"Can't you see? Henry's ESP exists! It's real, I tell you. It's real. He can read people's thoughts. He's probably reading all you'll thoughts!"

A male doctor, wearing gold-rimmed glasses, stared at Robert. "Did you say probably?"

"Yes."

"That's not good enough."

The physicians turned and walked away. Robert cried for help.

"Please don't go! Doesn't anyone believe me? I can't do this alone!"

The dream took Robert to a mental institution where he wore a straitjacket in an isolation room. A two-way mirror covered one of the walls. Robert yelled. "I'm not crazy. I'm sane. Please help me! Doesn't anyone believe me? P-l-e-a-s-e! I'm telling you the truth!" Robert cried.

Robert was now on the operating table. Doctors, assisted by nurses, perform surgery on his brain. Robert looked around the room in horror, terrified." Aren't you going to put me to sleep?"

A surgeon calmly said, "No need."

Robert screamed as his brain was opened after numbing the scalp and skull, revealing the frontal lobe. Another surgeon sliced the frontal lobe fibers on each side of his brain. Other doctors observe the operation. At the incision of Robert's brain, another surgeon held back the cut brain tissue with retractors. "Let's hope this will get rid of the illusory beliefs." The other doctors nodded in agreement.

The dream ended, and Robert awoke, staring at the

ESP book beside him. He checked his watch, and it was working. He realized it was all a bad, terrible dream. One he could not fully understand. But it was two series of dreams. The first series involved physics, and the second was about how ridiculous it was to believe in Henry's ESP. Perhaps the first set of dreams was an attempt to connect Henry's ESP to science, highlighting how physics plays a critical role. Paranormal events result from an interaction of space and time. Henry's ESP was a product of mind and matter, which were intertwined. However, as the physicians in the second set of dreams were telling Robert, Henry's ESP was just a fantasy. It didn't exist. So, which series of dreams to believe? Therefore, the questions pondered in Robert's mind. Is Henry's ESP genuine? And if it did exist, how did it relate to the surrounding universe?

Chapter 10 - IT'S JUST AN ILLUSION

A paper boy rode his bike past Henry's house, throwing a newspaper onto Henry's porch. However, the paper hit Gigi. She snarled at him. The paper boy continued down the street. He said, "I hate cats. They make me sick," peddling to his next destination. A few houses away, several mongrel dogs rested in the front yard. The boy rode past them. The dogs began to growl. Their sharp teeth show as they snap at the boy. Without warning, the dogs chase after him. The paper boy noticed and peddled faster, trying to outride the dogs. However, they gained on him. One mongrel bit his right ankle. The boy cried out in pain. Another dog bit the boy's left ankle. The boy cried out again. Suddenly, the crazy dogs stopped in their tracks. The boy kept on pedaling, blood dripping from his ankles.

Henry sat in his recliner in the den, sporting a devilish grin as his eyes focused on a soundless CNN broadcast. He mentally said, *"Good dogs."*

Meanwhile, Muriel walked to the front porch and picked up the newspaper. She addressed Gigi. "Come in, Gigi, before somebody hurts you." Gigi followed Muriel inside.

Muriel entered, with Gigi close behind. She sat on her usual chair, and Gigi curled up at her feet. Muriel read the paper, scanning the headlines. They spoke telepathically.

"So, what's that SOB Yellowstone up to now?"

"He's feeling sorry for himself again. Wondering if he should write letters to the FBI or CIA."

"You did not select him as a Single-Channeler. She turned to Henry. *"You should have ship him off to Tulsa."*

"I have it under control."

Muriel focused back on her paper. *"He also knows Linda is our daughter. And he wasn't supposed to know that either. Maybe he has some psychic ability himself?"*

"He got lucky, and Linda did exactly what she said she'd do. And she couldn't even last a week. Needless to say, she no longer finds him interesting. Besides, I won't let his greasy hands touch her anyway."

Henry and Muriel smile gleefully.

"Don't worry, dear. The law can't help him. You know that."

Muriel turned the page as Gigi brushed her groomed white coat against Muriel's ankles.

"The sooner I nail that Raul Torrez, the better."

"The IT manager is padding Desiree's paycheck for sex again, isn't he?"

Henry nodded.

"Crime doesn't pay."

"Not at Maverick."

Muriel continued to read the paper. *"Will Yellowstone go back to work?"*

Henry revealed a devilish smile, *"I am sure he will."* He looked at her. *"Tea."*

Muriel stood and placed the paper on the chair. She left with Gigi close behind for the kitchen.

Several hours later, Raul and Desiree were in bed making love at Raul's house. They made love like it was their first time together. Skin touching skin with exotic passion. Desiree's sexy black body suited Raul to a tee, and he was not about to let her go. He wanted more of her, and she wanted more money from Raul—fraudulent overtime money.

It was Henry's turn to make a move as he continued

to watch unemotionally from his recliner.

The following morning, the elevator door at Maverick opened, and Robert exited. He looked tense. Robert walked and decided to stop a short distance from Henry Honey's office. He stared at the closed door. A male employee saw him.

"Hey. Shouldn't you be in Accounts Payable? This is the management area."

Robert walked away.

Later that day, Robert and Wayne were busy at their desks in the Accounts Payable office. Wayne stood up and headed to the door.

"I am heading out for lunch."

"And Jim?"

"He's on medical."

"Uh... I'll join you."

"Are you sure?"

"Yeah."

Robert and Wayne sat outside at a downtown upbeat café. They finished their meals. "It's good to have you back. Jim and I were starting to worry about you. We don't want to be stuck doing all your work." Smirked. "You know what I mean?"

Robert and Wayne chuckle.

"Bill said you had a severe case of the flu."

"Yeah. That blasted flu. I couldn't shake it loose."

"Didn't you see a doctor?"

"That was after I was sick for a couple of days."

The waitress approached the table. "Can I get you gentlemen anything else?"

"No, thank you."

The waitress handed them their checks and left.

"Shall we?"

"Wait... I want... I need to ask you something."

"Sure."

Robert thought for a moment. "Do you believe in telepathy?"

"Reading someone's thoughts?"

"Yeah."

"Um, no... pretty sure that's not a real thing. Why?"

"I was just curious. Well… I've been reading up on it. I found a few interesting books…"

Wayne cut him off, "Those books are a pack of lies."

Robert gave him a deer-in-the-headlights look.

"Are you good, Robert? You seem... off."

"No. Everything's fine."

Wayne finished his glass of water as Robert stared at him intensely.

Wayne teased Robert. "So, do you think someone is reading your thoughts now?"

"Uh...Maybe..."

Wayne laughed. "Okay, buddy. You definitely need to see a shrink! The sooner, the better."

Robert appeared shocked, "Shrink?"

"A psychiatrist."

"I know what a shrink is." Robert cleared his throat. "It's just that... strange things have been happening to me at work."

"Like what?"

Linda sat alone at a nearby table, sporting a large pair of sunglasses. She watched Robert.

Robert looked away sheepishly. He stumbled on his words. "Well... The restroom thing, for instance."

"What restroom thing?"

"Surely someone told you?"

Wayne shook his head.

"Oh. Well... never mind then. It's not important."

"Then, why did you bring it up?"

Robert was lost in thought.

"Robert?"

"You know me, Wayne. I'm always worrying about stupid things."

Wayne glanced at his watch. "Yeah, okay. We'd better head back to work."

Robert and Wayne left with their checks.

Linda watched Robert leave as she sipped her tea. A sad expression was on her face.

The following day, Henry sat behind his desk, hands folded neatly. Linda sat in a chair across from him. He stared at her. They both refuse to speak. Linda finally broke the silence.

"It's my life. I can do what I want."

"Stop following him."

"Why?"

"I shouldn't have to explain that to you. Just obey my wishes."

"Or what?"

Henry replied with a serious stare.

"What was the promise we all made? Or have you forgotten?" Calmly smiled. "All I ask is that you don't torment him."

"Whatever makes you happy, dear."

Henry stood up and ushered his daughter out of the room. As soon as she was out, he displayed a slick smile.

Later in the afternoon, Robert worked at his desk in the Accounts Payable office. Behind him, Jim was back from an appointment. Sara entered the office and walked toward Jim's desk, leaning over him. They began to flirt. Robert turned around and saw her stunning looks. Unexpectedly, he felt pain in his right ear.

Robert touched it, "No…"

Robert tried to look away from Sara's perfect body. Robert squirmed. The pain intensified. Sara noticed him staring.

Smiling at him. "What are you looking at?"

Giving Sara a stern look. "Nothing."

Robert managed to tear his gaze away. Sara turned back to Jim as they continued flirting.

In his office, Henry sat alone as he leaned in his chair. His shoes were propped up on his expensive desk, and a smile came over his face as he monitored Robert.

The following morning, Robert ran towards the Maverick building. It was pouring rain, and he was the only person on the street without an umbrella.

Robert finally arrived at his working floor as the rain continued to slap against the windows in the Accounts Payable office. Wayne and Jim eat their donuts at their desks, working away as they did. Robert entered, soaking wet. Neither Wayne nor Jim looked up. Robert took off his coat and sat down. He began to go through the mail he brought from his apartment mailbox. To his surprise, he found a letter from his mother. He opened it. Inside was a note and a personal check. It read the following:

"Hello, Robert. I've tried calling you, but no

*answer. So, I assume your phone is not
working since I refuse to believe you'd
ignore your mother. The check for $600
should help cover your bills. Your Father
and I worry about you. When was the last
time you went to church?"*
Robert frowned. He continued with the
letter.
*"I thought so. Below is the address of a
nearby church. Give it a try. Love, Mom.
P.S. Call me when your phone is working
again."*
Robert read the church address.

Saturday night, Robert was watching television in his
apartment. Like most Saturday nights in Dallas, Robert
would stay in his apartment lusting at his porno magazines
or hitting up on coke from a local dealer unless he was out
socializing. But since the arrival of the strange idea (the
idea Henry was monitoring his mind), Robert stayed away
from such things. He tried hard to turn his mind away from
Henry's ESP, although Robert found it challenging. Like a
tape recorder, Robert kept reconfirming events that led to
his conception of Henry's telepathy. Robert often felt a
sense of gloom. Melancholy feelings, Henry found
agreeable in Robert's state of mind. But tonight, Robert felt
a little cheerful. Tomorrow will be a new day, and Robert
was going to try something different. Tomorrow's
expectations took Robert from his usual Saturday night
gloomy state of mind.

Chapter 11 - A NEW ROAD IS FORGED

The following Sunday morning, Robert was in the lobby at the nondenominational church. Robert shuffled into the church. Gospel music was playing. Robert was the only person in the lobby. It had been many years since he last visited a place of worship. When Robert was in grade school, he attended a Catholic church. His parents were staunch Catholic supporters. Robert was an altar boy for several years until his teenage years. At the age of thirteen, adolescence and sexual desires for girls in his school kicked in. So, Robert felt it was time to outgrow his altar boy image.

A little girl named Kim, who was only five and had golden blonde hair, decided to approach him. She startled Robert as she tapped him from behind.

"Hey. Do you have a dollar?"

Robert looked perplexed. "What?"

Her lovely face began to strain. "A dollar for the offering."

"Yeah, sure." Robert reached for his wallet and retrieved a dollar bill. He handed the dollar to the little girl and placed his wallet back in his trouser pocket. "Here."

Kim reached for the dollar and smiled at Robert. "Thank you."

Robert smiled back at her. He momentarily looked at Kim as she walked to the other side of the lobby. Robert then walked to one of the doors leading to the sanctuary.

Meanwhile, the little girl was spotted by her mother, Sally, who also had blonde hair and was about thirty. She called for her daughter in a loud voice: "Kim. Come here this very instant. I have been looking for you."

Immediately, Kim hurriedly walked to her mother,

holding the dollar bill for Sally to see.

"Look, Mommy. I have a dollar for the offering."

Sally rushed to her daughter and grabbed the dollar from her hand. "Who gave you this?"

Kim responded by pointing to a sanctuary door. "From the man who went in there, mommy."

Naturally, the mother looked in her daughter's direction but saw no one. Sally then jerked one of her daughter's arms. "I told you never to accept money from strangers." She spanked Kim several times on the buttocks. Holding her daughter's arm, Sally walked off with her as Kim began to cry.

Meanwhile, Henry and Muriel sat in front of their television, with Muriel knitting and Henry watching CNN. Again, he was following broadcast reports on events he was already monitoring. Suddenly, Muriel stopped knitting, alarmed at what she had just witnessed through Henry's ESP. They communicated mentally like they always do.

"Did you do that?"

With Henry's eyes glued to the television screen. *"No. The child just wanted a dollar."*

"I don't want him around kids. Especially if they look like our own kind."

Henry nodded in agreement. Muriel continued her knitting, and Henry was now watching a CNN broadcast on illegal insider trading practices on Wall Street. A subject Henry was all too familiar with.

Robert walked back to his car after church services. He spotted a well-worn Bible on the ground. He examined it for a moment. His first instinct was to walk to the church to turn in the Bible. But he decided to keep it. *"Finder's*

Keepers," Robert thought.

Later in his apartment that night, he began to look over the Bible as he turned the pages. He came across pages addressing Armageddon in Revelation. He read it for a while. He yawned and put the Bible down. He sat on the couch and flipped on the TV. He began watching what was on the screen. Unexpectedly, he turned towards the Bible on the table. He decided to walk over to the dining table and sat down to explore the Bible once again. He turned to a page and read, *"For we wrestle not against flesh and blood, but against principalities, against powers, against rulers of this dark age, against the superhuman forces of evil in high places."* Robert's face glowed as he read the passage.

Meanwhile, Henry, sitting alone in his recliner and stroking Gigi, shook his head as if talking to his cat, "Well, now, we can't have that. Can we?"

A cheese commercial was on Robert's TV. It featured a goat grazing in a field, promoting goat cheese. The commercial ended.

Henry smiled as he monitored Robert.

Unexpectedly, Robert went into a dream. He was in the countryside. A sheep had wandered off and was grazing in an open field, with blue skies above. A sheep herder was attending to the herd nearby. Robert watched the animal from a distance, wearing only his briefs. The sheep decided to stop and turn toward Robert. Robert began to take his briefs off. The dream quickly ended. Robert did not take the dream further. Robert dropped the Bible onto the table, shocked and confused. "What the hell was that?" Robert grabbed his left ear as he felt pain there. He did not know why he would initiate such a strange, bizarre fantasy as the tingling sensation in his ear lingered.

Robert decided to visit a medical doctor the following day about the pattern of pains he had been receiving in his inner ears. Sometimes, it will be in his left ear and, at other times, in his right. However, the physician could find nothing physically wrong. The doctor indicated it sounded like phantom pains, better known as somatization. The patient experienced prolonged pain, but showed no signs of any physiological problems. Robert thought. *"Maybe it's all in my mind. The problems aren't physical; they're mental."* The physician did mention they could be TMJ pains. Better known as the Temporomandibular Joint. Robert would have to see a dentist and wear a costly mouth splint for at least six months for treatment. However, there was no guarantee the treatment would help. Robert decided to pass on the treatment.

Chapter 12 - OH! IT'S THAT STRANGE FEELING AGAIN

It was the first working day of another new year. Wayne and Jim sat at their desks in the Accounts Payable office, chatting with Chase. They laughed hysterically just as Robert entered, carrying his lunch. Robert sat down at his desk. He learned to ignore them. He started to shuffle paper around his desk as he overheard their conversation.

Chase grinned, "... And they arrested Raul Torrez on the spot. Hell, he didn't know what hit him! I guess you could say he was caught with his pants down."

More laughter.

Jim looked concerned. "Hey. What about Desiree?"

"She was fired," Chase said nonchalantly.

"She wasn't arrested, was she?" Wayne said.

"No," replied Chase.

Jim gave Chase a serious look. "I wonder if she's available?"

An irritated Chase said. "Look, Jim!"

Jim produced a smile. "I was kidding. You know me, Chase."

"That's the problem," an exasperated Chase told Jim.

They laugh.

"Besides, I have someone else in mind."

Wayne chimed in. "We know about Sara."

Jim replied with a broad, satisfying smile.

"Sara? Do I know her?"

"No, Chase," a beaming Jim replied. "But if you saw her, you won't forget her."

"Wow! That hot."

Jim and Wayne nodded their heads.

Chase changed the subject. "What do you guys think

about Ed being transferred to Tulsa?"

Robert stared at his paperwork. Disappointment registered on his face.

Robert looked around. A thought ran through his mind. *"I forgot the Bible!"*

Suddenly, laughter from an adjoining office.

Meanwhile, the parking lot adjacent to the Maverick parking garage was full of cars. When the garage reached capacity, employees would park there. In his 70s, Harry, the parking attendant, stood inside his booth reading a magazine.

Two men in their 20s approach the booth. They shuffled on their feet and kept their eyes cast down. They were Flash and Lightning. Flash was the older of the two. They approach Harry. Flash face, lit up, "What's the word, old man?"

Harry looked up from his magazine and eyeballed a car. Flash and Lightning followed his gaze to a brand-new mid-size four-door Mercedes-Benz. Harry turned back to his magazine.

Flash smiled, his gold tooth shining in the sunlight. "Let's go, Lightning."

The two men strolled over to the Mercedes-Benz. Out of the blue, Flash and Lightning's faces went blank. They turned and walked toward Robert's car as if in a trance. They looked inside the vehicle. They saw the Bible in the passenger seat. Their eyes then rolled to the CD player on the dashboard.

Work was over, and Robert stood by his car with Harry. The driver's side window was smashed, and glass littered the ground. His CD player was gone, but so was the Bible.

"I can't believe this!"

" Yeah, I can't believe it either. They usually go for the

expensive cars."

"You know them?

"Ahhh... No. I'm just saying that thieves generally go for the luxury types."

"They even took the Bible."

The parking attendant scratched his head. "Maybe their churchgoers."

The following day at work, Robert walked into a small hallway carrying an invoice to a set of computer reports fastened by binders on metal racks against a wall. He retrieved a binder and laid it, along with the invoice, on a nearby desk. He attempted to reconcile the invoice with the computer report to determine if it was paid twice. Sara and two other male employees entered the open area from an adjacent office. They stopped a very short distance from Robert and began to chit-chat. Robert immediately noticed Sara and eyed her with interest. He had the following mental conversation. *"Why don't you ask her out? Asked her out? Are you crazy? I'll be the laughingstock of the whole department when word gets out that I asked Sara for a date. Not only will she turn me down. But she'll get a big laugh, and so will everyone else. No, thank you. I don't want to go through the embarrassment. I'll pass."* Robert's mind then went into a fantasy about her. Sara wore a skimpy bikini and conversed with male employees in the same hallway. The fantasy ended almost as quickly as it began. The two male employees immediately turned and gave Robert icy cold stares. Meanwhile, Sara looked at Robert with a sensual smile on her face. Sensing something was wrong, Robert retrieved the invoice and quickly returned to the Accounts Payable office.

Robert sat at his desk, as Wayne and Jim were too busy

at their desk to notice him. Robert stared at the invoice with a puzzled look on his face. He was confused by Sara's reaction and that of the two male employees. He then began to work on his computer. But as soon as he started, he decided to stop. He stood up and walked out of the office. Robert walked down the hallway. He then stepped into another hallway leading to Henry's office. He glanced at Henry's office door. Henry's door was closed. Robert then turned and continued to walk until he came upon a restroom.

Robert entered the restroom and noticed he was alone. Robert selected the middle stall to do his business. In the stall, he put down his trousers and briefs. In doing so, Robert continued to dwell on the recent events. Something his mind would do from time to time. *"That's strange that they would stare at me like that. It's as if they were aware of my fantasy of her."* Robert paused in thought and then wondered if Henry Honey had anything to do with their reaction towards him. Robert then touched his right ear. *"Wow! These pains sure do fluctuate."*

Two male employees entered, and his pain subsided. Since Robert was in the stall, he could not see their faces. One of the men occupied the left stall while the other went into the right stall. They both took their trousers and briefs off. Simultaneously, they both began to whistle. Robert felt very uncomfortable. It reminded him of an old joke he heard in grade school. "Hey, left ball. Hey, right ball. Who's that dick in the middle?" They whistled louder. Robert quickly cleaned himself and pulled up his briefs and trousers. He flushed the toilet and promptly left the restroom without washing his hands. Robert was a nervous wreck.

Robert walked very quickly back to the Accounts

Payable office. In doing so, he could see various employees milling around the hallway and snickering at him. Before he entered the office, he took another quick look at Henry's office. Henry's office door was wide open, with several employees talking to him from his doorway. Robert did not notice Henry.

Robert quickly sat behind his desk while Wayne and Jim told each other a joke. They continued to converse without paying any attention to Robert. Robert looked at the invoice on his desk. But his mind was not on the invoice. It was somewhere else. He looked afraid, with anxiety written all over him. *" No. No. Please don't tell me it exists!"* Wayne and Jim then burst out laughing. It was an uncontrollable laugh, which made Robert feel alone.

The following morning, Wayne and Jim engage in a lively conversation. Sara entered, looking as stunning as always.

What are you guys laughing about?

"Oh... nothing", Wayne smiled.

"Are you guys talking about cucumbers again?"

"No."

Robert entered with a new Bible.

He walked over and sat at his desk. He stared at Sara.

To himself, *"I would love to nail her just once."*

Meanwhile, Henry sat alone behind his desk, smirking at Robert. *"Cochise thinks Sara would be interested in him."*

Wayne, Jim, Sara, and the adjoining office laughed simultaneously as Robert placed the Bible on his desk.

Sara turned toward Robert. "Nice book."

"It's not a book. It's the Bible. The previous one was stolen."

Sarcastically, "Oh really? Stolen? How awful."

Wayne stifling a laugh, "Sara... don't spoil it!"

Sara took Wayne's advice and dropped the subject. She addressed Wayne and Jim. "Well, let me just say this."

Jim beamed, "Here she goes..."

"Women aren't interested in the size of one... cucumber. But bigger is better."

Wayne and Jim burst into laughter. Sara managed to maintain a straight face. Robert ignored them.

"Hey, it's true. I'm speaking from experience, boys."

Robert turned to face them but instead went into a fantasy. Sara stood over at Jim's desk. They talk and laugh. She leaned over to get closer to him. Unexpectedly, Robert walked from behind and slit her throat with a sharp knife. The violent fantasy ended.

Robert jumped. Wayne, Jim, and Sara laughed. Robert's expression turned to anger.

"Henry!"

He stormed out of the office. All turned toward Robert.

Wayne barked, "Where are you going?"

Robert did not respond. Instead, he walked toward the main hallway. He entered and sped down the hall. He noticed Henry's office door was open. Tom and Bill approach the office from the other direction. Before Robert could reach his office, Henry darted out and quickly walked away from Robert.

Robert muffled, "The elevator. Coward."

Robert made his way to follow Henry. Bill looked at Robert with concern, "Is everything all right, Robert?" Robert stopped.

Tom gave Robert a stern look. "What exactly are you doing over here? Shouldn't you be at your desk?"

"Oh... Ah. I... Nothing, Sir. I ... just forgot the voucher and made the wrong turn."

They both nodded.

Robert entered his apartment that evening and slammed the front door, Bible in hand. He threw his keys on the dining table, which ricocheted and landed on the carpet.

Robert spoke directly to Henry, "What the hell do you want from me?"

Meanwhile, Henry sat comfortably in his recliner, drinking a hot cup of tea, smiling. His eyes were on an old "Gunsmoke" episode in silence. Muriel was knitting in her usual chair. They both mentally heard Robert.

Robert walked over and tossed the Bible on the couch. "I know it's you, Henry. Everything! The laughing, the inner ear pains, these... mental images. Even with animals!" Robert took a deep breath, running his hand across his sweaty forehead.

Henry responded mentally, *"We all live in the yellow submarine."*

"You don't have the right to play with my mind. I'm not an experiment!" He began to paced, working off the anxiety Henry was giving him. "Am I to satisfy your mental pleasures?"

Henry and Muriel smiled at Robert's remarks.

"You're nothing but a psychopathic weirdo from the... Twilight Zone... or something, trying to pass yourself off as Superman! Well, news flash, you're not!"

Muriel laughed.

"And to top it off, you want me to know you're invading my mind!"

Henry yawned, bored by his tirade.

"I am not an animal, damn it! I'm a human being. And you..."

Robert's voice cuts out. Muriel looked up at Henry and

communicated mentally, *"Why did you do that?"*

Henry sips his tea. Shrugged. *"He was just droning on."*

Muriel continued knitting. Henry stared at the television, monitoring Robert.

The following day, Robert sat in front of a computer in the Dallas public library. He scrolled down a computer screen, searching a possible location for Henry's residence. A discovery. His face lights up. "Bingo!"

Robert drove down a lonely street, his eyes studied the addresses of the passing houses in a well-to-do neighborhood.

He drove on another street and decided to check his rear-view mirror. A police car followed him, its lights flashing. The siren blurted. Robert pulled over.

The patrol officer approached the driver. "Driver's license, please?"

Robert handed him his license.

The patrol officer studied it. "You stay put." He walked back to his car and called dispatch. After a few minutes, the patrol officer returned to Robert's car and handed him his license.

"Do you live around here?"

"Ah... No, sir."

"Why are you driving in this part of town?"

"I... I got lost! Oh! I know where I am going now."

"I suggest you get the hell out of here before you get yourself into a heap of trouble. Do you understand?"

"Yes, sir."

The patrol officer headed back to his car. Robert drove off, passing Henry's neighborhood. The patrol officer followed him. Robert turned left at a traffic light. The patrol officer followed. Robert kept on driving and made another turn. He looked in his rear-view mirror. The patrol officer continued to trail him.

Robert turned onto the expressway. He checked his mirror. The patrol car was gone. A sigh of relief registered on his face.

Robert entered his apartment and slammed the door behind him. He threw his keys on the dining table, which bounced and landed on the carpet. Robert then headed for the bedroom.

He went over to the adjoining bathroom. He turned on the water in the tub. He reentered, walked over, and sat on his bed. He began to take off his clothes. "Will try later." Unexpectedly, he felt pain in both ears as he dropped his head into his hands, as the pains intensified. Robert flinched. Dread filled his face as he held onto his ears. "No, no, no... please... stop!"

Henry mentally said," You *want a piece of me, Cochise? Don't you dare test me!"*

The pains intensified again. Robert cried out in pain. His knees buckled, and he fell to the floor. "God... oh god! Stop!" Robert screamed. He grabbed a pillow off the bed and used it to cover his ears. The water continued to fill the tub in the bathroom. "You're going to kill me! My eardrums are going to pop!" Hearing the water, Robert made a mad dash into the bathroom. Robert submerged his head in the water. He screamed underwater. The pain did not lessen. He whipped his head out, spraying water all over the walls. He stumbled back into the bedroom. Robert buried himself in his bed, covering his ears. "Stop! "Please! You have to stop! I won't come near your house ever again. I promise!" The pains persisted. "You have to believe me!" The pains finally stopped. Robert took deep, gulping breaths. Tears filled his eyes.

Chapter 13 - THOUGHTS, LAUGHTER, AND PAINS

A month had come and gone, and Robert was struggling with the anguish and torment caused by Henry Honey. At times, living with the idea that someone was monitoring his thoughts became so unbearable that he would sometimes think of committing suicide. As every week passed, Henry found new ways to provoke Robert into anger, guilt, and fear. Bombarding Robert with thoughts he was not accustomed to. Thoughts about having sex with animals. Racial thoughts towards minority groups. Violent thoughts relating to people Robert disliked. Thoughts about having sex with certain Maverick employees whom he would not dare want to have coitus with. The unwanted thoughts, or what Robert referred to as unfamiliar or negative thoughts, came daily now.

At times, Robert felt he was in London, being bombarded constantly by the Luftwaffe in 1940. Robert knew the thoughts were coming from Henry. How else could Robert explain the inevitable rash of unfamiliar thoughts? The unfamiliar thoughts pass through his mind like the wind passing through an open window. The thoughts coincided with his sudden belief in Henry's telepathy. Coincidence? Hardly. Robert knew his mind all too well. After all, Robert lived with his mind for twenty-three years before Henry got hold of it. In those first twenty-three years, Robert was never in trouble controlling his thoughts. His only sexual thoughts centered around attractive demoiselles. Now, Robert's thoughts branch to all new levels regarding sexuality. Thoughts he was not accustomed to. Like inserting his penis into the tailpipes of cars. Sex with significantly older women. Violent thoughts about women, he would fantasize about sexually. Thoughts about doing it with certain animals. It was as if Robert were going through a punishment phase. Punishing his lust for women, he deemed attractive. But that wasn't all. Robert worked on an invoice and added figures to his computer. But he keyed in the wrong number and totaled the invoice incorrectly. Wayne and Jim began to laugh. Wayne and Jim were not conversing. But someone or something caused them to giggle. After all, people don't giggle unless they have a reason to. Robert ignored their laughter and continued summing up the invoice. This time, the amount was correct. They ceased to laugh. It was as if someone was pushing their emotional buttons.

About an hour later, Robert left the office and walked to an open area of the small hallway to reconcile an invoice with a generated computer report. Standing several feet away were several employees chatting about the latest company gossip. Robert was not the focus of their attention. Robert realized he had retrieved the wrong report. Unexpectedly, the employees began to laugh as they stared at him. Robert felt their stare but paid no attention to it. He proceeded to retrieve the correct report and reconciled the invoice. Robert then walked back to the Accounts Payable office with the invoice.

Wayne and Jim were sitting and checking other invoices. Robert stood by his desk. His mind then remembered something. *"I forgot to journalize a payable transaction for the monthly voucher."* Suddenly, as if Wayne and Jim's emotional buttons were pushed, they both looked up at Robert and began to laugh at him. Not knowing the intent of their amusement, Robert said, "What happened?"

Wayne covered his mouth, trying to conceal his chuckling. "I don't know, but I had to laugh."

"Me too," Jim said. 'Don't worry about it, Robert. You're cool."

Wayne and Jim then sported their "get serious face" and continued working. Robert likewise did the same.

The laughing episodes involving Robert continued in the same mechanical, machine-like manner. Robert forgot to bring his comb to work. Results. Laughter. Robert forgot to bring his sack lunch to work. Results. Laughter. Robert computed an invoice incorrectly. Results. Laughter. They sounded like a pack of hyenas. Laughing at anything and everything physically or mentally, Robert did, which was remotely subject to error or flaw. Even a negative thought, like the one Robert experienced one morning while walking down management row. He imagined he was having sex with a 103-year-old nun. Or another thought involving an elderly lady in her 90s confined to her wheelchair, lasting several seconds. But there it was, a weird, grossly thought in living color. Several employees, milling in management row, turned and laughed at him. Robert did not know why he would have such a thought. But he did. So, there was the laughter, as if reminding him how dopey he was.

Robert would usually dismiss the sudden chuckles. "Oh, it's just a coincidence." But was it? Robert thought so. There was nothing wrong with people laughing. Laughing used fewer facial muscles than an ugly frown. "Laughing is good for the heart," as someone once said. Laughter breaks up the stress and tension that usually develops in the workplace. Laughing is just good old plain medicine. Besides, everyone laughs eventually. Therefore, what's the fuss about laughter, merriment, joviality, revelry, and glee? Nothing. Unless Henry's ESP caused it. It was as if Henry were trying to illustrate to Robert how unstable he was. How erroneous a person he could become. But Robert never said he was smart. That was an idea Henry put in his head. Robert just wanted to be treated fairly. Not special.

And who was Henry kidding? Henry was no bright one himself. Sometimes, he would draw wrong conclusions concerning employees' behavior patterns. Predicting events, they were supposed to happen, but never did. Forecasting false ideas into people's minds.

The previous week, it was Robert's turn to go to the Treasury office to deliver some checks and then head home. Vendors wrote checks payable to Maverick Oil for the purchase of salvage oil equipment. Thus, Robert went to the 14th floor to hand-deliver the checks. When Robert arrived at the office, the door was locked. Through the glass panel on the door, Robert noticed the office lights were off. He knocked for a moment more, but no answer. Naturally, Robert thought everyone in the office had left for the day. Therefore, Robert did what he could only do. He slipped the checks underneath the door. The checks would be retrieved when the employees entered the Treasury office on the next work day.

Robert did his job. He then left the office door and walked to the nearest restroom, a short distance away. He was in the restroom for no more than several minutes. He left the restroom and walked down the hallway to the nearest elevator. To his surprise, two young men left the Treasury office and headed to the same elevator. As the elevator went down, Robert was thinking. *"Why didn't they answer the door? Why didn't they hear me?"* Robert would stare into their faces. He eyed them for any clues he could find. But the two avoided making eye contact with Robert. Their eyes darted everywhere except in the direction of Robert's inquiring face. The elevator door opened, and the two young male employees quickly walked out and headed for the nearest exit door. Their quick walk indicated they were in a hurry. Something wasn't quite right. Then, it dawned on Robert that the two male employees did hear him. Was it a trap? A sort of sting operation to see if Robert would take the bait. However, taking the checks never entered Robert's mind. It was an automatic decision to deliver the checks without thinking about it. Apparently, someone thought Robert was capable of stealing company checks. But who? Robert knew. It was Henry Honey. He was monitoring Robert the whole time he had the checks. Hoping Robert would take the bait.

Henry had formulated ideas about Robert. False ideas. The kinds of ideas that put Robert in a bad light. Robert thought, *"That wicked bastard! So, he liked to bear false witness against thy fellow man. Huh."* Yes, Henry was with fault. He was a sinner, just like Robert and everyone else. But Henry carried on a facade of perfection, that he was without fault, and everyone else was a sinner.

And those pains. Oh, those nasty pains! The pains would sometimes remind Robert of blood-sucking ticks attaching themselves to his scalp and boring into his head and making his life miserable. Like a tick on an animal in the prairie, it constantly reminded him of its presence. And there was nothing Robert could do about it. The pains felt like a person continually nagging at him, laughing at him, and attacking him. The pains started to formulate their patterns. They coincided with Robert's unfamiliar thoughts. If the images were unaccustomed sexual thoughts, the pain would always be on his left side. They started in the neck area and then the inner ear or go directly into the inner ear. However, the pains were usually mild or a tingling sensation. At times, it was as if someone was tickling his ear. To Robert, the response to the pains suggested acceptance of such thoughts. Sexual thoughts relating to attractive women usually cause the pain to boom on the right side, ending in the inner ear. Unlike the pains on the left side, these pains were sharp and sometimes nerve-racking. His inner ear would sometimes ache for hours on end. Robert felt like Pavlov's dog, with the pains providing stimulus to the thoughts.

Robert wanted to talk to Wayne, his friend and co-worker, about the unfamiliar thoughts, the coincidental laughter, and those agonizing pains. But Wayne would inform Robert to visit a psychiatrist. And rather quickly, too. However, visiting a psychiatrist would be costly— money Robert didn't have. Considering the strain and tension he was going through, it was becoming increasingly difficult for him to continue working at Maverick Oil. But even if left Maverick, there were still those unfamiliar thoughts and associated pain patterns. Robert did not know if all the mental anguish would come to a halt if he worked with another employer. Robert even had ideas of moving back to live with his parents. Something he thought he would never do. But despite all he endured, Robert still kept up with his work. Trying to live an everyday life, the best he could.

Chapter 14 - A DREAM TO DREAM

On Saturday morning, Robert parked his car at a city park. Sitting alone, he closed his eyes and slowly tilted his face upward. He hoped Henry would be gone from his mind when he opened his eyes. But when he opened his eyes, Henry was still there like a determined albatross following a lost ship. Henry would not leave. The pains were still gripping his neck and inner ears.

An hour or so later, Robert wandered into the park. He would sometimes stop and notice the children playing, lovers kissing, and older adults feeding the pigeons. It all looked so innocent, so serene. No one would ever notice if Henry's octopus-like brain waves penetrated their skulls. But then Robert wondered if it would be better not to be aware of Henry's ESP. Sure, Henry would still be monitoring the individual's mind. But the person did not know, and that could be an advantage. Not knowing. It's best not to know everything. Robert then remembered what his father said to him years ago. "It was best God doesn't tell us everything. Because if God did, our brains would explode. We wouldn't be able to take in all the information. The information would be too overwhelming. It would be best to wait until we die." Robert realized his father was probably right. Robert's brain felt like it was exploding. He was overwhelmed with this knowledge of Henry's ESP. His mind struggled to adapt to this new way of life. Robert then squatted by a pond. He tossed several pebbles into the water. He then sat on a park bench, lost in thought.

Parents played with their children in an elementary school playground nearby. Robert drove hurriedly into the parking lot. He exited his car, his hands over his ears, and screamed silently.

The skies above turned to darkness as a downpour began. But Robert was walking on a sidewalk against traffic during the rain like a zombie.

In his apartment, Robert threw wild punches against his head. He then rams it into the living room wall.

Gathering his composure, Robert drove to a nearby grocery store. He shopped but looked paranoid, constantly checking his surroundings. He looked exhausted. Linda was nearby in the store. She watched him from a distance. She looked worried at his mental condition. She knew he was falling apart but kept her distance per her father's directions.

Later in his bedroom, Robert stared at the stack of Playboy magazines on a shelf. He began to reach out for one, then stopped as he touched his right ear in pain. He decided to walk to the living area. He reached for his coke tray underneath the couch. But it was empty. He ran around his living/dining room with his hands in the air, screaming for help.

Robert walked around in another park; gloominess filled his mind. He spotted a priest and a nun walking, engaged in conversation. He started to approach them, but stopped.

Robert stood on a street corner. Two police officers were chatting nearby. Robert looked at them, desperately seeking help, but decided to walk away.

Robert stopped in front of the FBI office and studied it briefly. He looked at the gloomy skies and drove off.

Robert returned to his apartment, realizing he had no one to turn to for help. He entered and laid his keys on the table.

Meanwhile, in the Honeys' den, Muriel and Henry watched Robert's mental activity as they sat in their respective chairs. Henry used his brain waves to jam Robert's neuron cells from firing. He felt Robert had had enough for one day, and involving law enforcement was not in Henry's plans. So, Robert became drowsy. He headed for the bedroom and fell asleep. Henry did not always interfere with Robert's REM dreams, though. Because Henry believed Robert's sleepy dreams were the only way to determine if Robert's mental state was still somewhat normal. Henry was afraid Robert might go off the deep end. Not that Henry cared. However, Robert was the first person outside Henry's Inner Circle to be aware of his ESP, and Henry was curious to see how Robert could function in society. Function with the knowledge of Henry's ESP in his mind. But an even darker side of Henry was anxious to determine how much Robert could take before breaking. Even Muriel did not know this. Everyone has a breaking point. What was Robert's? After all, Robert was an Outsider. He was not supposed to have this information. He wasn't someone Henry would approve of. He was also what one would call a Negative Wave Reaction. Someone whose human brain activity was faulty. A complete loser. Opposite of a Positive Wave Reaction.

Robert went to REM sleep and then into a dream. He was in a pitch-dark place, wearing his T-shirt and jeans. However, an aura surrounded him as if he were in a sukhasana position. He seemed confused about his whereabouts. Unexpectedly, a beautiful woman, Angel, dressed in a white gown, descended to Robert. Naturally,

Robert was startled by her appearance. She, however, calmly reached for his hand. Robert stood and gave her his hand. They immediately began to fly upright, still surrounded by darkness. They then flew faster, with the wind blowing against their hair.

Darkness turned into light as they approached a heavenly place. Flying slowly now, they pass spiritual beings, all dressed in colorful gowns, waving at Robert as they continue their flight. The spiritual beings stood behind a beautiful gate made of pearls, attached to jasper walls. They approach another lighted area. The woman Angel stopped her flight. Still holding Robert's hand, they stood before several dozen Angels, both men and women, all dressed in white gowns. They represented the various races of the world. They were singing a song, in which Robert heard the last chorus. "Yes, we must love. Yes, love. We must love one another. We must love one a-n-o-t-h-e-r now."

Unexpectedly, Robert awoke from his dream. He looked out the bedroom window as the sun settled in the west.

Meanwhile, Henry and Muriel closely monitored Robert's dream in the den. Muriel was surprised by Robert's dream and asked Henry for an explanation. But Henry himself was just as confused. His ESP had nothing to do with Roberts's REM dream.

Robert quickly left his bed and went over to the dresser mirror. The dream appeared to uplift Robert's tormented life. A smile came over him. Henry, not wanting Robert to feel so festive, administered sharp pains in Robert's right neck area as a sign of disapproval. But the pains did not dampen Roberts's cheerful mood. Henry's pains gave Robert even more reason to smile. Despite the mental struggles he was facing with Henry every day, Robert had something to live for. Robert had value. Spiritual value. Robert's smile grew into a happy grin. He left his bedroom for the living/dining area. Robert opened the front door and observed the beautiful sun. Robert then laughed hysterically as he stood outside the front door.

Robert's laughter made Muriel very nervous. It was as if Robert was possessed by something very evil.

He was laughing at the setting sun and laughing at Henry. Robert was high, all right. He felt like breaking out into a happy dance. His high spirits were based on the belief that the dream was a spiritual sign. Robert was not alone. He was being watched. Henry was being watched. Something or someone was watching both Robert and Henry. There was still hope for miserable Robert. The adrenaline Robert felt from the dream did not let him sleep that night. So, a little after midnight, Robert put on some clothes and walked about the apartment complex. He was remembering his REM dream. The beautiful woman Angel holding hands with Robert and entering a spiritual world. Heaven. As the Bible calls it. Then, recalling the tail end of a song, the other Angels sang. The Angels represented the various races of the world. "Yes, we must love. Yes, love. Yes, we must love one another. Yes, we must love one a-n-o-t-h-e-r now." How the song was so true.

Robert realized he must quit working at Maverick—quit now! The love is not there at Maverick Oil for him. And if employees did express sincere feelings for Robert, Henry would take it away from their minds, like a thief in the night. Yes, leave! Please leave!

Meanwhile, Henry and Muriel heard everything Robert was thinking loud and clear. They both laughed. Never taking Robert seriously for the intelligent things he would sometimes think. But deep down inside. Henry was angry. Very angry. *"How dare that half-bake son-of-a-bitch!"* But Henry could not let his true feelings show. He did not want his wife to know Robert was starting to get to him, irritating and frustrating him. So, Henry just laughed along with his wife. Yes, Henry and Muriel had a nice long laugh.

Chapter 15 - EVERYTHING MUST LOOK CLEAN

Henry, Tom, and various managers sat around a conference table as a speaker gave his lecture at Maverick Oil. However, Henry's eyes were fixed on Peter Grission, a fair-haired 40-year-old rising star at Maverick. The meeting was over, and everyone began to file out.

In the hallway, Henry stopped Peter. "Peter."

"How can I help you, Henry?"

"I've heard you're being considered for the new VP of retail."

"You've heard correctly."

"A word of caution. Be careful how you conduct yourself outside these walls."

"I'm sorry?"

Henry stared at him.

Peter stepped back. "Henry, I don't know what you're implying here. But neither you nor anyone here at Maverick controls what happens in my private life."

Henry answered him with silent, piercing eyes.

Peter became edgy. "Good day."

Peter left. Henry was not amused.

It was a beautiful day at the White House, sparkling in the sunlight. The President exited the West Wing alone with the Vice President. They approached a staircase. A Secret Service Agent stood vigilant, wearing an earpiece.

The Vice President reached over to the President, "Today's the day, sir. It's finally our moment to stand against those corporate oil tycoons."

The President beamed back, "It is indeed. The offshore drilling companies won't be happy, but this has been a long time coming."

The President and Vice President climbed down the stairs. The President, followed by the Vice President, entered the Rose Garden outside the Oval Office. Dignitaries awaited him at the signing table. In front of the table, media personnel began snapping pictures. Cameras flashed. The Secretary of the Interior greeted the President and Vice President.

The Secretary greeted the President, "Good day, Mr. President. And to you, Mr. Vice President."

"How is the Secretary of the Interior doing this fine day?"

"Doing very well, Mr. President. We're all very excited. This is a big move."

The President nodded. A Senator pulled the President's chair.

"Thank you, Senator Packman."

"My pleasure, Mr. President."

The legislation and various pens to sign the bill were on the table. The president stared at the document and looked up at the cameras. He picked up one of the pens. Unexpectedly, the light from the atmosphere was blocked, as dark clouds appeared overhead.

A brain wave from the White House had already linked to a skull in the Rose Garden—the wave connected to other skulls, creating a network. But no one noticed the waves.

Meanwhile, Henry sat alone in his office at Maverick, sporting a wicked smile as a wave extended from his head.

Bright sunlight then broke through, filling everything with color. The President stared at the document, hovering his hand over it. Suddenly, dread filled his face. He placed the pen down and faced the cameras.

"I regret to inform you and the citizens of this great country...." He took a deep breath. "As President, I cannot sign this legislation."

Audible gasps from the audience. The Vice President and the Secretary were shocked. Cameras flashed.

Senator Packman asked the President, "What are you doing, Mr. President?"

The President stood and gave the Senator a somber look.

"The Senate will have my veto message tomorrow."

Media representatives exploded with questions. A Media Representative, "Why are you vetoing the bill, Mr. President?"

Another Media Representative, "Mr. President, why are you changing your mind?"

The President did not return any questions. Instead, he returned to the Oval Office with the Vice President.

Robert decided to leave Maverick Oil and head back home. It was best to leave while he could. Robert began to suspect Henry was monitoring him while he was asleep. He also firmly believed Henry could monitor people practically anywhere. Reading those dusty ESP books in the library convinced him of that. But before doing so, he wanted to expose Henry. For all the awful and nasty things he had done to him. So, Robert sat at the dining table in his apartment, working from a recently purchased small laptop and portable printer. Robert's first thought was to send correspondence to the FBI. However, it was decided that it was best to send letters to the Maverick authority and let them decide on the best course of action. So, there were two anonymous letters inside envelopes next to him. One of the letters was addressed to the Maverick Oil Human Resources office. Still, another letter was addressed to the company's CEO. Robert grinned, "This will teach him."

The following day, Robert moved boxes out of the bedroom. This included his stack of Playboy magazines. He threw them in the trash. He also got rid of his cocaine paraphernalia, such as snorting straws, snuff bullets, and small mirror boards. The dream with the Angels gave him a new lease on life. A fresh start. Something to hope for. However, he needed to get rid of the things holding him back. So, he looked at those things in the trash bag and proceeded to haul them to the dumper. He gazed at the parking lot to see if Linda's car was there. But it was not to be found. *"I wondered what happened to her,"* he pondered.

It was nightfall at the Pleasure Palace Gentleman Club in downtown Dallas. The club's neon sign proudly flashes atop the building.

Inside the place, scantily clad female dancers performed arousing routines to the beat of pounding music. The club was packed with male customers. Among them was Peter, sitting at a corner table. Crystal, an attractive young black dancer, was with him. She was teasing and taunting him with her seductive moves. Peter was a family man with three beautiful children. Peter met and married his wife, Bobbie Jo, in Oklahoma when they were high school sweethearts. But lately, Peter's heart was with Crystal. Peter had deposited at least $500.00 in her tight thong every time he visited her, which was now often. When Crystal danced for him, she would bring her thong very close to his aroused face. So close, he could stick his tongue out and lick it. He was horny every time he left Pleasure Palace. He tried several times to lay her. But Crystal would have none of that. She was linked to a drug dealer, and besides, Peter wasn't her type anyway.

"Oh, Crystal... You know, you're the reason I come here. If you weren't here... I'd sue them!" Peter laughed. Crystal replied with a sensual smile.

Later that night, Henry sat alone in his recliner, the muted TV on CNN as usual. Going inside Henry's brain, one can see new neurons growing as sprouting axons and dendrites create new synapses in the synaptogenesis process and strengthen Henry's existing neurons, resulting in greater neuron complexity in his vast neuronal network. Henry received various forms of mental activity inside his visual cortex, such as streaming visuals from the many electrical impulses that streamed data. The left and right visual cortex of his brain signal to each other.

For example, Henry witnessed worshippers in a mosque somewhere in the Middle East.

An NBA game was in full swing somewhere on the West Coast.

Tom practiced his putting game in the living room.

Jim and Sara kissed passionately and then began to make love in his apartment.

Wayne was having a late dinner with his male friends at a restaurant.

Peter stumbled into bed beside his wife, who was fast asleep after his time with Crystal.

Henry was also busy monitoring Jack, who was in his sixties. He was face down and strapped to his bed. He wore only his briefs. On the bed with him was Jessica, a young white prostitute in her thong with a spanking paddle board.

In his recliner, Henry smiled at Jack's predicament. He forwarded a mental message to Jessica.

Jessica began to paddle Jack as she heard Henry's voice inside her head, *"Spank Maverick's contracts manager for being a naughty boy for not being with his sick wife in the hospital. He needs to retire. Spank him until he bleeds."*

Jessica spanked Jack harder. "Yes, I am going to spank you, sweetie. You should be with your wife. She is very sick. You need to retire."

He moans in pain. She hits him more times. Each time, Jack cried. "I thought you were going to cosplay with me? The dirty professor and the horny student? Is that not what we agreed to?"

She continued hitting him as Jack continued yelling in pain. "I like this better." Jessica pulled off his briefs. His ass was bruising red with blisters forming. Jack cried out for mercy as Jessica continued.

Meanwhile, Peter was fast asleep in his bedroom next to his wife. Soft moonlight spilled onto a photo of Peter, his wife, and three lovely children, sitting on the nightstand beside his heart pills by the bed. One of Henry's waves had penetrated a nearby wall and into Peter's head.

Henry's voice can be heard inside Peter's head. *"So, Peter, you want no one to control your life. Because you will always be what you choose to be. Nothing more. I expected more from you. You were being groomed for better things. Or should I say, you were..."*

Peter went into a dream. He was in a vacant room. It was lit. He was sporting a business suit and bound to a metal chair, his arms and legs shackled, with duct tape across his mouth.

The room became foggy. A soul-burning song began to play. Someone in bare feet padded across the room towards him. It was Crystal, as she emerged through the fog, wearing a sexy white teddy. She moved seductively towards him. Peter was aroused. She rubbed her body against Peter's arms and back. Peter's face started to turn red as Crystal was stimulating his sexual hunger for her. She moved in front of Peter and sat on his lap. Not saying anything, a grin came over her face as she started to untie her teddy. Peter became hot as his forehead began to perspire. Continuing in her silent, coquettish manner, she removed her teddy, tossing it to the floor. Her well-firm breasts were exposed, and her black nipples were pointing toward Peter's chest. Peter's eyes were so wide that they appeared as if they would come out of his sockets. She began to massage her breasts slowly as her tongue slowly worked its way to his left ear. "So, you want me. Ah?"

Peter responded by nodding his head several times like a woodpecker pecking on a tree. Still grinning, Crystal stood before Peter and began to run a hand slowly inside her thong. By now, Peter was sizzling. If he didn't relieve his sexual urge soon, he would explode like an overheated teapot. Crystal put a foot on his lap and slowly rubbed a hand up and down against her shapely leg. Peter felt he was being tortured. Seeing and feeling Crystal's sexy body against his business suit, and not being able to screw her.

With her foot resting on his leg, she caressed his steaming face. She bent forward and placed a gentle kiss on his sweating forehead. She then stood in front of him and turned around, with her small, tight buttocks looking at him. She then bent over, with her hands touching the floor. The thong was stretched so tight around her buttocks that Peter could see her thong being engulfed by her sexy ass cheeks. She then sways her tight ass for Peter, slowly and rhythmically, which seems to be in sync with the pulsating beat of the song. Oh, how Peter desired to reach over and lick her buttock with his hot tongue.

Several moments later, Crystal stood up and faced Peter. "Now for the final act." She reached over and began to unbuckle Peter's belt. Peter's face glowed with pleasure as Crystal yanked the belt from his waist. She then moved the belt like a whip, causing it to make popping sounds. She then moved around Peter, holding the belt.

Behind Peter, she then placed the belt around his neck. "Well, it's time, Peter." She then began to strangle Peter viciously. Tightening her grip on his belt, she pulled ever so hard. Peter's face was turning from red to blue, as he was losing oxygen fast. Holding on to the belt, she laughably said to Peter, "Yes. It's time for the kill."

Peter awoke from his nightmarish dream, coughing harshly as he held his neck. It appeared Peter was out of breath, fighting for his life. He reached and clutched his heart as he touched his chest. Peter pounded his fist against his heart.

Inside Peter's anatomy, Peter's heart was beating fast. Henry's wave had altered Peter's autonomic nervous system. It interacted with the thoracolumbar region of the spinal cord and traveled to the medulla oblongata. A signal flowed to the cardiac nerve. The sound of the heart became faster. The right and left ventricles pumped wildly.

Peter tried to reach for his pills. But it is too late. He's dead, as Henry's wave was no longer attached to Peter's head.

Chapter 16 - GOING HOME

Robert hated to leave Dallas after quitting his job at Maverick. But Robert felt he had no other choice. He also noticed that the inner ear pains he had been experiencing had stopped. Although the pains had stopped, Robert wasn't sure if Henry had stopped monitoring him. But the optimistic part of Robert felt he had. His sanity appeared to be back. Maybe those letters he forwarded concerning Henry's ESP might have done the trick. Unless, of course, it was simply wishful thinking on Robert's part. After all, Maverick Oil could dismiss Robert's accusations as pure fantasy or mere coincidence, especially if Henry ran interference with his ESP.

Robert also felt that only a few people knew about Henry's ESP besides his wife and Linda, such as Margaret and Kyle, who worked in Projects Management. Robert labeled them the Inner Circle. Therefore, only a few knew about his coke episode in the Maverick restroom stall. Robert was convinced that Henry mentally channeled Robert's misconduct to one of the Inner Circle members, who might have then spread his misdeed to non-Inner Circle members. But all this was behind him now. Robert felt the pressure of Henry's constant mental attacks was over—no more Henry and no more of his strange ESP behavior.

It was a nice, pleasant day in late February, and Robert was driving down I-35 with a small U-Haul trailer hitched to his car, thinking about his ordeal. The invasion of his privacy, the pains, the unfamiliar thoughts. The torture, the suffering, the torment. The guilt and fear in Robert's mind seem to have a hold on him. A grip he could not escape. It was as if Robert was being squeezed by one of Henry's octopus wave tentacles, squeezing his very life out of him.

It was maddening. It all seems so unreal. So, unbelievable. The worst part of his whole ordeal was that there wasn't anyone who could understand what he was going through. No one he knew was experiencing those sorts of problems—at least, no sane person. People with personal crises can seek help. But who was going to help Robert from Henry Honey? All the psychiatrist would say was that it didn't exist and prescribed him some pills. What was a prescription going to do when you were confronted with the likes of Henry Honey? Nothing. Not a damn thing. Yikes! However, the pains had stopped, but the bad memories remained. So, his mind was still asking the same question, a thousand different questions. *"Why me? Why me, oh Lord? I don't understand. Why?"*

Tears began to run down his dark brown eyes. The tears he could no longer hold back. In his despair, he said, "I know everything has a place in the universe, of Lord. I'm nothing special. But here I'm crying to you. Crying in my shame. Crying in my embarrassment." Robert's tears were now flowing like a river. He looked at his rear-view mirror to see if anyone was noticing. No one was. Robert then looked at the orange-reddish setting in the southwest. He now saw the city limit sign of Oklahoma City. Robert's tears now became tears of joy. Behind all those tears, a smile radiated from his olive face. He then shouted, "I'm Home. I'm Home. Thank God I'm home." Robert honked his car horn.

Yes, Robert was home at last. But to what? His parents' house? Was that what his celebration was all about? To come to his parents' home with some furniture and the clothes on his back? Was that his crowning glory? His destiny? Or was it because he was in the city where he grew up? Where he felt safe, and a terrible burden had been lifted off his shoulders. Robert's face then became blank as he pondered the implications. *"Where do I go from here? What will I do? I feel safe. But what now?"* The sun waved goodbye to Robert.

His whole family waited for him in the Yellowstone house as Robert carried a piece of luggage to the living room. There they were: Mr. and Mrs. Yellowstone, in their 50s, and their two daughters, Margie, just a couple of years younger than Robert, and Tammy, who had just turned eighteen. They all sat on the couch. Every one of them expressed a look of disgust. Their attitude was in sharp contrast to Robert's festive mood.

"I'm home." His parent said nothing. Not a damn thing. His sisters likewise did the same. Robert's mother was the first to speak. "I can't believe you did this!"

"Did what, Mom?"

Margie echoed her mother's concerns, "Come on, Robert. How could you?"

Robert was confused. "I don't get it. Why is everyone so upset?"

Mrs. Yellowstone turned to anger, "Henry Honey! That's what's wrong!"

"Who told you about him?"

"The private detectives at Maverick Oil company. They didn't mind telling us about the asinine letters you mailed concerning this Henry Honey person, and the cocaine you took at work!"

Robert's father chimed in, "Why would you do that? No one can read your thoughts. That's only in the movies."

Tammy looked at her older sister, "He definitely needs to see a shrink."

Mr. Yellowstone gestures to her, "Clam up, Tammy!

Margie was not finished. "What do you have to say for yourself?"

Mrs. Yellowstone turned to Robert with a softer expression, attempting to ease the tension." Darling, if the pressure at Maverick Oil was causing you to have these... weird ideas, why didn't you tell us?"

Robert stared at the floor and shrugged. Mrs. Yellowstone approached him and placed a comforting arm around him. "No one can read your mind except God, Robert."

Robert looked at his mother. Margie and Tammy left in disgust.

"The Maverick detectives were here?"

Mr. Yellowstone searched for answers. "Did he work with you?"

"Not really."

"Then, why him?"

"We'll save it for Dr. Brandt."

Robert looked at his mother. "Dr. Brandt?"

"The psychiatrist."

"I'm going to see a psychiatrist?"

"Yes. Or they will press charges on you."

The following week, Robert was in Dr. Helen Brandt's office. She was in her late 30s and rather attractive, with long brown hair. She sat across from Robert and took notes. She looked and smiled at him. "I want you to be honest with me."

"Yes, Dr. Brandt."

"You can call me Helen."

"Okay, Helen."

"Because if you are not honest, I cannot help you." She jotted something on her notepad. "We cannot analyze your personality until we tackle the belief that someone is reading your thoughts. Because it will be difficult to improve yourself if you believe someone is always reading your mind. However, I do want to discuss the restroom incident first. Was that the only time at Maverick Oil?

Robert fumbled with his response, "Y-e-a-h."

Dr. Brandt wrote," So, you never attempted to retake it at work?"

"No."

"Would you agree that indulging in cocaine in the workplace or any other place is not appropriate? And this habit needs to stop?"

"Yes."

"And, you will never do this again?"

Robert nodded.

She wrote a quick note. "How about your pains?"

"Oh...The pains in my ears? It hasn't occurred since I have been back."

Again, Helen wrote something down.

"When did you first believe Mr. Honey was reading your thoughts?"

The session continued as she probed.

Several weeks had passed, and Robert was seeing Dr. Brandt twice a week. Robert was unemployed but feeling no pain—no Henry Honey pains. He spent most of his time reading, jogging, or watching television. Dr. Brandt changed her schedule with Robert to weekly visits and decided he was ready to return to work. So, Robert began job hunting. But he was not having much luck.

This afternoon, he was lying on his bed watching a television rerun of "Gilligan's Island." His mother came into the bedroom as she stood by the door. "How did that accounting interview with the door company go?

"Not so good."

"Why?"

Robert's eyes were glued to the television set. "Just a hunch."

"How about Ford Air Force Base?"

"That went okay. But I don't want to work there."

"Your father and I work there. And it suits us fine. If you have worked there when I told you to. You have never gone to Dallas and got caught up with that cockamamie mind-reading stuff."

Robert said nothing with his eyes on the Gilligan episode.

"I knew you were headed for trouble."

Robert turned to his mom. "So, you're a psychic now?"

"Just like Grandpa."

They both giggled.

"Look," Mrs. Yellowstone said in a stern voice. "You haven't found that accounting opportunity yet. And it might take some time before you do. Just take this buying job for now. And before you know it. The right job will come along. Now, how about church?"

"I'll go this Sunday."

"Good." Mrs. Yellowstone then walked away. However, she went back to Robert. "Remember, you're seeing Dr. Brandt again next week."

Robert nodded in agreement while focusing on the television. Mrs. Yellowstone responded with a smile and left.

The following Sunday, Robert, Mrs. Yellowstone, and Margie attended church. Tammy stayed home with her father as she was battling the flu. When the service ended,

Robert, his mother, and Margie left the church and walked down some concrete steps.

Robert then turned to his mother. "Mom. I'll go ahead and bring the car around."

"Okay."

Robert left for his mother's car, which was parked a short distance away.

"You know Margie. I think Robert is finally turning around. He even said he's controlling his thoughts better."

"Let's just keep our fingers crossed, Mom."

Another month had passed, and Robert was still without a job. Robert didn't mind the unemployment. After all, he needed time to reflect on his future and forget about the horrible past at Maverick Oil. The pains stopped. However, he sometimes felt as if the pains were like a sleepy volcano waiting to erupt at any given moment. But Robert should not have those kinds of ideas. He should think positive thoughts. But sometimes, his mind would tell him it was not over.

Once in a while, Robert would read the Bible. It gave him some comfort, a reassurance that all was not lost. Just have faith, and your prayers will be answered; at least, that was what his mother told him.

Robert was reading the Bible and biting on an apple, hoping his prayers would be answered. Then the phone rang in the dining room. A moment later, his mother, who was not working that day, called out for him.

"Robert, you have a call."

Robert put down the Bible and left the bedroom with his apple. He then picked up the phone receiver.

"Hello."

He listened.

"Yes."

Listened.

"That sounds fine."

Listened.

"Okay. Bye." Robert then hung up the receiver. He called out for his mother, who was in the kitchen cleaning the oven. "Hey, Mom."

Mrs. Yellowstone left the kitchen and made her way to the dining room. She entered as she wiped her hands with a dish towel. Robert bit into his apple before nonchalantly delivering the news his mother had been waiting for: "I got the job."

"Which one?"

"The one at Ford Air Force Base."

A smile came over her face. "That's great. So, when do you start working?"

"This coming Monday."

"Do you know where to report?"

Robert bit into his apple again. "Building 243. But the pay is $5,000 lower than what I was getting at Maverick."

"But at least you have a job."

Robert bit into his fruit as he neared the apple core. "I suppose."

His mother then hurried back to the kitchen. "That's great, Robert."

Meanwhile, in her office, Dr. Brandt was reviewing her summary report regarding Robert's mental condition, sitting behind her desk on the computer. She just finished her daily morning visits to the state mental hospital, where she checked several of her more perilous patients. She read the report to herself.

"After two months of sessions with patient Robert Yellowstone. It is apparent he was suffering from a

mild obsessive-compulsive thought disorder. He was experiencing somatization pains, mainly in his inner ears, which reinforced his belief that a sadistic psychic was reading and attempting to control his mind. His constant fantasies that this illusory psychic was causing his persisting pains indicate this. It would appear that the thought disorder triggered his pain disorder. The pains also contributed to his random, unusual thoughts. His thoughts are now controllable. This, in effect, caused his pains to have less impact on his mental conditions and thus ceased."

Satisfied with her findings, she saved the report on her hard drive under a folder labeled "Robert Yellowstone."

It was decided to see Robert only if necessary.

Chapter 17 - COMMON DENOMINATOR

Linda was well aware of Robert's sexual virginity. Like Robert, she was also a virgin. She was caught up in her father's ESP. Wandering at times, how it would feel for a man to make love to her. A real man. Someone who could pick her up and gently lay her on the bed. And then passionately love her. Love Linda. Wanting every inch her man could give her.

But who was she fooling? Her constant reminder of her father's ESP would even make an intimate kiss seem embarrassing. Making love to a man was out of the question. Because of her situation, she at times felt sorry for Robert, as her parents labeled him a "pervert." Robert Yellowstone, that is. She knew how desperate and lonely Robert was. In some respects, she was in his shoes. She didn't have chronic pains or frequent unfamiliar thoughts, but she knew—the knowledge of Henry Honey.

Henry knew her daughter's sentimental feelings for Robert. Her kind heartiness. Therefore, Linda needed to be acquainted with Robert's constant lust toward women and those unfamiliar thoughts. Thus, her father would sometimes transfer Robert's thoughts to Linda, especially the unfamiliar ones. Henry wanted Linda to know firsthand how perverted Robert Yellowstone was, how her Lone Ranger daddy had to deal with such slime every damn day. How disgusting! However, Linda was not all naive to her father's ways. She knew firsthand what her father's ESP could do. She knew her father, at times, could transform a sane person into a kooky bird.

Once, when Linda was only eight, she wanted to prove to her parents that she was capable of being self-sufficient. So, Linda set up a stand in front of her parents' house.

Complete with 10 oz. paper cups, she was selling cool, delicious lemonade cups for twenty cents each. But the first hour of business was slow. Linda only had several thirsty customers. It was a hot, humid day. *"Surely there should have been more customers,"* she thought. Linda was crestfallen at the poor turnout. Her father, of course, also knew how her daughter felt. So, Henry went to work. Within ten minutes, several dozen or so neighbors came over to Linda's lemonade stand. Then, several dozen more. Linda raised her price to forty cents a cup after she sold the first three pitchers of her delicious lemonade. Before Linda knew it, she had collected $76.20 that day. Muriel wanted to help. But Linda said, "No." She planned to do it all by herself—no assistance from her parents. However, several years later, Muriel informed Linda that her daddy had brought the customers to her lemonade stand. Linda was upset, all right. However, as the years passed, Linda let it go and moved on to more pressing events in her life. (But what choice did she have?) Therefore, she sometimes wondered if some of Robert's mental problems concerning his thought pattern stemmed from her father's ESP.

She wasn't supportive of the chronic pains she knew her father was administering to Robert. She sensed that the pains might have caused Robert to conceive the unfamiliar thoughts consciously. Linda was not on the battlefield, feeling the machine-like pattern of pain her father was pulverizing Robert with. But she knew what her father could do to the human mind. And she felt sorry for Robert. She was merely an observer. Henry's blitzkrieg was eating away at Robert's mind, and Linda wondered what his breaking point was. Will he commit suicide? Will he go on a rampage and kill innocent people? Will he even attempt to go after Henry himself? Not that Linda was concerned, since Robert was not a threat to Henry. (No human was a threat to Henry except for Henry.) Yet the questions passed through her mind. But for now, there was peace. Robert felt no pain from Henry. His unfamiliar thoughts were kept to a minimum. Robert only had normal problems to deal with, such as finding a job, which he eventually did. But how long will the peace last for Robert? Only Henry knew.

Chapter 18 - SOME THINGS ARE WORST THE SECOND TIME AROUND

Robert drove into a sprawling military base. Various aircraft, people, and vehicles were everywhere. Robert stopped his car as two Airmen walked across a pedestrian crosswalk. He then proceeded to his final destination at Ford AFB. The military installation was established as a supply and maintenance depot at the start of World War II. The military base occupied over 5,000 acres of space, where 25,000 military and civilian employees worked various jobs. From above, one could observe the sprawling base below with its machine shops, aircraft hangars, office buildings, and landing strips. Of course, no building could be more than several stories high because of aircraft traffic.

An Air Control Wing of E-3 Sentry aircraft was stationed there. The base was also home to cyberspace activities and the Navy's Strategic Communications Wing. Ford AFB was also a vital logistical center. When Heads of State, like America's Commander-In-Chief, arrived in Oklahoma City, they usually arrived at Ford AFB rather than Will Rogers Int'l Airport. This was primarily for security reasons. Even the space shuttle piggyback ride from Edwards AFB back to Cape Canaveral would sometimes refuel at Ford AFB along the way. Now, Ford AFB would be home to Robert Yellowstone. He was going to work at a place where his parents, uncles, aunts, and cousins also worked. At least some of his uncles, aunts, and cousins. Yes, Ford AFB was vital for the Yellowstone's, as it was for the economy of Oklahoma.

In the main hallway of building #243, people were milling about. In fact, the area looked like a beehive of activity. Everyone had a purpose and knew where they were going, like automobiles driving down a vast highway.

Everyone except for Robert. He was walking around and looking like a chicken without a head. He was lost all right. But this was his first day on the job. The procurement job. The job he didn't want. After fifteen minutes of wandering, Robert finally asked an employee where the Automatic Test Equipment (ATE) for the B-1 buying section was. The B-1, better known as the B-1 Lancer, is a strategic bomber. The aircraft first entered service as a nuclear deterrent. However, it was later switched over to a conventional bombing role.

Robert walked past an array of small hallways. He took a right turn here and a left turn there. The maze of partitions gave the appearance that building #243 was a massive labyrinth for mice—a maze where paths and turns led to the cheese. In Robert's case, his cheese lay in the B-1 ATE purchasing section. Of course, he would have to work to earn his little piece. Robert finally entered the ATE procurement section, like a timid little boy attending his first class day of the new school year. His supervisor's office was right at the entranceway to the section. Robert immediately went to his supervisor's office, Mary Lou Anderson.

Mary's office was small but cozy, with her nameplate proudly displayed in front of her desk. She was sitting and writing. A portrait of her family was proudly displayed on a credenza behind her. She was in her 40s and would not be considered the type of woman Robert thought attractive. However, she was smart and knew her job well. And now she was Robert's boss. She was also a mother of two teenage children. Her husband was employed in the public sector as a maintenance chief at a local school district. She looked up at Robert and then laid her eyes back on the paper as she continued to write. Mary was not thrilled with her newly assigned buyer.

"You must be Yellowstone?"

Robert cleared his throat. "Yes, Ma'am."

"All right then." Mary Lou stopped writing and looked up. She managed to show a smile. "You can call me Mary Lou."

"Okay."

She stood and shook his hand. "Let me show you around."

"Okay."

They both began to walk past the empty desks of other employees. The section looked relatively deserted.

"As you can see, my section looked like a ghost town. That's because a major Contractor flew in and wanted to meet with my buyers. So, they'll at the conference room."

They both continued to walk as they turned a corner. Robert and Mary Lou then came to Naomi Carter. She was the only one at her desk. Naomi, twenty-three, had brunette hair and was rather attractive. She was Mary Lou's procurement clerk. As soon as Robert laid eyes on Naomi, he smiled at her, taken by her looks. Out of politeness, Naomi returned the smile with a "how do you do" grin.

"Naomi. I want you to meet Robert. He is going to be our new contract specialist."

"Hi, Robert."

"Nice to meet you."

"Naomi has been my procurement clerk for, let's see..."

As Mary Lou continued, Robert touched his right ear with dread. His face went into a startling reaction. He felt numb and disorganized, like a military soldier walking into a trap in the Vietnam jungle. His mind was in panic mode. *"Oh, Shit! The pains! They're back again!"* The pain was sharp and clear. It was if someone was poking him with a needle. A very sharp needle.

Mary Lou noticed the change in Robert. "Are you alright? Is it something I said, Robert?"

Robert quickly withdrew his hand. "No. Not at all."

"Well, let me show you to your desk."

Robert followed Mary Lou to his desk.

"Here you are."

Mary Lou left. Robert sat down. His hand found its way back to his right ear. An employee across a partition whistled. Another employee let out a cat-like meow. Hysterical laughter followed.

Meanwhile, Henry and Muriel laughed in their house as they sat in their usual recliners. Gigi was on her lap, and the cat meowed.

In a panic, Robert exited his desk and frantically walked down a hallway. He entered another hallway and saw a vacant telephone booth. He proceeded toward it. A young male employee flashed a smile as he walked by.

Unexpectedly, Robert had a wicked vision. He was standing behind Mary Lou at her desk, holding her tight with one hand, and placing a knife to her throat with the other. The vision quickly ended.

Robert clenched his ear as the pain intensified in his left ear. Two other employees gave Robert an odd look as he entered the booth. He heard several employees laughing loudly as he placed a call.

"Hello, Mom."

Listened.

"Yaw. The buying section is okay."

Listened.

"I don't know. Look. Something just came up."

Listened.

"The pains are back."

Listened.

Robert raised his voice in exasperation. "Hell! How do I know? I wasn't doing anything stressful."

Listened.

Robert said sharply to her. "Yes, I'll calm down. I just want a fresh start."

Robert listened as he ran a hand through his hair.

He said patiently, "Dr. Brandt can tell me something when I see her again."

Robert listened for a moment longer.

"Okay. Bye." Robert hung up the receiver, perplexed at the idea that Henry could attack him again. He stayed in the booth and momentarily stared into space, lost in thought. Robert finally realized his answer. Henry was monitoring him and stringing him all along. Now, the unfamiliar thoughts were back. The irritable laughter was back. The pains were back. And now Robert realized Henry Honey was back. Robert said defiantly, "I'm going to fight this." Several employees walk past Robert. They laughed at him as they walked by.

Later that day, Henry and Muriel sat on their chairs as usual. She was knitting, and he was watching the muted TV. Henry gave her a mental message. *"She's coming."* Moments later, Linda entered and sat next to her mother.

"Are you kidding me, Dad? You just had to, didn't you? Hasn't he been through enough?"

Henry replied mentally, *"I thought I told you to back off."*

"Stop with the mental talk!"

Muriel stopped knitting. "Fine, darling. If you want to talk, we'll talk. Now… His mind has to be redirected.

Lusting all the time..." Clicked her tongue. "In fact, he often fantasizes about having sex with you."

A broad smile came over Linda. "Really..." Linda changed her expression as she realized her parents' disapproval. "I mean, gross! But, still. Haven't you done enough? With all the thoughts? The mind game pains. He's been tormented way too much."

Henry added, "Those violent thoughts are coming from him. It represents a confused part of him. He doesn't know if he wants to have sex or kill them instead."

"He claims those thoughts initially came from you, Dad. Is that true or not?"

"Do you believe a pervert like him?"

"He never experienced a woman. He even goes to church." Paused. "Unless those thoughts are a diversion or mind game his subconscious is playing..."

Muriel interpreted, "His mind is twisted. Period!"

Henry gleamed, "You have to understand. I dealt with his kind back in Oklahoma. They're all the same. He can't even clean his ass half the time."

Muriel laughed.

"It's just personal, racial, and vengeful."

Henry said warmly, "Plus, there's another reason."

"What?"

"The firing of his neurons."

Linda looked confused.

"You see, dear, some neurotransmitters are excitatory, while others are inhibitory. If your brain is turned on by something it is receiving, let's say from the visual cortex, the neurotransmitters would be firing excitatory. In Yellowstone's brain, he appears to fire a lot of excitatory neurotransmitters when he has violent thoughts. Or unfamiliar thoughts, as he so conveniently puts it.

Therefore, his sexual hormones are speaking through his thoughts."

Linda answered back. "Thoughts can also be caused by underlying factors in our environment. And do you see anything in Robert's environment that would cause him to have those unfamiliar thoughts? Because I do. And that's his discovery of your ESP in his head. Besides, thoughts alone don't mean a thing. If I think I'm a bird, does that make me a bird?"

Muriel replied as she knit, "Now you're being ridiculous, child!"

"Just because Robert's brain might get excited if he has those thoughts doesn't mean he sexually prefers beating or killing women. Anxiety and excitement are both aroused emotions, and..."

Muriel interrupted, "Didn't he have thoughts of killing you?"

"He just wanted to see if Dad was reading his thoughts."

Henry said calmly, "Sex and violence do share some of the same neural circuits, neurotransmitters, and hormones of arousal. And both activities strongly stimulate the brain's reward and pleasure systems."

"I have friends who are into S&M..."

Muriel interrupts, "We know about your friends."

"And if they knew Robert like I do. They'll say he's not the sadist type."

Henry and Muriel smirk at her comments.

Henry snapped back. "You don't even know him as well as you think you do. And besides. How come you don't have trouble controlling your thoughts?"

Linda thought for a moment and looked at him sternly. "He didn't have to learn to accept your ESP like I did. I was raised in an environment where ESP was an everyday occurrence. But not him. If I had a problem understanding you, I could confront you or Mother. But who does Robert have? If he came to you, you would laugh at the poor guy and label him a schizophrenic, just like you did with the Maverick detectives. Now, tell me if that's a normal environment for him?" Linda touched her head. "I feel a headache coming on. Or wait... are you giving me this headache, Dad? What nasty images are you picking up now?" She stormed out of the room.

Muriel communicated mentally, *"The pains are not working. She has grown too attached to him, affecting our relationship with her."* She stopped knitting. *"He's going to be hard to eliminate from her mind."*

Henry, watching the TV, replied, *"I should have never allowed her to channel him."*

"You created a Dedicated Wave Connection," Muriel replied as she continued to knit.

Henry took a deep breath at her last words. Establishing a wave connection, which led to an emotional bond between Robert and their daughter, was something he did not want.

Chapter 19 - HENRY'S VICIOUS CYCLE

Robert saw Dr. Brandt several days after the chronic pain episodes began again. Dr. Brandt was surprised by the recurrence of the pains. She was sure the so-called somatization pains would not recur, especially when Robert was able to control his thoughts and was no longer consumed by his belief in Henry's ESP. Dr. Brandt was confident that Robert's pains were brought on by his delusions of Henry Honey's ESP again. But Robert insisted his thoughts concerning Henry's telepathy were minimal until the relapse of the pains. Now, Robert thought about Henry's frequency. Dr. Brandt believed that Robert was probably truthful about disassociating himself with Henry's ESP, at least on a conscious level, when he returned to Oklahoma.

However, with the regression of the pains, she felt Robert was still contemplating Henry's fictitious ESP on a subconscious level. Therefore, she began to change her diagnosis of Robert. His hallucinatory perception of Henry's ESP was more serious than she first believed. Especially if Robert's hallucinations of Henry's ESP were habitual in his subconscious. Dr. Brandt decided to put Robert on Stelazine (now only in generic form) to combat Robert's delusions of Henry. Dr. Brandt was not aware that Henry had started the vicious cycle again. But how could she if Henry's ESP was an illusion? Henry would usually begin with unfamiliar thoughts and then proceed to the pains.

A pharmacist handed Robert a prescription. He looked at the container to read the inscription. It read, "STELAZINE". He studied the label for a moment and walked off.

There were times Henry disapproved of Robert's

unfamiliar thoughts. This was due to Robert's manufacturing of unfamiliar thoughts without direct stimulus from Henry, which were inappropriate when they occurred.

For example, if Robert recalled a previous image of having sex with a sheep (initiated by Henry some time ago) in a pasture with human supervision, Henry would indicate his approval by administering pain on Robert's left side. Since in Henry's state of mind, Robert would not perform such an act with people observing him. So, that kind of sick, unnatural thought was acceptable in Henry's mind. However, if Robert imagined having sex with the same sheep without adult supervision, Henry would indicate disapproval with pain in Robert's right side. Muriel's attitude reflecting Robert was based on Robert's thoughts. It did not matter how outrageous or unfamiliar the idea generated by Robert was. Muriel would take all of the thoughts Robert received from Henry seriously. Which, of course, suited Henry and his mind control methods.

Applying negative (unfamiliar) thoughts to Robert's mind was not meant for him to act on those thoughts, per se. But meant to throw fear and anxiety in Robert's mind that he could act on such thoughts, given the right circumstances. That is, his mind was becoming unstable. If Robert had planned to act on unfamiliar thoughts, such as committing violent acts toward individuals, Henry probably would not have stood in the way. Depending, of course, on who the individuals were. He might even encourage it. But that was not Henry's intent. His goal was to illustrate how mentally unstable Robert was to his Inner Circle, such as Murial and Linda, by allowing them to channel in on Robert's thoughts.

Henry's frequency level of pain applied to Robert did

not alter Robert's unacceptability of the unfamiliar thoughts, nor did it keep Robert from thinking such thoughts either. (That is, Henry's mind control or brainwashing techniques involving pain were not successful in altering Robert's established personality or were effective stimuli in keeping Robert from having unfamiliar thoughts after the guilt/fear flight was established.) Therefore, utilizing pain to punish Robert for thoughts Henry disapproved of only further increased Robert's guilt/fear flight. As a result, Robert produced more of the same kind of unfamiliar thoughts. Hence, the catalyst for Robert's frequent unfamiliar thoughts produced by Robert was the guilt/fear flight. The flight was caused or increased by a high degree of anxiety, guilt, and fear. The pain was one way of establishing this state of mind in Robert. Although at times, if Robert were in a very relaxed or uplifting mood (which was not very often), the pains would not contribute to causing such a flight.

Henry's pain stimuli could create such a flight in Robert's mind. Depending, of course, on the severity of the unaccustomed thought and Robert's emotional state. But once the guilt/fear flight existed in the human mind, the flight determined the level of guilt and fear in the person's brain. It was natural for Robert to express some regret for experiencing unfamiliar thoughts. However, reacting to such thoughts in such a way as to harness the guilt/fear flight only added to the increased level of unfamiliar thoughts. And it was apparent that Henry knew the negative side effects the pains caused, but not Muriel. Of course, Henry would not let on what he already knew. Henry performed his usual acting and became just as concerned as Muriel was. "Why would Robert produce such ghastly thoughts?"

Henry also did not let on; he initiated most of Robert's unaccustomed thoughts. Robert had an idea that some of his unfamiliar thoughts had been created by Henry. The problem was, which ones? Therefore, a part of Robert's mind took on the responsibility that all unfamiliar thoughts were caused by himself, thus causing the guilt/fear flight.

What was the guilt/fear flight? The guilt/fear flight meant a state of mind in which the person believed they were capable of committing the very act that every thought would indicate, no matter the circumstance. Thus, all thoughts must be taken seriously. Thought and not action determine the person's true personality. The action was simply a by-product of the thought. So, the underlying principle was that the thought, and not the action, reflected the individual's true self. No matter how the thought was generated. Never mind if a person received an outlandish thought of blowing up Mount Everest. In the mind of a person who was under the flight, he or she would believe they were capable of doing so, even if the person did not have the means to perform such an act.

The filtering process, or as the Disney movie "Pinocchio" called it, conscious, had little impact in controlling fear induced by an unwanted thought if the individual was experiencing the guilt/fear flight. Under this flight, all thoughts should be taken seriously under every circumstance. Therefore, "Let your conscience be your guide" did not exist for a person under the guilt/fear flight. And if a person was under this terrible flight, it was very easy for Henry's ESP to manipulate the human mind. In other words, Henry would replace that person's consciousness. People under the flight would have difficulty utilizing their consciousness to convince themselves they could not perform evil acts based on evil thoughts. Instead, the flight would convince themselves they were just as capable of committing evil acts as well as good ones based solely on thoughts. Of course, it would be inevitable that the same person could develop a compulsive thought disorder. The kind of disorder Robert was experiencing. Someone once said, "You cannot stop birds from flying over your heads, but you can stop them from building a nest there." But to a person with the guilt/fear flight, any bird flying over a person's head will be able to build a nest there.

In a classroom at Ford AFB, Robert stood alone in front of a chalkboard. With a piece of chalk in hand, he finished a flow chart. The top of the chart is titled: "<u>HENRY'S VICIOUS CYCLE</u>"

The diagram featured various symbols commonly found in flowcharts. It attempted to explain the process of unfamiliar thoughts stemming from Henry's ESP, which created the guilt/fear flight in Robert's mind. The flowchart was as follows:

"HENRY'S VICIOUS CYCLE"

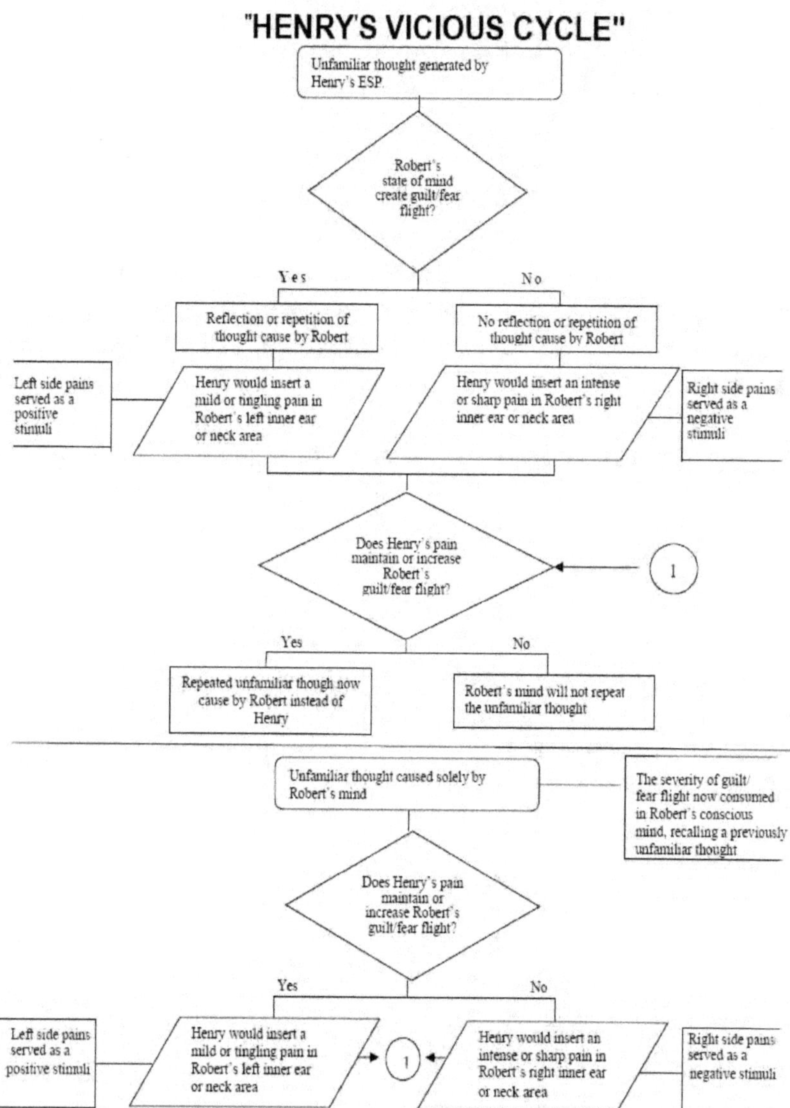

Robert saw a beautiful baby girl in her mother's arms at the checkout lane at a grocery store a week later. Robert was standing behind them. Suddenly, Robert had a bizarre feeling of wanting to hurt the baby. Robert didn't know why. Maybe Robert's paranoia came from previous unfamiliar thoughts, which seemed to build up over time—one on top of the other. Perhaps the endless barrage from Henry's senseless aerial attacks was finally taking its toll on Robert and was thus causing Robert to engage in delusional paranoia of hurting people. Or maybe the guilt came directly from Henry himself. Regardless, the guilt/fear flight was there, and Robert immediately tried to shake the guilt out of his mind. But it was too late. Once Robert had the awful guilt, Henry kept the guilt floating in Robert's mind by using pain to serve as the stimulus. Robert's guilt was now a heat-seeking missile. No matter how hard Robert tried to shake off the guilt, the heat-seeking missile would not elude him, as it came closer and closer in penetrating his mind to create a negative or unfamiliar image. Robert would change his state of mind to go through tunnels of sexual thoughts with women, roads of recreational images of the past, and the highways of ideas floating about his current career. But it didn't matter; the missile came closer and closer to achieving its objective. Oh, so ever closer. Robert's palms began to sweat. His heartbeat was pumping faster. His nerves were feeling the strain from the oncoming missile. Oh, how Robert wished he could avoid the guilt of hurting the little child. Oh, how he wished he could destroy the heat-seeking missile. And Henry, guilty as charged, loved to see the missile sink him again. Robert tried to maneuver the missile. But this time, the missile was very fast and very slick. And then, finally, the missile of guilt took over. And the horrible guilt about hurting that small child sent an image in Robert's mind. Robert produced a positive thought of not hurting the baby to counter the guilt. But Henry switched that thought into a negative one. Because Henry loved to switch positive thoughts with negative ones, as he had done so many times before. The Switching Technique was one of Henry's ways of confusing another person's mind. The negative image lingered for several seconds before fading away. Followed by a tingling pain in his left inner ear. And now the flight took off, and Robert repeated the negative thought of hurting the child again and again and again. So, the damage was done. Robert then closed his eyes. Feeling hurt and feeling ashamed by the thoughts.

Henry won, as a happy sigh of relief came over his wicked face. And, of course, Henry made sure the jury, consisting of Muriel and Linda, also received the horrible thoughts. Robert was a potential child abuser. Robert cannot be trusted around children.

Robert wanted to cry. He walked outside to the parking lot with his small bag of groceries. His eyes then cast over to the gray clouds hovering overhead. Guilt like this could last for days. And Henry knew it. But then the clouds broke, revealing sunlight that hit Robert like falling bricks. The light seems to tell Robert not to worry. Just forget about the damage and negative mental images, and continue with life. "I'm with you, the light was saying." So, Robert was like a damaged vessel, with mortar wounds in its bow and stern, but he kept sailing. Robert shook off the idea of hurting the child and went about his business, as the repetition of negative thoughts stopped to the dismay of Henry. Not happy with the desired outcome, Henry hit Robert with a sharp pain in his right inner ear. Robert touched his ear but kept his composure as he entered his vehicle and drove away. Henry's missile penetrated Robert's consciousness, but he survived the aftermath. Robert would then hope he could survive the next heat-seeking missile. The next negative thought, the next time around. Because there will be a next time. Robert doesn't know when.

Chapter 20 - CONSCIOUS DOOR

Several weeks had come and gone since the recurrence of the pains, and Robert was very tense indeed. Robert sat at his desk in his procurement section, aggressively biting on a pencil. On other days, he wandered on the grounds of Ford AFB, fighting off the increased anxiety he was experiencing. He sometimes looked like a frightened raccoon up a tree, with several vicious dogs growling below. Their teeth were snarling and ready to tear him apart. Robert was suspicious of everything around him. The employees, the phone calls. Anything resembling or sounding remotely human. Robert didn't trust anyone. He even started to distrust himself. Those unfamiliar thoughts. *"Was I capable of doing those nasty things? Have sex with animals? Masturbating in a public street? Committing violent acts against individuals? Hurting children?"*

Sitting behind his small desk, Robert would think his unfamiliar thoughts, which had been regenerated from his guilt/fear flights caused by Henry's Vicious Cycle. Over and over again. Yet Robert still managed to look sane. He did not socialize with anyone at work. However, he miraculously performed the duties required of him. But it was difficult at times, especially with those blasted pains and those Stelazine pills he was consuming. The pains sometimes cause Robert to think he was on a long leash, stretching miles from Henry's mind. Henry yanked on the leash every time Robert did something wrong. Any little item, Henry did not care for. Physically or mentally, it did not matter. Henry was mixing those pains with the unfamiliar thoughts. This caused Robert's mind to be in a sea of trouble. Like trying to navigate a small vessel in a terrible storm. And the pills, adding to the havoc in Robert's state of mind.

The phone rang at his desk. Robert immediately answered the phone in a suspicious manner.

"Hello. Contracting. Who are you, and what do you want?"

"Robert, is that you?" The concerned voice was that of Mrs. Yellowstone. She was calling from her work desk.

Robert sounded downcast, realizing it was his mother. "Yaw, it's me."

His mother sounded concerned. "How are you feeling this morning?"

"Oh. Okay, I guess."

"How're the pains?"

Rubbing the right side of his neck. "They'll still there, Mom."

"But you can still work, can't you?"

"Yaw, mom. I'm still hanging on. But these pills…."

"Everything will be all right. I have been praying for that. And remember. No one is reading your thoughts. You understand."

The pain on his right side flared into a ringing sound. The employees around him began to laugh hysterically as if they were laughing at Robert.

"Robert, are you there?"

Robert ran a hand through his hair. "Yes, Mom, I'm still here."

"I'll see you when you come home."

"Yaw, mom."

His mother hung up the receiver, and Robert hung up his. The laughter ceased.

Several weeks later, Dr. Brandt decided to take Robert off those Stelazine trick-or-treat pills. It turned out that Stelazine was an anti-psychotic medication prescribed to patients usually diagnosed as schizophrenic. Robert was experiencing an obsessive-compulsive disorder and not schizophrenia. All Stelazine was doing was giving Robert anxiety attacks. And there were days when Robert did not want to get out of bed. And when he did appear at work, he sometimes just sat behind his desk, chewing on an eraser stick to relieve the anxiety he was going through. He even wanted to quit and came close in during so. During his Stelazine days, Robert wrote a resignation note and placed it on Mary Lou's desk one morning, but returned to retrieve it an hour later. Robert changed his mind, and Mary Lou was at a meeting all morning. So, she never read the note. Therefore, Dr. Brandt decided to stay with psychotherapy. Mrs. Yellowstone was delighted at the decision. But Robert was too tense to rejoice.

Robert knew Henry wanted him to be aware that he was monitoring him, for there was nothing Robert could do to stop him. At first, Henry did not relish the idea. After all, Robert was an Outsider. But after a while, Henry favored the relationship. This was something new for Henry: having someone connected to the knowledge of his ESP who wasn't supposed to know.

With the knowledge of ESP in his mind, Robert started to believe there was more than one conscious level. In textbooks, Robert was familiar with the theories of the conscious, preconscious, and unconscious areas first introduced by Freud. However, Robert felt that Henry could not always control an individual unless the individual being monitored was aware of his existence and accepted how he utilized his ESP. In other words, Henry's mind control would be less effective if that person could not accept him. But how could that person accept him if he or she was unaware of Henry's ESP? As a result, controlling individuals who were not aware of Henry's ESP was not always possible. For example, if Henry placed a message in a person's mind to jump off a bridge into the river, who was unaware of his ESP, it would not necessarily mean the person would jump. Henry would have had better luck if he had persuaded that person to eat a turkey sandwich instead of a hot dog for lunch, because Henry needed to create the right environment for him or her to take the plunge down into the river. And that was not always easy. Placing messages using his telepathy to have people perform tasks they were accustomed to was quite different than placing messages in people's minds to perform tasks they considered strange unless they accepted Henry's application of his ESP.

Therefore, creating the right environment was essential to achieve the desired results. If Henry wanted to achieve a divorce or even domestic violence, he would have to create the right atmosphere. If a spouse has a high emotional tolerance, it could be challenging to provoke that person to lash out at their spouse during an argument. The outcome would probably result in a difference of opinion, as the husband would attempt to defuse the issue before his wife became emotionally irritated. However, if the husband with a low emotional tolerance level engages in a heated argument with his wife with an equally low tolerance level. The results could be disastrous for the couple. Henry had to create the right situation using telepathic messages, negative thoughts, and visual distractions, among other techniques. The result: Divorce. Domestic Violence. Broken Family. Music to Henry's ears if the spouse was a Negative Wave Reaction.

Of course, if Henry wanted a task to be performed, and his mental techniques were not working. He always had the option to locate another person to do his dirty work.

Some believe there are as many as seven levels of consciousness. There is also the theory of quantum consciousness, which explores how it is used to determine our own consciousness. However, all would agree that brain wave behavior determines different conscious levels. Or, to put it another way, different conscious levels determine the brain wave activity. Henry usually monitored an individual's brain activity without that person's awareness, as he occupied the person's consciousness unless he or she was a Single-Channeler. Therefore, there was no awareness interaction between Henry and the person he was monitoring. But if that same person was aware of his ESP existence, Henry had achieved total conscious awareness. Total Conscious Awareness in Telepathy means all conscious levels become aware of a specific entity. And that entity was interacting with the total consciousness.

The entity in Robert's case was Henry's ESP. For Henry, Total Consciousness Awareness meant the possibility of controlling all the conscious levels. Henry was occupying Robert's consciousness before Robert was aware of it. However, when Robert became aware that Henry was reading his mind, he opened his conscious awareness to his ESP. Therefore, Henry saw an opportunity to control Robert—provided, of course, Robert accepted Henry's ESP in his life.

If Robert had never accepted the book from deceased psychic John Derick, he probably would have never encountered Henry's ESP. All Henry could have done was to attack Robert. Unfortunately for Robert, Henry had achieved total consciousness awareness. Now, Henry wanted total control. Attacking and harassing Robert was just part of the plan. Therefore, the relentless pains, unfamiliar thoughts, and irritating laughing were tools Henry was using to control Robert. To be his Pavlov dog. The result was the awful guilt/fear flights Robert was now experiencing.

When Robert started to toss the Henry's Vicious Cycle in his mind concerning his unfamiliar thoughts, Henry was furious. Henry wanted to prove to Muriel that Robert was insane. A danger to society, abnormal, and anything else Henry could think of. Developing Henry's Vicious Cycle theory portrayed Henry in an evil light. Henry did not want to be viewed as the instigator of Robert's unfamiliar thoughts. Either directly or indirectly. Henry wanted to wash his hands of initiating the whole unfamiliar thought matter. Henry insinuated he had nothing to do with Robert's thoughts. All Henry was doing was monitoring the asshole. All the blame for Robert's thoughts rested squarely on Robert's shoulders. When Muriel mentally asked, *"How did Robert's thought problems develop?"* Henry would say (mentally), *"Robert is mad at the world. He is an angry man. Angry at my pains, angry at his failures. So naturally, he has to release his anger in some way. So, he has these violent thoughts. Weird sexual acts. Those unfamiliar thoughts, as he called them. How else could you explain it?"* Naturally, Muriel accepted Henry's rationale. After all, if anyone knew Robert's mind, it was Henry.

However, who would not react angrily to Henry's ESP? The way he was utilizing it? To control Robert. How in the world could Muriel think for one moment that Robert would accept the raping of his mind in a calm, rational manner? *"Oh! It's okay, Henry. Invade my privacy and destroy my career. I'll tie-toe through the tulips. For everything is fine with me. I won't get one bit angry that Henry is trying to destroy my sanity. Who would get mad at a person like Henry? Oh, Tweedledee. Oh, Tweedledum. I like Henry invading my mind."* Of course, Robert was angry. He wanted to kill Henry and thought about it often. Who could blame him? But Robert was not going to take it out on the world. Henry desired to create such an environment for Robert to display such hatred. Maybe become an active shooter. Fortunately, Robert abstained from such behavior. *"Why is the world to blame for Henry's evil acts on me? Henry is probably monitoring their minds too. They'll simply not aware of it".* However, as long as Robert had unfamiliar thoughts, Henry looked really good in the minds of his Inner Circle.

Believing in Henry's ESP felt like a curse for Robert, an evil curse. Like the guy transforming into the werewolf when the moon was full. The problem was that the moon was always full for Robert. Robert remembered something a Catholic nun told him when he was quite young. "The devil will knock on your door. But he will not control you if you do not let him in." But Robert opened the door for Henry and was now fighting to control his mind. Robert would sometimes experience negative thoughts of employees at Ford AFB hanging him by a rope on a tree and executing him for believing in something so weird. So, grotesque. Robert could hear them say, "Come on, gang, let's hang that bastard. Yaw, let's hang him." So, the employees put a rope around Robert and dragged him until they came to a tree by the parking lot. Tied the rope to a steady branch and then let Robert hang. They were hanging him for believing in something so ridiculous. As Robert's corpse swags on the rope, he would then imagine them, saying, "Hey, we don't want Henry knocking at our conscious awareness door. Keep Henry Honey to yourself. You bastard."

While Robert was sitting at his desk and caught up in his thoughts of being hung by his co-workers, Henry took a particular interest in Harold Thompson's consciousness.

Harold was a black employee who sat several desks from Robert. He was a relatively large man, aged forty-five, and had been employed as a contracting officer at Ford AFB for five years. He was a veteran, proud to have served for the U.S. Army during his tour of duty. Harold was also married with no children and made friends at Ford AFB.

Harold stood with a paper and walked away from his procurement section. Harold continued down a hallway until he came across a copier. As he copied the paper, an attractive female employee walked past him. Harold eyed her as he thought to himself. *"Hmmm. What a delicious-looking fox. The things I could do with her in bed."* Harold retrieved the papers from the copier and returned to his buying section. Harold sat at his desk while Robert was still sitting behind his. Robert looked tense as he attempted to work on a small contract buy.

Later in the evening, Harold opened the front door and entered his house after another day at work. Harold lived in a modest subdivision on the outskirts of the city. As always, he closed the door loudly. "Joann, I'm home." However, he did not hear a response from his wife, a woman he had been married to for almost ten years. Harold then decided to walk over to the dining room.

To his surprise, the dining room table was barren. His wife walked in from the hallway. She was a thirty-year-old brunette woman. She was petite, with big hazel eyes.

Without looking at his wife, Harold said, "Where is my supper?"

Nonchalantly, Joann replied, "I didn't cook anything."

"Say what?" Harold said sharply.

"I was busy doing other things."

Harold's dark eyes were now clearly focused on Joann. "What things?"

Joann grinned. "Shopping."

"Shopping:" Harold then walked closer to Joann, almost standing on her toes, as he looked down at her angrily. "You know I like supper to be ready when I come home from work. Besides, who said you could go shopping? My unemployed housewife!"

"I did," Joann said defiantly. "And for now, on. You prepare your supper."

Joann's remarks angered Harold to a higher level. He responded by slapping her hard across the face. Harold stormed out of the dining room as Joann began to cry.

Harold then entered the master bedroom and immediately went to a dresser drawer. He retrieved a porn magazine. He then walked over to the adjoining bathroom and started to talk loudly to himself. It was as if he wanted Joann to hear his every word. "Damn that bitch! I should have never married that piece of white trash in the first place."

Harold walked over to turn on the light switch in the master bathroom. He slammed the door behind him, unbuckled his belt, and dropped his pants. He then sat on the open toilet seat with the magazine in his hands, deciding which pictorial he would fantasize about for the evening.

Several hours later, Harold was sleeping alone with the moonlight shining through the window curtains. Joann had packed a suitcase and decided to spend several days with her mother until Harold cooled down. But not until Harold threw a few more curse words at her.

So, Harold was sleeping, dreaming his dreams before another new day at work. His heartbeat was steady at 72 beats per minute.

Meanwhile, a serious-looking Henry was monitoring Harold from his bed. Henry and Muriel slept in different bedrooms, and Henry preferred it that way.

With Harold fast asleep, Henry's brain wave touched and felt parts of Harold's autonomy. It was Henry's turn to apply his brand of justice. Harold was an abusive husband and should have been charged with domestic violence and served time in jail. However, Henry wanted more. So, like a skilled surgeon, Henry was now ready to operate. Henry's wave penetrated Harold's right ventricle and connected to the left ventricle of his heart.

Harold was still fast asleep, appearing comfortable in his bed. His heart continued to beat a brisk 72 beats per minute.

Inside Harold's anatomy, both ventricles were sending electrical signals rapidly. Without warning, Harold's heart took off like a rocket, beating furiously.

Harold began kicking in his bed, his heart beating over 140 beats per minute. He opened his eyes and grabbed his throat as his heart accelerated to an even 200 beats per minute. Harold then began to regurgitate while Henry increased the frequency of his wave. Harold's heart was going through contractions. Suddenly, Harold's bodily functions stopped as his heart beat no more. His face was lifeless, as his eyes and mouth were open. Harold was dead.

Several days after Harold's untimely death, Robert sat at his desk, reading a sympathy card addressed to Harold's wife, Joann. Other employees' signatures were also on the card. After reading the card, Robert signed his name.

With Henry, Robert experienced the same antics involving sexual desires he encountered in Dallas. Henry would do everything he could to make Robert feel guilty for every temptation he had with women. For instance, someone unexpectedly coughed, laughed, or stared at him. And, of course, the usual pains. These sorts of things made it difficult for Robert to cope with.

An hour after he signed the sympathy card, Robert was waiting to make a copy of a memo. He was standing behind Naomi, who was busy at the copying machine. Robert stared at her as he eyed her shapely legs. Henry did not like that at all. So, one of Henry's waves traveled into Naomi's inner ear area and made contact with the diaphragm muscle. Naomi then began to cough horribly. Was she coming down with something awful? But Robert kept on staring at her, oblivious to her sudden ailment. Naomi suddenly stopped coughing as Henry had her turn around and gave Robert an annoying glare. Robert expressed guilt for his staring and smiled back at her. She then continued copying as he stood timidly. He did not want to look at her anymore. He felt ashamed, admiring her beauty—that awful stare of his. Two employees walked past the copier and stared at Robert sternly. Robert could feel their stare as he turned in their direction. Robert then turned back to look at his memo. He kept his eyes on the memo and would never stare at Naomi again. No matter what the situation was.

Robert was clear enough to know he had to do something about his lack of relationships with women. It might sound like that would be the last thing he should worry about. Considering that no woman in her right mind would want to date a man if she knew he was being tormented by Henry. But that was precisely what Robert felt he had to do. Since Henry was trying to drive Robert away from them. Robert remembered walking to his car with a small bag of groceries. An attractive woman in the parking lot was walking to her car from the store. She immediately caught his eye. A pain then traveled the right side of his inner ear. The pains were very irritable, biting into him. Henry mentally told him, "I am *monitoring you, so beware!"* Robert's mind was now more concerned with the pain than the attractive woman in the parking lot.

Robert needed help dealing with Henry's ESP. He realized at Maverick Oil that Henry was psycho. And it was his ESP that allowed him to act out his psychopathic behaviors. But where to turn to? His psychiatrist was no help. All she would do was lock him in a mental hospital and throw away the key. No, Robert needed to try something different. So, a desperate Robert drove through town until he came across a parapsychology organization, "Mind Science Institute," two weeks later. He called earlier to make an appointment with them.

Robert walked into the Institute. He approached the young receptionist.

"Can I help you?"

"I came to see Brad Lance, the parapsychologist."

She looked at the appointment log and smiled back at him.

"Have a seat. I will call you when he's ready."

Robert sat down on a vinyl cushion chair. Beside him was a magazine rack with various issues. Robert retrieved the latest issue of Time magazine and began to leaf through it.

The receptionist looked up at Robert. "Mr. Brad Lance will see you now. Just go straight down the hallway. His office is the second door to your right."

Robert forced the issue back into the crowded rack, partially crumbling the magazine cover in the process. He stood and proceeded to walk. However, he stopped by the receptionist's desk. "Thank You."

She again smiled back at him. "You'll quite welcome."

Robert then continued to walk down the hallway.

Brad, a large man in his 50s, sat behind his desk. He had a booming voice and a bandholz beard. He wore a business suit. He heard a knock on the door.

"Please come in." Brad stood as Robert entered. They shook hands.

"Hello. I'm Brad Lance. You must be Robert Yellowstone!"

"Yes."

Robert sat. Brad closed the door and took a seat behind his desk. Behind him were bookshelves filled with materials about parapsychology. Diplomas certifying Brad as a parapsychologist hung on a wall. Robert's gaze fell upon an unusual painting above Brad's desk, also on a wall. Brad noticed his interest.

"It's a copy called HIDE-AND-SEEK by Pavel Tchelitchew. It's supposed to capture the interplay between the mind and the environment."

Robert continued to stare at the painting.

"So, you're interested in becoming a member of the Mind Science Institute?"

Robert turned his attention to Brad. "Uh...Yes. Yes, I am."

Brad retrieved a pamphlet and handed it to Robert. "This will explain the history, purpose, and goals of the Institute, as well as the dues."

Robert glanced at the pamphlet.

"So, what's made you interested?

"Oh... I can't say."

"Well, is there any particular branch of PSI that interests you?"

"Telepathy."

"Is that so? Well, it's considered one of the most widely reported parapsychological phenomena. Have you ever experienced a telepathic episode or some other form of PSI phenomena?

"Well...When I was sixteen.

"Really? Tell me about it."

"I was in a car accident about a mile from my mom's. And about ten minutes later, my mom drove to the accident. But, no one told her about it."

"You don't mind if I smoke my pipe?"

"Oh, no. Not at all."

Brad pulled a pipe out of his desk drawer. "Go ahead, Robert. Don't let me interrupt you."

"My mother had a precognition about the accident. It's like she knew the accident would happen before it happened. And it's not the only time with my mom."

Brad lights his pipe and puffs on it. "What your mother was experiencing is what I call premonition. It is usually associated with some form of crisis. It serves as an early warning signal." He puffed his pipe. "Anyone else had other experiences you would consider PSI?"

"Ahh... No. Just my mom. Well... There was my deceased grandfather. He made his money as a psychic. You know, one of those who can tell you your future.

Sometimes, he will use tarot cards. He claims he can sometimes pick up other people's thoughts." He shrugged. "He said I, too, have this in me. But I don't believe in any of it."

Brad puffed on his pipe. "Your grandfather was a clairvoyant."

Robert looked confused.

"Fortune Teller."

Nodded. "Oh…Sure."

Have you ever picked up on someone's thoughts?"

No… No way."

"Clairvoyants are not Telepathic. But with your grandpa. …Who knows… Well... Concerning telepathy, society is not able to see it for what it is. Because we exist in it. It is not separable from our perception of it." Puffing on his pipe. "Tell me, do you think the experience with your mother was unusual? Or, to put it another way, abnormal? Because that is how society generally views parapsychology. As something..." Brad gestures, waving an arm in the air. "Supernatural."

"So, it's possible for someone to monitor another person's thoughts all the time while monitoring the thoughts of others? Could they hack into a person's nervous system and manipulate it?"

"What do you mean, manipulate the person's nervous system?"

"Attack the nerves, causing things like neck or inner ear pains. Excess bowel movements."

Brad smiled. "I don't believe so."

"What about the monitoring?"

"Random telepathy exists, but constant monitoring, no. After all, the psychic would eventually have to sleep. Now, dream-telepathy, where an individual would randomly transmit images to a sleeper during rapid eye movement, does exist. But even the best psychics cannot communicate all the time, and certainly not to multiple people simultaneously."

"So, what advice would you give a person who believes such a person exists?

"Go see a psychiatrist."

"A psychiatrist?"

"Do you have any proof that such a person exists?"

"Ahh... Well no. Not exactly. But he torments me. Taps into my brain at will, wreaking havoc. God knows how many other people he is doing this to."

"So, you know the person's identity?"

"Yes. And I would do anything to see him dead!"

Brad's face lit up. "Why don't you document your experiences? Gather facts. A discovery like this, if proven, would have a huge impact on the medical and scientific community."

Robert was dumbfounded.

"Find out how electrical impulses in this person's neurons travel as they receive signals from other neurons from other humans. Find out how the various neurons communicate with each other through axons as electrical impulses send messages back and forth concerning other people's brain activity. Like a huge fiber optics network that lit up, data transfers to various parts of his brain. The electromagnetic fields will be extremely active, creating negative and positive charges. And it's this energy force that aids this individual, as you put it. Tap into your brain and wreak havoc with the nervous system."

He grabbed a lighter from his pants pocket and re-lit his pipe, as Robert looked like a confused child learning about the birds and the bees.

"No. Instead of wanting to kill him, I would embrace his unusual gift and learn from it." He smiled. "But, of course, you have no proof. And therefore, it can be safe to say your mind is playing games. And in conclusion, as I indicated before, you need to see a shrink." He puffed his pipe and grinned at Robert.

Robert exited the Institute, threw the pamphlet into a trash can, and walked away. He was visibly upset as he drove. He turned on the radio. A song from a musical group entitled "INTERCONNECTIVITY" began to play.

"See a psychiatrist! I probably know more about telepathy than he or that damn Mind Science Institute." He took a deep breath. "But I should write about this. This will be my goal." The singer began to sing the song on the radio.

"With one thought and one call
 You will be, within interconnectivity
 It binds you, as it links you
 For it tells you, like synchronicity
 Interconnecting principle, psychic intellectuals
 Connecting into the invisible
 With data so incredible
 Institutions are insensible
 Yet the knowledge is so accessible."

As the singer sang the first verse, Robert visualized Henry sitting alone in the den, watching the muted TV on a CNN newsreel. Suddenly, everything faded into black and white. Henry's skull transformed into a magnetic resonance image. Simultaneously, a bright gold, hair-thin laser wave protruded from his skull and extended through several walls. His wave now produced other waves as it connected to other brains nearby. Now in full color, one of Henry's waves was on the Eiffel Tower at the Observation Deck.

Several people enjoy lunch. Once again, everything turned to black and white as one of Henry's bright gold-colored waves penetrated everyone without their knowledge.

The second verse began
"Interconnectivity will touch you, as you act
This interconnection
This universal spirituality
It will connect, as it binds
This unknown human mystery."

During the second verse, Robert visualizes himself inside a woman's brain in the tower. An array of colorful neurons flashes electrochemical messages to each other. A bright gold wave from Henry entered her brain, latching onto a firing neuron and penetrating it. When the neuron fires to other neurons nearby, Henry's wave latches to the neurotransmitters of the firing neurons.

Robert nodded along with the piercing words from the singer singing the third verse.
"Interconnecting principle, psychic intellectuals
Connecting into the invisible
With data so incredible
Institutions are insensible
Yet the knowledge is so accessible."

The song went into a short instrumental. Robert visualized a movie theater with a comedy playing on the big screen. In the audience, Jim slipped his arm around Sara. They eat popcorn by the handful, laughing away at the movie. A single gold-colored wave originating from an exterior wall was in Jim's head. The wave traveled in and out of his head and then did the same to everyone else in the theater. But everyone was oblivious to the waves. While visualizing this in his mind, Robert pondered, *"Then, it came to me. All the waves in and out of Henry's head were created by energy all around us. The waves interconnect with each other, producing a wireless brain network that can create a Brain Wave Network. All our brain waves can be interconnected with each other. We just have to know how to tap into it."*

The singer continued with the fourth verse.

"The energy network knows me as it knows you
For it will create interconnectivity
An atomic cause that placed the call
An interaction law that started it all
Interconnecting principle, psychic intellectuals
Connecting into the invisible
With data so incredible
Institutions are insensible
Yet the knowledge is so accessible."

As Robert heard the fourth verse, he visualized a single wave from the movie theater entering the lobby. Like before, it infiltrated everyone's minds as the Brain Wave Network expanded.

Robert now observed a NASA space shuttle travel through space, passing by Earth. Then, the planet turned black and white as one of Henry's gold-colored brain waves from Earth was monitoring the astronauts in the NASA space shuttle. The wave continued to travel through space.

The song went into another instrumental. Robert's mind visualized two cosmonauts doing their daily work at the International Space Station. Everything turned to black and white as Henry's wave penetrated and entered each of the cosmonauts' skulls. Everything turned to color as they laughed and talked in Russian. The cosmonauts were unaware of Henry's wave. Robert pondered the following as he visualized the cosmonauts in space. *"And once the wave travels through time and space, connecting with another wave, it increases in frequency. And then when two waves meet, their amplitudes add. Wave energy then goes as amplitude squared. Therefore, the wave energy is quadrupled when the wavelength amplitude is doubled. And Henry is the master server in the network. He has access to the flow of waves. The brain waves.*"

Robert sweated, exhilarated. This discovery blew him away. The singer continued.

"The connectivity is vast, as it expands
We try to understand what we did not plan
Quantum mechanics talks creating electrical thoughts
For this is human interconnectivity, human interconnectivity…"

Robert pounded his fist against the steering wheel, matching the beat of the remaining song with the singer.

"Interconnectivity. Interconnectivity.
Interconnectivity. Interconnectivity!"

Robert ran a hand across his sweaty forehead. He shouted, "Yes, Interconnectivity!

The song continued with the final instrumental. He pondered, "*And since Henry can mentally move within the network at will, he could expand his waves through the network, increasing his wave energy as he absorbs other brain activities. And thus, he never has to sleep. Always on the ESP high. Transferring data like the Internet and even creating a synchronicity event.*" A puzzled look came over Robert. "*Henry wasn't just another psychic. He was something much more.*" Robert grinned as he talked to himself. "I called him a... Wave Master." Then, a worried look came over his face. "Oh God, how could you?" Robert's foot pressed down on the accelerator.

His car sped down the street as the song ended.

Meanwhile, Henry and Muriel sat in their recliners, the television muted, as they observed Robert in their minds.

Muriel was fuming as she spoke to him in anger. "How did he figure it out? How?"

Henry shrugged his shoulders, "I wouldn't know."

"This degenerate knows more than he should."

Muriel turned to the television, which was now showing a live broadcast of the White House. Henry smirked as he closed his eyes.

Robert was correct about the link between the Brain Wave Network, which Henry could create with his ESP through interconnectivity, and produced synchronicity events. The elements of the network were always there based on science. It just needed a Wave Master to connect and move data in and out of various brains. And Henry was that source. And when it came to synchronicity, he would do things where a person, clergy, or even a scientist would think synchronicity-type events were caused by chance, or God directly caused those events to unfold. Within this vast network, a Wave Master can affect many individuals without their knowledge. The Internet seems primitive when compared with the Brain Wave Network.

Some time ago, Henry came across a young woman named Mary. She was young, attractive, and from Oklahoma. Henry was initially taken by her because her physical features resembled his mother's when she was young. In fact, Mary could pass for Henry's mom. Over time, Henry looked upon her in a favorable light. And as a result, she could do no wrong. Henry would utilize his ESP to make

Mary's path easy for her to achieve. Her looks and personality created a Positive Wave Reaction. Because in the eyes of Henry, she was as perfect as they come.

When Mary turned twenty-five, she was engaged to a young fellow named Sam. Henry saw Sam as a good choice for Mary. He was about the same age as Mary, Caucasian, hard-working, moral, and handsome enough to win Mary's heart. As the wedding approached, Mary desperately sought to purchase a particular wedding dress she had seen in a magazine. Mr. Wave Master knew precisely where the dress could be located and utilized ESP in the Brain Wave Network to direct Mary to a particular older lady. The lady owned a dress shop in Tulsa and had the specific wedding dress in her inventory. Mary was a tax preparer, and the lady needed someone to prepare her taxes. Therefore, Henry had the lady contact Mary to prepare her income tax return.

Neither one had ever met before and, therefore, were strangers. As they began to chat about tax-related issues, the subject of the wedding dress came up. Of course, the lady informed Mary she had the dress for sale.

To Mary, it was a miracle. After all, she prayed to God at her local church in Broken Arrow to locate that particular dress. To others, it was a mere chance. And to a few, it was synchronicity at work. But in actuality, Henry acting through the Brain Wave Network caused the two unrelated events to occur together to create a meaningful conclusion. And neither was the event of the lady meeting Mary to prepare her taxes by chance. However, not all synchronicity events are caused by a Wave Master through the Brain

Wave Network. Other forces may also contribute to these occurrences. Something Henry could not or did not want to explain.

Chapter 22 - WHO CAN I TRUST?

The following nightfall, Henry sat alone in his recliner in the den. The family cat, Gigi, sat on his lap. Henry's eyes stared at the muted TV. However, his mind was on other important matters he had been monitoring. The trap had been set.

He was monitoring a 1968 Plymouth GTX, which rolled into the parking lot of a three-story office satellite building owned by Maverick Oil on the outskirts of town. It parked military-style in front of the facility. In her late 30s, Jana was the first to exit the car from the passenger side. She wore a light jacket and carried an over-the-shoulder duffel bag. In his 40s, Max was next to exit the vehicle, followed by Joe, the driver, in his early 30s.

A worried look registered on Max's face, "You're sure it's empty?"

Jana responded with a self-assuring smile, "Relax, would you? I told you everyone leaves by five."

"Even security?"

Jana shook her head in frustration, "Yes."

Jana headed up a small flight of stairs, clearly unconcerned. Max and Joe followed, nervously checking their surroundings. Jana swiped her Smart Card in a magnetic stripe reader by the door. It flashed green. She opened it, and they entered. Max and Joe looked around. They both noticed an apparent lack of surveillance cameras. Jana led them confidently, frustrated by their timid actions.

"Focus. There are no surveillance cameras, alright."

Max responded, "You sure? You'd think Maverick Oil would want to... I don't know. Protect their assets? They are one of the largest oil and gas outfits." Paused. "They're not stupid, right? I mean, no security? No cameras?"

Jana answered, "Maverick doesn't bother with security. Not

here."

Joe was equally surprised, "That's wild."

Max looked around. "So, where are the prints?"

Jana motioned to them, "Follow me." Jana walked to an elevator, which took them to the third floor. It opened, and they exited.

Max asked Jana, "Why don't they keep this stuff in the main corporate office?"

Joe echoed his concern: "Yeah."

Jana ignored them as they walked toward another door. A sign posted next to it read, "RESEARCH & DEVELOPMENT." She swiped her card in the reader, opened the door, and they entered.

Jana switched on the lights. The floor was a maze of empty desks and a scattering of suboffices. Jana approached a series of file cabinets as she had done many times before as a Maverick employee. She entered a code on an electronic lock in one of the cabinets and pulled on the lever. The cabinet opened. She retrieved a set of folders. She opened one of the folders and laid out the schematics, blueprints, and other related materials on a nearby desk. "Here are the technicals for the next-generation reciprocating gas compressor."

Max glazed over the material. "And the patent hasn't been filed yet?"

"Nope." She then handed the folder to Max. "Here. Go make copies."

"Where?"

"The photocopier is right over there." She gestured toward a copier. "Or do I have to walk you there too?"

Max headed over to the photocopier.

Jana looked at the contents of another folder and handed it to Joe. "Here. Be careful."

Joe nodded and left.

After making the copies, Jana rechecked them and placed

them inside a catalog-size envelope. Satisfied, she then put the envelope in her duffel bag. After refilling the folders in the cabinet, they quickly exited the Research and Development department and reached the elevator.

Jana turned to Max. "When will we get paid?"

"Once the Chinese get the info."

The elevator door opened, and they entered. The elevator lurched and then dropped smoothly.

"Remember, I get half the cut."

Max answered Jana back sarcastically, "Really?"

Joe responded with a grin.

The front door of the satellite building opened. They exited. Max and Joe appeared nervous. They looked around for anything suspicious. Jana ensured the front door was locked as Max and Joe quickly entered the vehicle. Joe started the engine as Jana jogged over. Just as she opened the car door, several security officers with guns drawn appeared from around the corner of the building.

One of the security officers shouted, "Stop and back away from the vehicle!"

Jana smiled, "Officer, I work here. I just came to finish up some paperwork.

The officer was unfazed. "Again. Back away from the vehicle, now."

Jana glanced at Joe. He nodded as if he understood. Jana then quickly jumped into the vehicle. The tires screech as the car roars off. The officers responded with gunshots as bullets hit the vehicle. A few of the bullets manage to hit the back window, shattering glass. Joe headed for the entranceway but was blocked by a patrol car. With no other option left, Joe drove through a fence. The vehicle escaped from view. Joe's car was barreling down the street.

He was frantic, "You said there wouldn't be security! What

the hell was that?"

Jana was equally surprised. "I don't know Joe. Someone must've tipped them off."

"I didn't get involved to get caught. I've been in the slammer one too many times. I'm not going back!"

"Hey! I didn't want you to get involved. That was Max's idea. Right, Max?" Max did not respond. "Max?" She turned to him. But Max was lying dead in the seat behind them. She noticed a gunshot wound to his head. She screamed, startling Joe, who nearly lost control of the car.

"What the hell?"

"Max is dead."

"Shit!"

"Pull over."

Joe swung the car to the side of the road, grinding to a halt. They both look at dead Max.

Joe ran his hands over his hair. "Those fuckers."

"We've got to get him out."

"What?"

"There's a dead body in our car!"

"You mean my car?"

"Who cares, Joe? Do you want the cops to find him dead in your car?"

Joe exited the car and pulled Max's limp body out. He dumped him in the grassy area near the vehicle. Sirens can be heard in the distance. Joe hurried back to the car. Joe hits the gas, and the car lurches forward, skidding back onto the road.

"How fast can it go?"

"This GTX has a 440 Super Commando. It's not as fast as the Hemi, but it'll do." Joe's GTX sped off into the night.

About twenty more miles later on a state farm road, Joe slowed down as he approached an intersection. The road was otherwise empty, and the sirens had ceased. He decided to run the red light and kept going. "I think we ditched them. "

Jana checked behind them. Satisfied, she turned toward Joe. "Now what?"

"I know a nice wooded place not far from here."

As Joe drove, Jana gently touched his shoulder. "You handled yourself well back there."

"Yeah? ... Yeah."

 "Max told me you were sort of a nerd."

"He did?"

"But... I can see he was wrong."

Suddenly, sirens were heard again. Joe looked into his review mirror as Jana turned to see what was behind them. Two police cars were approaching fast. Joe slammed his foot onto the accelerator. Jana tightened her seat belt.

"Where did they come from?"

"Don't worry. I'll lose them."

Joe spotted a side county road. He took a quick left turn onto the road. There was silence. A few moments later, both police cars were approaching. Joe made a quick turn onto another county road. He came to a fork in the road and took the right route. He decided to turn off his headlights. Joe and Jana watched the police cars follow another road. They both fell back into their seats, relieved.

"They went the other way."

Joe stopped his vehicle. With his car lights back on, he quickly turned around. He decided to drive hard back to the main road.

Joe was baffled. "It's like they knew where we were going."

Suddenly, Henry's voice was heard in Joe's head. *"It's time to sleep, Joe. Sleep forevermore."*

Unexpectedly, Joe became very drowsy and quickly fell asleep at the wheel. His head hit the steering wheel.

Jana tried to pull his head from the steering wheel. "What

the hell!"

But the car swerved to the right and headed for a traffic sign. Jana yanked on the wheel to avoid the collision. But it was too late. The car smashed into the sign. And the engine went dead. Jana violently jerked forward and was rattled by the impact. Joe, meanwhile, was slumped over and appeared unconscious. The sirens were heard again. She turned and saw several police cars fast approaching with blaring lights. She unlatched the seatbelt, exited her car, and hurried with her bag. She noticed a wooded area off to the side. She decided to make a run for it.

Jana ran through the woods under the moonlight. She then crawled through the woods, clutching her bag. She heard the sounds of dogs and footsteps as law enforcement officers drew near. She decided to hide behind a tree. She took the large envelope out of her bag and tucked it behind her back into her pants. The officers and their dogs finally approach her. She kicked her purse toward them and raised her hands. The officers aimed their guns at her. The dogs snarled and drooled, their leashes held tight by the officers.

The first officer barked a command, "Step away from the tree, and you won't get hurt. Alright, Jana?"

Jana obeyed.

The second officer spoke. "Where are the technicals?"

"How do you know my name? Who told you about me?"

The first officer smiled and replied, "Now, Jana, don't make this hard on yourself. Are you armed?"

"You didn't answer my question?"

The second office became agitated. "Lay face down. Now!"

"You want the damn drawings! You can have them." She reached for the envelope behind her back.

The second officer, as well as several others, misread her action and opened fire. Jana fell. The officers rush over to her.

The first officer felt her pulse. "She's dead."

Another officer reached over and retrieved the envelope. The second officer took the envelope from him and examined its contents. "Yup. This is it."

The first officer was with one knee beside her. "She wasn't even armed."

The second officer then looked at Jana lying dead on the ground. He became angry that she had to die. "Damn it."

Meanwhile, Henry, monitoring the situation, gently stroked Gigi. A wicked smile appeared on his face. "Good."

That same night, Linda emerged from her bathroom wearing skimpy lingerie as she entered her spacious bedroom. She continued to live with her parents despite having thoughts of moving out. She went to the queen-sized bed and turned on the wide-screen TV, which was anchored to the wall. A murder mystery movie was on the screen. She began watching it with interest. It was about a vicious serial murderer. A man in his thirties. His victims were young, attractive women. It was relatively easy for him to lure his victims into his apartment using his good looks and clever charm. The detective assigned to solve the serial murders was a young female in her late twenties. The conscientious detective followed every lead and thoroughly studied the forensic evidence from each victim. She was determined to get her man—the heartless serial murderer. In the end, she almost became a victim herself. However, the detective apprehended the cutthroat criminal. While watching the movie, Linda sometimes saw herself as a detective pursuing truth and justice.

As time moved on, Linda saw less of her father. Linda knew very little about the individuals Henry was monitoring, except for Robert. She wanted to seek the truth about her father. What does he do with his ESP? She knew her father occasionally liked to watch sporting events—especially the annual Texas vs

Oklahoma Red River rivalry. And even though Heney lived in Texas, he was always a big OU fan. However, she did not know that her father had a hand in the outcome of such events. He would sit there and watch the game and decide who would win. It could be a college football rivalry, a hockey match, or a basketball game. Henry would ensure a team won if he did not care or dislike the other team or a particular player, and enjoyed watching how fans and players reacted when their beloved team lost. He would use his brain wave precisely to cause the team to make mistakes. In football, for example, the quarterback would throw an interception. The receiver would somehow drop a pass. Defense linemen jump offside. His invisible wave would penetrate the player's head, and mistakes were made. It was so easy. The mafia, notorious for fixing sporting events, had nothing on Henry. Therefore, Henry would decide on sporting events like Super Bowl games, NBA outcomes, and even the Triple Crown if he wanted to. Yet, Henry never collected a dime from fixing sporting events. Henry was doing exceptionally well. Therefore, determining the outcome of sporting events was part of Henry's mental pleasures. It made him feel he was the Lord of all sporting creation, for he and he alone could determine the fate of a sporting event. And if, by rare circumstance, the team that Henry wanted to lose won. He would make that team pay dearly. For example, one year, a college team won the national title. But they were not supposed to. Henry was using his ESP to have the other team win. But for some weird circumstance, the team that was supposed to lose won. The reason was that the quarterback frequently changed the plays after snap by running with the ball. Henry knew what the play would be before the snap and used his ESP to have the other team defend for that play. However, with the quarterback changing the plays at the last minute, it did not matter what Henry knew before the snap. Well, the college team that won the national championship experienced an awful off-season. Two of the running backs were arrested on DWI charges. One of the star linebackers was killed in an auto accident. The coach was fired after he was accused of sexual harassment, even though there was no substantial evidence to support the fallacious charges. The quarterback who led his team was put on waivers after being drafted in the NFL and was never allowed to play for another NFL team again. All of these tragic events were caused by Henry. Talk about being a sore loser. Of course, Linda knew none of these shenanigans her father pulled.

Henry did not let her daughter know about his world of dark secrets. The world Henry knew all too well. He kept her daughter away from receiving mental images of such things. Occasionally, he did give Linda little bits of information he thought would be safe for her to know. "The President ate beef Wellington when he had dinner with Britain's Prime Minister at the White House the other day. Singing star Sapphire has a small tattoo of a red rose on her left buttock. Some married fellow at Maverick was fooling around with his secretary."

Even Muriel did not know who her husband was monitoring at times. Due to his unique multi-channeling abilities, Henry could simultaneously monitor and perform mental activities on other people around the world. How many? No one knew for sure. Henry told his wife he could easily monitor many individuals simultaneously, but no one knew precisely how many.

Linda continued to question some of the things Henry mentioned about Robert. The unfamiliar thoughts. The use of chronic pains. From her father's ESP, the only person whose thoughts she could access on a somewhat regular basis was Robert. Henry needed Linda to receive Robert's thoughts to illustrate how unbalanced Robert was. The problem was that Linda did not know why Robert received those weird thoughts. She did not know the true origin of such thoughts. *"Maybe some of Robert's unfamiliar thoughts were generated by my father?"*

In any event, Linda continued to receive Robert's mental images from time to time. Sometimes, several hours a day. Other times, only several images a week. The times fluctuated based on Linda's schedule. Like working out at the gym and entering fitness contests (despite her father's wishes not to). Socializing with female friends. That sort of thing. Unless it was a mental activity, Linda needed to know immediately.

Henry wanted Linda to know what kind of person Robert was. All those assorted accusations Robert was accusing her father of were simply unfounded. Henry will tell his daughter, "It was Robert who was unstable. He can't be trusted. I'm not sneaky or manipulative. How can you take the word of an unbalanced screwball like Robert Yellowstone?" Yet Linda continued to dwell on some of Robert's ideas about her father. And it worried Henry. However, Henry did promise he would not interfere with Linda's choice of men, which was one of the conditions for her moving back with her parents. After a couple of weeks of arguments with her parents, she was able to get access to Robert's email.

Chapter 23 - LET'S TALK

A week later, Robert was on the computer in his bedroom searching the Internet as he always does, when his mother came to the door.

"Darling. Supper will be ready soon."

"Okay, Mom."

She left. Robert decided to check his emails. They were mostly spam, but one email grabbed his attention. It was from Linda. He decided to read it.

*"Hey, Robert. Do you miss me? I'm sorry you
had to leave, D. I want to talk and get to know
you better. I attached a photo. Meet me at
ChatLive.com. My profile name is FreeBird.
I will be waiting."*

Robert was stunned. Linda Honey was reaching out to him. He clicked the attachment, and there was a photo of Linda. She was wearing a blue cut-out crisscross crop halter top and tiny tight daisy-duke shorts in front of her car, her lengthy hair blowing in the wind. Robert was in awe of the photo. He immediately went to ChatLive and searched for her using "FreeBird." And there, he found her photo. ChatLive indicated she was online. He clicked her profile photo, but first, he must register. So, he registered and provided his email address. He clicked on Linda's photo, and he's in. Linda began chatting with him.

"Hi Robert, I am glad you're interested in me. Let's do a video."

Robert responded, "Sure." However, the site requested that Robert add money to his account. "I need some credits."

"No worries. I will initiate. Just have your camera on."

Robert clicks his camera. Robert and Linda were now on video.

Linda flipped her hair over her shoulder. "Hey. Was I keeping you from something?"

"No…Not at all. You'll … Linda?"

"Here I am, FreeBird. You remember me. Right?"

"How can I forget."

"I want us to feel comfortable."

Robert became edgy. "And your father? His ESP? How do you expect me to feel comfortable? Did your father put you up…"

"Robert. If we continue, I need to set up some ground rules. First, we don't mention anything concerning him. This is between us. My father has nothing to do with me communicating with you. If he had his way, I would not be here chatting. Second. I am not responsible for his actions. If anything, I am trying to persuade him to let go of you."

"And If he doesn't?"

"His mind is twisted. He has issues."

"He's monitoring us now. Isn't he?"

"Robert, enough of him. Alright." She managed to smile. "How is your life in OKC?"

"So, you are interested in me? And no one put you up to this?"

"Why is that so hard?"

"Look at me and look at you. Jack the Ripper has a better chance of dating women like you than me. So, why?"

"You lack confidence."

"Am being realistic."

"Let…me say. I find you interesting."

"Because of my knowledge of your father's …"

"Robert! I am telling you for the last time. Do not mention my father. Or am I ending this."

Robert took a deep breath as he composed himself. He rubs his hand across his forehead.

"I know how you must feel."

Robert did not respond as he appeared lost in thought.

Linda tried to ease him. "What do you do for physical activities?"

"Ah?"

"Exercise? Do you have a fitness program?"

He nodded his head. "Oh no. Not at all. Well…I do occasionally jog… And you?"

"I stay in shape."

"Well… You look healthy. I imagine you spend time at the gym."

"I love working out. It makes me feel free. It's an adrenaline rush."

"Hmmm. Free like FreeBird."

Chuckled, "Yes."

They stare into each other's eyes.

"Am sure people give you compliments on your looks."

Shrugged her shoulders. "I get my share."

"You could pass for a model."

"I don't know about that. But I have entered a few fitness contests."

Robert's eyes widen." Oh. How did you do?"

Without saying another word, Linda forwarded a photo. Robert opened the photo on his computer. Linda was posing in a mini swimsuit with her contestant number attached to her thong. Robert was impressed.

"Wow… You look like a winner!"

"That was a contest I entered here in Dallas last month. I placed third."

"I don't know about the other contestants, but I would have given you the trophy."

Linda warmly smiled. "Did you play any sports?

"I used to play tennis in college."

"You played for your school?"

"No. I played to pass the time."

"What was your degree?

"Accounting?"

"Mine was in marine biology."

"You like the sea?"

"That has always been my passion. To explore the mysteries of our ocean ecosystems. To better understand how our oceans play with weather. To study the marine resources like the food we eat."

Robert nodded.

"It makes up about 70% of our planet, and there is still so much to learn."

"You'll a marine biologist?"

"I need to get my graduate degree."

"So, you live with your parents."

"Just like you."

They both chuckle.

"Well. At least we have that in common."

Linda seriously looked at him, "I think we have more in common than you realize."

Robert did not respond. He was mesmerized by her eyes staring at him as if they were trying to tell him something more.

"Robert. I like our talk. Can we talk again?"

Robert took a deep breath, digesting all that had transpired. "If you want."

"Until later."

"Wait. How will I know?"

"FreeBird."

Nodded, "Oh yeah."

"Bye, Robert."

"Bye."

The video chat ended. Robert stared at the computer screen. He decided to take another look at the photo Linda forwarded. He stared at it with lust. "She's a hot tamale." He downloaded the picture on his portable hard drive. His mother came to the door.

"Supper is ready."

"Okay, Mom."

Robert again took one more look at the photo and left for supper.

The following day, Robert checked his computer, but there was no email from Linda. He went to ChatLive and clicked on her profile, but she was not online. Her profile did not reveal too much about her. It stated her age and physical data, such as height and weight. It also mentioned her bachelor's degree and interest in marine biology—information Robert knew.

Chapter 24 - ANOTHER DOOR

It was afternoon the following day, and Robert was in bed reading a book in his bedroom. The book was entitled." WAVE DYNAMICS IN MOTION." A book he checked out from a branch library. Suddenly, a noise from the carpenters next door distracted him as they worked on Tammy's room. He opened the door. One of the workers was pulling sheetrock across the hallway.

Later in the evening, Robert searched for Linda on ChatLive but was out of luck. He decided to do a few errands for his mom and then drove to a nearby church for some quiet time with the book. He parked his car under an archway on the church grounds to continue his reading. After a few minutes, he exited and jogged some sixty meters to a wooded area to urinate. He made his way back to his car to continue reading.

Unexpectedly, a short time later, a police helicopter shined a searchlight down on the spot where he urinated. Robert looked up from his book, surprised by the helicopter. He looked around wildly.

Henry's voice entered Robert's mind. *"All those stupid letters, and where did it get you? And now you want to write a book about me. Well... I'll make sure they cage you for any slip. And that includes pissing in the wind."*

Robert laid the book down on his lap. He closed his eyes, lost in thought.

Later that night, Robert sat up in bed, moonlight spilling onto his face. He pondered, *"I knew I had to write about Henry. For all the shit am going through."* He paused in thought. *"But there's Linda. I want her. But her fuckin father gets in the way. He's like a damn psycho machine!"* He took a deep breath to calm down. He laid his head back on the bed and stared at the ceiling. *"She's beauty and brains."* He searched for an answer to prove he was right for Linda. *"I need to prove to Henry I am worthy for her. That am no mindless asshole."* Then, his face illuminated. *"The CPA exam!"*

Robert came to his bedroom from work the following day and went directly to his computer. Anxiety was written all over his face as he clicked on ChatLive. Bingo! Linda was online. He clicked on her profile, and they began to video each other.

"Hello, FreeBird."

How's everything, Mr. Robert."

"Just another day at the Air Force."

"You like it there?"

"Oh…It will do for now."

"Because your degree is in accounting, yet you'll in procurement."

"Yeah…But… Wait…How did you know about my job…Oh yeah. I forgot. Your father."

"What about him?"

"He told you. That's how you were able to get my email."

"He doesn't tell me anything unless I ask. And I was just curious about what you do."

"So, you asked him to spy on me?"

"No. I did not. And I told you not to speak about him in here."

"You seem to take up for him, knowing how he treats me. Yes, I understand he's your father. But his ESP…."

Suddenly, her video was gone. Robert quickly clicked her profile again, but the site indicated she was offline. Robert was upset. He muttered, "I should have known."

Later that night, he went to the computer and searched for her in ChatLive. He found Linda's profile, "FreeBird." However, her profile was disabled. He then accessed his emails and searched for Linda's previous email. He found it! He emailed her back with the following message. *"Linda. Look, I am sorry if I upset you. Let's talk again."* He forwarded it. However, an automatic email returned indicating her email address was invalid and could not be sent. Robert was surprised and disappointed. With his elbows on the desk, he raised his hands and rested his head on them. His face stared at the surface.

The following day, Muriel was standing on a chair, dusting the photograph of Linda above the cabinet. Henry was sitting on the dining table, sipping his tea. Muriel turned toward him.

She and Henry engaged in their mental conversation. *"You need to let him find a woman!"*

"That's not in the plan."

"As long as he's unattached, she will always be interested in him. And we will eventually lose our daughter."

"But you forget, Cochise is not popular with the ladies."

Muriel replied with a cold stare. Henry frowned.

A week later, Robert drove to a parking lot at a Mexican restaurant, "Pancho's." He exited his car and purchased a newspaper from the vending machine by the door. He entered and sat at a nearby table. He looked around and decided to read the news. His mind wandered, *"I've got to get my mind off of Henry Honey."* He continued to read the paper. He flipped the page, and the glaring headlines stared right at him. "SONOMA. A BIG BONANZA FOR MAVERICK". The headlines hit him like a bolt of lightning. "Wow." He read the article. *"Maverick Oil's stock shot up 50% after news that the Sonoma Ridge Offshore project will generate oil reserves equal to a quarter of their worldwide crude holdings. This was after the President withdrew his support to halt offshore drilling."* Robert looked up and thought. *"Henry was probably behind this one."* Robert touched his right ear as he received a sharp pain. *"Well, I guess that answers that question."*

Maria, the waitress in her mid-30's arrived. "Do you need to see a menu?"

"I've never been here before. But I will take a glass of iced tea. Do you have chicken enchiladas?"

"Of course."

"I just take that with beans and rice."

Maria replied with a smile and left.

Robert continued to read the paper. But his mind turned to Linda. *"I wish I could see her. Tell her I miss her. Hold her. I wonder if she will try to contact me again. Then there's him. I must keep my mind off of him. Not communicate with him."* Maria arrived with the glass of iced tea.

"Your enchilada plate will be ready shortly."

"Thanks."

She left. Robert felt a soft, ticking pain in his left ear. He touched it. As if directed by Henry, he turned his head toward a young woman in her 20s walking over to clear some tables. She was Elizaveta. She was brown-haired and rather tall like Linda, although not as fit. She was slender with a fashion model look.

Maria approached her. "Liza, hurry up! You have to make the tables ready for the party room."

Elizaveta responded in her Ukrainian accent, "Yes, Maria. I will do this."

Maria left. Robert stared at her. Elizaveta looked up and caught Robert's stare. To Robert's amazement, she replied with a smile. Elizaveta finished and quickly left. Robert's eyes follow her with lust and with surprise. He reached over and took a sip from his tea. *"And no disapproving pains from my evil Jiminy Cricket."* Robert smiled and took another drink.

Later, Robert paid for his dinner and left. He walked to the parking lot and headed for his car when he noticed Elizaveta dragging a trash bag to the dumpster. She hauled it in as Robert approached her.

"Wait. Liza right? My name is Robert. How long have you been working here?

"Several months ago."

"Where are you from?

"Ukraine."

"Ukraine?"

Elizaveta smiled.

Jose, a manager at Rosita's in his 40s, observed Robert and Elizaveta from a distance. But neither Robert nor Elizaveta was aware of him.

"What did you do in Ukraine?"

"I was a lawyer. Everyone calls me Liza. But my real name is Elizaveta."

"Es-la-veta."

"No, Elizaveta."

"Okay." Gestured with his hands, "But, why are you clearing tables?"

"In America, I have to start over. So, it will take time."

"Why here?"

"My mother married an American, so I followed her here."

Maria opened the back door. "Liza. What are you doing? You have tables to clean."

Maria went back inside. Elizaveta quickly followed.

"Es-la-veta. I meant Liza. Maybe I can see you again?"

Elizaveta smiled. "Sure." She left.

Jose also decided to leave.

Chapter 25 - A DAY IN THE LIFE OF A MENTAL CRISIS

Robert sat at a kitchen table as he studied for the CPA exam the next day. Around him were various accounting books. Robert flinched, touching the side of his head. Two weeks had gone by, and Robert managed to visit a neurologist to receive treatment for his migraines. He only experienced migraines when he studied for the exam. He took drugs like Cafergot (a mixture of ergotamine and caffeine) orally. Also, another drug called Inderal was used in Robert's regimen of beta-blocker medications.

So, there he sat at the dining table, attempting to study with his headaches. The CPA exam was already difficult without those blasted headaches. Robert felt Henry was behind those migraines. He took several pills from containers next to him and swallowed them with a glass of water. The beta-blockers should work against Henry's ESP.

Later that day, Robert sat at the same table with a bag of ice on his head as he tried to study. The drugs were no match for Henry's ESP.

A month had already gone by, and Robert sat at his desk in the morning, writing on a notepad at work. Dr. Brandt continued having sessions with him, from time to time to cope with his anxiety, as well as convince Robert that Henry's ESP was all in his head. Well, she was right about one thing. Henry Honey was undoubtedly in his head. But not in the way she intended. And for fear of ending up in a psycho ward, Robert inform her he was convincing himself that Henry's ESP was just a fantasy. A sick joke he was playing on himself. But Robert knew better, as Henry continued with his cruel mental games on him.

So, there was Robert, sitting on his desk, attempting to spell a word in his mind, "Price Negotiation Memorandum-m-m-m. How do you spell memorandum?" Several employees laughed loudly. Robert stopped and went to a search engine on his computer for assistance. "Where's that fucking word?" Again, they laughed. Mary Lou walked over to Robert's desk.

"How are you doing on that PNM?"

"I'm working on it now."

"I need it by the end of the day. Understand?"

"Yes, Mary Lou."

Mary Lou left. Robert became worried. He quickly began working on the document on his computer. Robert felt a sharp pain on the right side of his neck as he was just on the first sentence. Robert tried desperately to ignore such pain. Then, in the second sentence, Robert misspelled a word. Immediately, the quiet buying section was interrupted by laughter. Maybe someone said something quite humorous. But Robert knew better. The laughter grew to a feverish pitch as Robert ignored the sudden jollity.

Henry then injected a fantasy of Robert having sexual overtones with Mary Lou. They were both naked and embraced in a delicious kiss in front of his desk. But one of his hands was holding a large knife. He slowly ran the tip of the pointed knife against Mary's backside. Just enough for Mary to feel the blade. She began to kiss his neck as she softly said. "I like it like that. Give me more." Robert then stopped the fantasy dead in his tracks. He looked away from the computer screen with the laughter continuing. He was mentally frustrated. *What the hell was that?* " Robert then shook it off. *"I got to finish this damn PNM."*

Robert was now in the last paragraph. *"Thank God I am almost finished."* He added a signature block at the end of the document. And that was that. Or so Robert thought. Robert forwarded the document to Lisa, his contracting officer, through the computer for her final signature. The PNM was for a small purchase, so it was simple enough. Robert had already prepared enough of these simplified PNMs. However, the contracting officer was not satisfied. She marked the document and returned it to him with enough comments to fill a coloring book. Henry had instilled his version of the dos and don'ts of preparing a simplified PNM in Lisa's head. Robert had corrections to make. Robert's pain then traveled to his right inner ear. It was a sharp, stabbing sensation. Then, the pains were vibrating in his eardrum. *"Damn, Henry. What the hell doesn't he leave me alone!"* his mind wondered.

Meanwhile, Muriel laughed as Henry grinned at Robert's mental remark. Both were sitting and drinking their tea while watching CNN. Henry decided to take the day off from an otherwise busy schedule at Maverick. Henry was also monitoring various other people. Some very important people. However, Robert was a unique specimen for Henry and Muriel. Yes, Robert made the day gratifying for them. The day would not be the same if Henry left Robert alone. *"The hell with dignitaries. The hell with child molesters. The hell with the murders. The hell with the mad rapists. To hell with them all. I want Robert."*

Henry began to see Robert as a form of entertainment in the most wicked way. Since Robert resented Henry's treatment of him, it influenced Henry and Muriel to cast Robert as their court fool. A silly, stupid simpleton, and the butt of their sick jokes. This form of amusement was new to them since it was rare for someone to pick up on Henry's Wave Master's abilities and wasn't part of the Inner Circle. Therefore, Henry judged Robert differently from practically everyone else. It was a very unfair method. But that's the way Henry wanted it. Like a mental parasite inside a person's head, it was his duty to record every error Robert made. Physical. Mental. It did not matter. And criticized him for it. *"Oh, you dialed the wrong phone number today. You misspelled a word in your draft letter. You used "are" instead of "is" in your conversation an hour ago. You press the wrong keystroke when using the computer. I didn't like that image in your brain."* A parasite like that could make anyone go crazy. It was Henry's objective to create constant misery in Robert's life. To make Robert aware of every error/mistake he made, or any mental activity Henry did not care for no matter how trivial it was. He was their fool. To use as they pleased.

It was Henry's way of justifying Robert's appraisal at Ford AFB. Yes, Henry controlled Robert's appraisal through his telepathy. But he had to justify it to his Inner Circle. (Although Linda wanted nothing to do with it.) So, the parasite found a way. It was too bad Henry did not apply his misguided analysis to other Ford AFB employees. Other employees could be dumb-like shit floating in the toilet. However, those employees received better appraisals and were promoted. Henry did not judge them the same way he did Robert. Muriel never knew the quality of work of other employees at the Air Force base. So, Robert had to be perfect in thought, word, and deed to be recognized as an excellent employee by Henry's misguided standards—an impossible task for any employee to satisfy. Robert had to meet his standards to be considered for any promotion. Henry would torture Robert if he couldn't fulfill a task that could never be satisfied in the first place. With laughter, frustration, and pain. Similar to what he went through at Maverick Oil. Therefore, Robert could never be promoted at Ford AFB as long as the parasite demanded that Robert satisfy the impossible.

Another week went by, and Mary Lou decided to give Robert his first appraisal. Mary Lou's appraisal of Robert could have been better indeed. His raw score was just enough to label him a marginally adequate employee. Robert thought Mary Lou was pulling a joke on him. Unfortunately, that was not the case. Robert was steamed after Mary Lou gave him a poor grade on his first review. Mary Lou would not detail the reasons for his mediocre performance. Other than to say in general terms, Robert was too quiet. Did he not openly discuss contracting issues with fellow employees. He showed a lack of interest as a contracting specialist due to his passive attitude. He was not a team player. As she said all those wonderful things to Robert, questions were going through his mind. *How about my productivity? I exceeded my goal by awarding more small contracts this month. What about the situations where I assisted other buyers with their pricing problems when they approached me for help? How about the times I volunteered to work late without pay?"* When Mary Lou was finished, she smiled at him and asked him to sign the review.

"This does not mean you agreed with the review. It simply means I went over your review and adequately explained why you received the score you did."

Robert did not bother to ask her the questions he had in mind. He did what he was told and signed the review. "Sure, Mary Lou."

"Thanks, Robert. I'll make you a copy later."

"A copy?"

"Yes. For your records."

"Oh." Robert then stood and left her office dejected. This, of course, made Henry and Muriel very happy. Well, at least Mary Lou was right about one thing. Robert could, at times, be passive. Let's put it another way. If the police wanted Robert to confess to a misdemeanor he committed years ago, Robert would confess. It would be so easy.

Robert strongly suspected Henry was behind Mary Lou's appraisal. After all, good old Henry could manipulate activities connected to his job at Ford AFB. The problem was that Robert could never prove it or stop it. Mentally sending messages to the human mind was child's play for Henry, like stealing candy from a blind baby.

But if Robert had stopped and thought about it for a moment. It was pretty remarkable that Robert managed to receive his marginal rating, considering the ordeal he was going through. Many times, Henry bombarded Robert with unfamiliar thoughts. And those nagging pains. Always those nagging pains. He was playing games with his mind and putting Robert through enormous stress and tension day after day. Most people probably couldn't endure the mental anguish Robert was going through. Yes, Robert should consider himself lucky. He was fortunate to be able to blend in with the other employees. He was managing to perform his job despite the mental turmoil he was experiencing.

After the appraisal, Robert returned to his desk and was about to head home. It was time to punch out. However, Mary Lou gave him the task of faxing a letter ASAP. During this time, facsimiles were preferred for sending documents to outside parties. So, on his desk was a letter that needed to be faxed immediately to a Contractor. But Robert was ready to go home. Before the restaurant closed, he thought he might have enough time to visit Elizaveta at

Pancho's. He tried to meet with her the last several weeks, but was unsuccessful. puzzled

Robert stood with the letter in hand and walked to the fax machine, a short distance away from his buying section. He already had a big chip on his shoulder because of the appraisal. However, a coworker named Rhonda quickly approached Robert to use the fax machine. She had a lengthy document, some forty pages. Rhonda cut right in front of him, and the letter Robert needed to fax had to be in the Contractor's office ASAP. This infuriated Robert. Especially since Robert and Rhonda never got along. They tend to ignore each other as much as possible. Rhonda made a conscious effort to disassociate herself from Robert and only him.

Henry had been monitoring Rhonda and waited for the right moment to spring her loose. Henry liked putting salt on Robert's wound. It made the flesh taste so much better. Henry now wanted Robert to explode. Put Robert in hot water with the Ford AFB employees. Have him fired from his job. Say something nasty to Rhonda. "Hey, you fat, ugly ass bitch! I was here first. Look, horse's ass. I'm in a bad mood. Don't make it any worse." Robert's pain was sizzling in his left inner ear and was needling him, and wanting Robert to break. Break down mentally. It was Henry's way of saying. "Remember. I'm your worst nightmare."

Robert was angry, all right. But not at Rhonda. He was furious at Henry. He had a strong inclination that Henry had a hand in this. With Rhonda, Robert was frustrated with her for only a moment. Henry then had her whistle while she continued to fax her documents. This made Robert more irritated. But he kept his cool and took a deep breath. Without warning, Henry inserted a nasty mental image of

Robert attacking Rhonda. The image had Robert stand behind Rhonda and plunge a knife into her back. He then stabbed her in the neck. Quickly, the image left him. Robert stood there with dread written on his face as Rhonda continued whistling. It seemed to get louder. Robert turned and headed back to his desk as the guilt of that violent image overtook him. He decided it would be best to fax the letter after Rhonda returned to her desk. As for Elizaveta, he would try to see her another day. So, he sat, running his hand over his head as he stared at the desk. He was feeling remorseful for the homicidal thought of murdering Rhonda.

Robert knew antics like the one Henry pulled with Rhonda aimed to portray him as unstable. It was essential to describe Robert in a negative light. A real stinker. A loose cannon. Henry played it well, like a skilled poker player, but with a marked deck of cards. He was placing Robert in certain situations among people with the intent of causing instant irritation. Hoping Robert's reaction would be adverse. Even criminal. But Robert never reacted the way Henry hoped he would. Robert never faltered. Never waved. Situations like the one involving Rhonda did remind him of a passage he read in the Bible back in Dallas, *"For we wrestle not against flesh and blood, but against principalities, against powers, against rulers of this dark age, against the superhuman forces of evil in high places."*

Robert finally had an opportunity to see Elizaveta. It was a Friday, and Mary Lou decided to leave early that day. It happened to be her birthday, and a big birthday party was planned for her, so Robert drove to Pancho's.

Maria brought Robert a glass of iced tea. Robert was not paying attention. His eyes were squarely on Elizaveta, who was exiting the kitchen. She cleaned a nearby table. Jose watched her from a distance.

"Eslaveta?"

Elizaveta turned and smiled at Robert.

"It's me, Robert."

"Yes, I know. And it is Elizaveta."

"So, how is everything?"

"I cannot talk to you."

"Can I have your number?"

She finished the table.

"Eslaveta? Or should I call you Liza?"

Elizaveta ignored him and walked to the kitchen. She placed the dirty dishes on the dishwashing rack. Jose entered and grabbed Elizaveta's arm.

"What are you doing talking to him?"

"I not talk to him." She pulled her arm away from Jose.

"He's talked with you before."

Elizaveta continued her work. Jose cupped one of her breasts.

"You belong to me."

She pulled away from him. "I have work to do."

"If I see you mess with him, I will make sure they deport you back to Ukraine."

"Jose, I no mess with him. And I need to go back anyway."

Jose attempted to kiss her, but she pulled back.

Maria walked up and communicated with him in Spanish, "Jose. I need to see you in the office right now. It is important."

Jose stopped, his eyes on Elizaveta. "Si."

Elizaveta left. Jose watched her with a hungry look.

Elizaveta entered the restroom and looked in the mirror. She cried.

Another day at work, Robert looked at the clock on the wall. Robert then touched his buttocks as he sat at his desk, gathering his thoughts. *"These hemorrhoids. I wonder if Henry is causing them?"* Employees laughed as Robert tried to focus on his work. *"At least I'm out of here soon."* Robert found it hard, struggling with the pain and noisy chatter everywhere. *"I wish the military knew about him."* Unexpectedly, the employees stopped their laughter. One employee let out a terrifying cough. An eerie silence filled the area. Mary Lou walked over to Robert's desk with a small file. She handed it to him.

"Robert, I have an urgent requirement that must be awarded by the end of the week. So, I want you to do an oral solicitation."

A puzzled look came over him. "Oral?"

"Yes. I need an oral. You have been familiarizing yourself with the FAR?"

"The FAR? Oh…Do you mean the Federal Acquisition Regulation? Yes, I have."

"Good. Then, get busy." She left.

Robert momentarily examined the purchase request (PR) in the file. He quickly retrieved the list of Contractors who qualified for the solicitation. It was just what Robert needed: an emergency PR with fifteen qualified Contractors. Henry wanted Robert to receive the PR before he was scheduled to go home. Robert would have to work extra hours on this PR. After that, the day was over. Robert could finally say that another frustrating day with Henry had come and gone at Ford AFB. As Henry would sometimes say, "Those are the breaks."

That night, Robert planned to study hard for the CPA exam. He needed to catch up on his studies, and the first exam day was only two weeks away. But his mind had other ideas. He went to his bedroom and retrieved the book, "WAVE DYNAMICS IN MOTION" from the library. He began to read the following passage to himself. *"Flux and fluxion mean a flowing of fluid. A rate of flow of neutrons; the number of neutrons passing through a unit area in unit time. The motion characteristic of the neutrons flowing."* Robert looked up from the page as his mind tried to understand Henry's Wave Master abilities. Robert thought, *"Using principles of flux and fluxion, Henry, as a Wave Master, can measure and manipulate the neurotransmitters in terms of how they fire and the rate of firing."* Robert left his bedroom with the book and headed for the kitchen table. He found a notepad and a pen. He sat at the table with the book and wrote a concocted formula as follows:

"TWR = BWA x BE" Where: T=Telepathy, W=Wave, R=Rate, A=Activity, B=Brain, E=Energy, W=Wave. Robert stared at the formula. He was trying to understand everything and how it worked in Henry's brain. Robert looked up. He pondered, *"But if Wave Masters exist, there must be good and evil ones."* He became belligerent. *"And if a Wave Master decides to destroy a good person's life!"* He calmly concluded, *"Then, I would call that person an Evil Wave Master."* Robert continued to study the formula and labeled it the "Telepathy Wave Rate Formula."

Chapter 26 - LET'S GET PHYSICAL

The following night, Robert stared in the mirror in the bathroom. He had the urge to talk to Henry directly. It was something Robert refrained from doing. He did not want to give the impression he approved of this Twilight Zone relationship with him. However, he needed to make a stand. Change his life, and not be afraid to face the consequences. Even if it meant confronting Henry face-to-face. So, he stood in front of the mirror, talking directly to him. "I have no hope in confronting you. For I am not a Wave Master." Robert cast his melancholy eyes downward and looked up again. "And that's where it lies. A so-called pervert in your mind. And an Evil Wave Master in mine. I realized that if I was going to overcome you and accomplish my goals, I had to quit thinking about it and do it. And with God's help, I will."

Robert smiled in the mirror and flinched as the pain started up in his right inner ear. He touched his right ear for a moment and pulled his hand away. "And the pains will no longer help you anymore, Henry."

The following Saturday morning, Robert drove his car to a park on a beautiful day. He decided to park his vehicle on a hill plateau. He opened his door and walked. He went over to the edge of the area and slowly looked down. Below, he saw various children and adults of all races and creeds engaged in recreational activity. Yet not one of them had any knowledge of Henry and his ESP. To his right, he saw dogs playing with their owners. Above, he observed a biplane fly overhead. To his left, he saw young and old couples holding hands as they walked. He observed children playing a game of hide and seek. He shook his head as he could not figure out how and why he came up with this knowledge, for he did not consider himself different from anyone else. He contemplated, *"So what was I to do with this knowledge?"* A smile slowly came over him. *"Maybe it's a gift of some sort. But I am sure Henry would not like to hear that."* Again, he witnessed numerous people having fun under the sun. Robert looked at them with a sincere look. *"I do not know what God has in store for me concerning him. This must be some purpose. I couldn't figure out what it was. But whatever path lies between him and me. It won't end here."* He slowly smiled at the various people and bowed to them, as they were unaware of Robert's presence. He turned and walked toward his car. He entered and drove away.

It was evening, and Henry sat staring at the silent CNN broadcast as Muriel knitted a nice sweater for Linda. Both Henry and Muriel realized Robert's attitude was changing. He was displaying courage in the face of overwhelming odds. He wasn't the easy pushover they thought he would be. "Cochise," as Henry would like to refer to him, was not to be underestimated. He could figure out things. He was gaining an understanding of Henry's personality and ESP. Robert was not the dumb-minded court jester Murial wanted him to be. In other words, Robert was no longer fun, and Linda was bitter at her parents for how her relationship with Robert turned out. Muriel hoped the sweater would cheer her up. They communicated mentally.

"Linda does not want to communicate with us anymore because of him. And the Ukrainian thing is not working out."

Henry agreed. *"He's becoming too cocky for his own good."*

Muriel looked up at Henry." *No more messing around. He must be eliminated.*"

Henry nodded.

"*But it must look like an accident, or she'll catch on.*"

A week later, Robert sat at a table, sipping his iced tea at Pancho's. He saw Elizaveta. To his surprise, she approached him. "Have you ordered yet?"

"No."

"We talk more in private."

"Really?"

"It is good for you?"

"Sure." Robert stood and followed her.

Elizaveta and Robert entered the empty party room, found a table, and sat across from each other.

Jose entered and observed Robert and Elizaveta. However, they did not notice him. He became upset and left.

"So, how is everything?"

Elizaveta was downcast. "Fine."

"Is something wrong?"

"Nothing is wrong."

"Be honest."

"My mother and her husband are to divorce."

"Why?"

"Do not know."

"You live with your mother?"

Elizaveta nodded.

Meanwhile, Jose and Juan, who was in his 20s, walked over to Robert's car. Juan carried a small cloth bag. "His car is over here."

"Are you sure, Jose?"

"Si.".

Juan walked over to the driver's door.

"Make it fast."

Juan proceeded to retrieve a jimmy from the bag.

Back at the restaurant, Elizaveta looked at Robert sadly. "We are flying back to Ukraine the day after tomorrow."

"Don't leave. You can find something else here."

"My grandmother is dying, and she needs us. We will be there until she passes. And then we can come back. Hopefully, things will be better."

Robert reached for her hand. "Things will be better. You'll see."

"You are so confident."

Robert responded with a smile. "You have an email address?"

"I had to discontinue the one I had. But no worries. When I come to my country, I contact you. And I will be back soon. You be patient? Yes?"

"Of course. So, you're returning here?"

"No. Not here. Not safe for me here."

"Why?"

"No worries. I will be fine. But you can give me your email address and phone number? Yes?"

"Sure." Robert retrieved a paper handkerchief from the table and wrote his information. He gave it back to her with a smile.

She smiled. "I want to ask you. What is last name?

"Yellowstone."

"Is that a Mexican name?"

"I'm mixed." Chuckled. "Mexican."

"Did I say something not correct?"

"No, it's just the way you say it. With your Russian accent."

"Ukrainian."

"Sorry. Ukrainian." Robert chuckled again.

"You're laughing at me."

Robert gestured no.

"You do."

They became quiet as they gazed at each other.

Robert attempted to strap on his seat belt in his car at Pancho's parking lot after his conversation with Elizaveta. But the buckle did not lock. After a few more attempts, he gave up. "I don't need it." He started the engine and drove.

While driving, Robert listened to the radio. The traffic light changed to green. He drove another block and stopped his car at an intersection as the light turned red.

Later, on the expressway, Robert decided to exit to merge onto the feeder. Meanwhile, a 9,000-gallon fuel truck drove on the feeder toward Robert. The fuel truck driver saw the yield sign. However, he ignored the sign as his foot pressed down on the accelerator. The fuel truck drove right in front of Robert's car. Robert hit the brakes to avoid a collision. He honked his horn. "You asshole! You could have killed me!" The fuel truck driver was surprised to see Robert in the sideview mirror.

Later, Robert approached an intersection with a green traffic light. However, a vehicle from the other direction sped through the red light. Robert slammed on the brakes. His car stopped as the other vehicle flew past him. Robert was upset. "What the hell is going on with the drivers today?"

The traffic light in front of him then turned red. He waited for the green. Holding hands, a woman and her little daughter walk in front of Robert's car. They stared at Robert in shock as they continued walking past his car. Robert noticed their eerie stare.

A short time later, Robert finally entered his parents' driveway. His car slowly rolled behind his mother's car. However, when Robert applied the brakes, the vehicle did not stop. It made contact with his mother's car. Robert jerked forward from the impact, hitting his head on the steering wheel. He was visibly rattled.

Meanwhile, Henry and Muriel sat in their den. Muriel let out a scream in frustration. Henry remained calm.

"How? How did he manage that?"

"He must have nine lives," Henry replied in a calm voice.

The following day, a mechanic in his 40s looked under the hood of Robert's car in his parents' driveway. Robert and his mother stood nearby, watching. The mechanic turned toward Robert. He held up a piece of paper towel with a pair of pliers. It was dripping with brake fluid.

"Here's your problem."

Robert looked confused, "That looks like a paper towel."

"Yep. And it was stuck inside the brake reservoir hose, which leads to the brake line."

Robert and his mother replied with a blank look.

"In other words, this trash prevented the brake fluid from flowing into your brake line." The mechanic reached into his pocket and pulled out a penny. "And this penny was inside the seat belt buckle. This is why the clip wouldn't snap into the buckle." He scratched his head. "Somebody wanted you dead. Unless you just had terrible luck with the car. When you think about it, you're lucky to be alive."

Robert and his mother exchange a glance.

The following day, Robert was driving in a hurry as he whipped into Pancho's parking lot. He left his car and walked to the backside of the restaurant. He found Elizaveta by a back door.

She said warmly. "I am glad you came."

"You said it was something important you wanted to say before you leave."

She embraced him. Her eyes widened as she screamed, pulling away from him. "Jose!"

Robert turned. Jose was approaching, holding a 6" blade.

Meanwhile, Henry sat alone in his recliner, his legs crossed, sipping hot tea. A smile on his face. "This should be interesting."

Jose had hate written all over his face. "Are you ready to die for your love?"

Robert slowly backed away from Elizaveta and Jose. "She's not your property!"

Jose laughed. "So, she's yours, amigo?"

"She's free to choose whom she wants to be with. And it's not you."

Henry's smile disappeared. He commented mentally, *"Get him!"*

Jose charged Robert as Elizaveta screamed. Robert grabbed Jose's arm, holding the knife, and kicked him. Jose lost his grip on the knife, which fell to the ground. Jose tackled Robert to the ground and straddled him. Robert hit him across the face several times and managed to get Jose off him. Robert and Jose were on their feet, facing each other.

Henry set his cup on the saucer. He mentally talked to Jose. *"Come on, Jose. Do you want Cochise to take away your prize? You're the man."*

Jose grabbed the knife from the ground. He charged at Robert again. Robert grabbed Jose's arm again, holding the knife, and kicked him in the abdomen. Jose buckled, and Robert flipped him over on his back. Jose fell hard on the ground. Robert slammed against Jose hard, his elbow striking him in the face. Jose grunts. Robert hit Jose repeatedly across the face. Jose's face began to bleed. Robert got off him and walked over to Elizaveta.

She saw Jose gaining his position. "He's getting up!" Robert turned and saw Jose raise his head. Robert moved and quickly kicked him across the face. Jose hit the ground again, this time without moving.

"You killed him!"

Robert went and took his pulse. "Nah. He'll live." Robert approached Elizaveta with hungry eyes. He pulled her in and kissed her with a passion not seen before. He looked into her eyes. "I hope you want me as much as I want you."

Jose began to moan.

"Let's go, Liza."

"No."

"You like him?"

"I like you. And very much so. That is what I want to tell you before I fly to my country. But I will be in big trouble if I do not stay and call emergency."

"What will you say?

"He slipped."

Robert smiled, then glanced away. He gently touched his head.

"Maybe it is possible."

"I no understand?"

He looked at her with a gleam in his eyes, "It's hard to explain, but we are all surrounded by this energy. Used correctly, we can make the right decisions, like the love in front of me."

They kiss again.

A short time later, Robert drove off with a smile. His confidence was beaming. "No one is going to take her away from me."

However, Henry was not finished, as he sat alone in his chair mentally speaking to him. *"Let me entertain you."*

Unexpectedly, Robert became drowsy. His head was drooping, and his eyes started to close. He desperately tried to fight it off. But he began to swerve his car and veered into the opposite lane. An approaching car honked. Robert jolted and was awake. He steered his car back to his lane just before the approaching vehicle passed him. Robert then looked in his rear-view mirror. An 18-wheel truck was fast approaching from behind on the next lane. Robert struggled to stay alert. However, the truck did not slow down as Robert moved into its lane. Robert brushed his hand across his forehead and ran it over to the top of his head. The drowsiness stopped. He swung his car to his lane just in time to avoid a collision with the 18-wheeler, as it passed him. Robert pulled his hand away from his head. He became drowsy again. He placed his hand back on top of his head. He became alert. Now, the drowsiness reappeared. Robert moved his hand to another part of his head. He was alert again. "I don't understand!" A startled look then came over him. Robert became angry. But Robert felt drowsy again. He responded by moving his hand to another part of his head. The drowsiness stopped. His Hand Technique was working. "It's Henry! I should have known. How many people have you killed this way, my Evil Wave Master!"

Robert continued driving in his lane with his hand over his head.

Meanwhile, Henry sat in his recliner, looking out the window.

Chapter 27 - MOVING ON, SO LET IT BLEED

Linda was studying at the university library. There were books around her as she took notes. The library was now Linda's second home. She spent most of her free time there, unless she was attending classes, working out at the gym, or staying at her parents' house. Enrolled in the marine biology graduate program, Linda was devoted to her studies. She wanted to get away from her parents. But she needed a job. But a job she would love. So, she enrolled full-time, including summer semesters. Her goal was to graduate in just 18 months. Find a job in her field and split. To get away as far as she could. To move on with her life.

Linda was well aware of what Robert was doing. She was channeling Robert's relationship with Elizaveta through her father's ESP. She was disappointed. She wished it were her who had this relationship with Robert. At first, Linda's initial desire for Robert was to get back at her parents, knowing they would not accept Robert. However, as time passed, she began to develop strong feelings for him. Something she wasn't expecting. But she now concluded Robert's knowledge of her father's ESP would not be beneficial. Robert and Henry's relationship had built to such an emotional state that there would be no hope of Robert and her having any romantic connection. Linda did not know how long her parents would continue with Robert this way. The constant torture of Robert's mind. The endless mind games her father was playing on dejected Robert. Linda thought that at least Robert's relationship with Elizaveta would end her parents' obsessive behavior towards him. So, she thought. Linda also realized how difficult it would be for her to have a normal relationship with any man unless her parents approved it. So, she blamed her failed attempt on Robert squarely on her parents' shoulders.

But the last thing she wanted was for her father to eliminate Robert. Linda knew her father had murdered a few people. So, if Robert's sudden death were attributed to an aneurysm or a stroke, Linda would immediately blame her father. However, she felt the few (actually, there were many) individuals who met their untimely end were dishonest people. Vicious criminals. They were a threat to society. At least, that's what Muriel would say if she confronted her. But Robert was none of these. Her father had told her he had no intention of murdering Robert. Therefore, Linda believed him. She trusted him. After all, Robert was not a threat. But she also knew her father could break promises.

Robert and hundreds of others were ready for the first day of the CPA exam at the convention hall in the first week of November. Exam proctors closely observed them as they took their seats.

Robert sat and lined his pencils, eraser, blank sheet of paper, driver's ID, exam identification card, and exam booklet in front of him. Melissa, in her 20s, sat next to him.

"Are you ready?" she asked.

"I hope so."

She sighed, "Only 25% will pass the exam."

"Really...?"

"Yep." She frowns. "It's too bad we're not allowed to use a calculator."

A young female proctor approached. "There is to be no talking among the candidates." She walked away. Melissa gave Robert a nervous smile.

The large clock on the wall in the convention hall indicated noon. The head proctor behind the podium spoke into the microphone, "You may begin."

The proctors move around the hall during the examination, watching the candidates like hawks. Robert concentrated on a series of questions in the exam booklet. A young female proctor walked up to him. She retrieved and compared his exam ID card with his driver's ID. Satisfied. She placed them back on his desk and left. Robert felt pain in the back of his neck. He ignored it and continued with the exam. He came upon a question. "CONSTRUCT A BALANCE SHEET AND INCOME STATEMENT FOR AJAX CORPORATION BASED ON THE FOLLOWING EVENTS BELOW." Robert continued to read. Unexpectedly, Robert's mind came upon a fantasy. He mentally visualized a sizeable purple elephant running around the convention hall, stomping its large feet, and eating peanuts on the ground with its large trunk. The fantasy ended as it started. A surprised look came over Robert.

Meanwhile, Henry sat behind his desk at Maverick with a smile. He forwarded a mental message to Robert's brain. *"Purple is my favorite color."*

Another female proctor was approaching Robert. Robert looked up at her like a frightened child. He quickly turned his attention back to the booklet. The proctor stood in front of him. Robert entered another fantasy as the sizeable purple elephant ran around the convention hall, stomping its large feet and eating peanuts on the ground with its large trunk. The fantasy ended.

Robert smiled at the proctor as she checked his exam ID. She returned his smile with an icy-cold stare. Robert looked down at his exam booklet as the proctor walked away. Robert's eyes began to droop as if falling asleep. He placed his hand over his head. Alert now, he continued. He became sleepy again. He moved his hand around to another part of his head. Robert was alert again. He continued this process as he prepared to answer the balance sheet and income statement questions. Finished. He turned the exam booklet page and decided to stand.

Robert went to a restroom and entered a stall as a male proctor watched. Robert urinated with stress written all over his face.

The exam day ended, as the large clock on the wall indicated 4:29 P.M. Robert continued with the exam, hurrying to complete the last set of questions.

The head proctor walked up to the podium. "It's time to put your pencils down. The AICPA exam for today is over."

Pencils hit the desks throughout the convention hall. Robert took a deep breath. He stood up with his exam booklet and turned it in.

The next day of the exam, the large clock on the convention hall wall indicated a time of noon. The head proctor stood behind the podium and talked into the microphone. "This is the second day of the AICPA exam. You may begin."

Robert quickly opened the booklet. A question read, "What is Process Cost used for?" Robert began to choose his answer. He flinched, touching his head. Robert continued, but his face was twisting in pain. He quickly waved down a male proctor.

He approached. "Yes?"

"Do you have any aspirins?"

"No."

"Does anyone sell anything like that here?"

"No."

The male proctor left. Robert struggled to manage the pain. He took several deep breaths. He began to relax. He continued with the examination, taking more breaths. Suddenly, his face registered anxiety. He placed his hand on the back of his head. He felt pressure on the right side of his head, leading to dizziness. Robert pondered. *"Is he trying to give me an aneurysm?"* He stopped and took deep breaths. *"To overcome Henry, I must be a mental warrior."* Robert closed his eyes. *"I must reflect on the principles of wave energy and how it relates to the flow in the brain. The principles of flux and fluxion."*

Inside Robert's brain, Henry's wave already latched onto Robert's neurotransmitters and traveled to various parts of the brain. The wave branched out into the frontal lobe area. It began to apply pressure to an artery. The artery wall began to bulge. *"Apply the force by focusing your energy to the point where Henry's wave is applying the pressure. Meet his wave with your energy."* Robert generated electrical energy, and the electrical impulses from his neurons traveled up from the axons to meet the point in the brain where Henry's wave was applying pressure to the artery.

In his chair, Robert appeared to be in a trance.

Back inside Robert's brain, the energy flowing in Robert's axons was strong enough to weaken the part of Henry's wave that was applying the pressure.

In his chair, a smile came over Robert's face as his mind spoke. *"I'll call this the Wave Binding Technique."*

Meanwhile, Henry was alone behind his desk at Maverick. A look of shock wore over his face. "This can't be?"

On the next and last day of the examination, the head proctor stood behind the podium and talked into the microphone. "This is the third and final day of the AICPA exam. You may begin."

Robert was busy with the exam. He breathes deeply, his eyes slightly open. *" My techniques are working."* A female proctor walked over to Robert. She looked at his ID and addressed him. "Excuse me. But are you alright?"

"Yes, just fine."

She gave Robert a look of concern and left.

The day continued, and Robert was with his exam. He appeared relaxed, not allowing Henry to interfere with the rest of his performance.

The head proctor finally approached the podium and talked into a microphone. "It's time to put your pencils down. The third and final day of the AICPA exam is over."

Pencils hit the desks throughout the convention hall. A confident Robert slammed his pencil down as well.

Meanwhile, an unhappy Henry sat alone behind his desk and slowly nodded.

Robert drove his car home after completing the exam. He clenched his fist against the steering wheel. He spoke as if a triumphant warrior. "Henry gave me his best shot. And I ace it!" Robert looked at himself in the rear-view mirror. He grinned. "I won, and Henry lost." Unexpectedly, Henry communicated with him mentally.

"Don't you finally want to meet your Evil Wave Master?"

Robert's eyes widened in disbelief. He looked again at himself in the mirror. "Henry?"

"Don't be afraid."

Robert entered an intersection without looking ahead, as the light was red. When he finally saw the light, Robert slammed on the brakes. His body jerked, and his seat belt pulled him back in his seat.

"What the hell?"

Robert heard Henry's laughter. *"You're a complete fool."*

"If I could kill you, I would!" Robert answered in anger.

"Now you're chance."

"It's a trap."

"Linda thinks about you often."

"Linda?"

"She's keeping you alive."

"What?"

"She wants you more than you ever know."

"Why didn't she approach me when she had the chance?"

"She was not allowed to."

The traffic light changed, and Robert drove.

"I know your desires for her are still strong."

"I have Elizaveta."

"I know you want to move on with your life with her. But you still have sexual thoughts about my daughter."

"Get out of my head!" Robert waited for Henry's response. Instead, an eerie silence engulfed the car as Robert drove. Robert took a deep breath and continued driving.

Later that night, Robert was fast asleep in his bed. He entered REM, and a dream fast approached his mind. Robert was wearing only a T-shirt and trousers, attempting to repair a small boat on the shore beneath some coconut trees on a small island. The day was beautiful, but it was hot. He wiped his hand across his forehead to brush off the perspiration. Out of the blue, Linda approached. She was barefoot, wearing only a loosely knit dress, and her long blonde hair shone in the sun. Robert turned and noticed her.

"Linda?"

"You're surprised to see me?"

Robert was lost for words. He gathered his composure. "I am working as fast as I can."

Linda was not interested in the boat. "Don't you desire me?"

"Of course I do. But what about your father?"

"Don't you mind him." She took off her dress, exposing only her thong.

Robert's eyes widened as he dropped his tools. He stood and went to her. They began to kiss with passion. He laid her on the sand, and they began to make love. His dream suddenly ended.

Robert awoke in a cold sweat. He stood up, lost in thought.

Robert entered a gun shop the following day. He was searching for a 9mm. He needed it if he was going back to Dallas, where Henry would be waiting for him. If he wanted to see Linda, he needed to confront him first. The Evil Wave Master. Where a showdown would probably occur. Robert was not a Wave Master. So, he needed something to try to even the odds. He thought he should not go. But Heney was right. Robert's lust for Linda was intense. He desired her like no other. Sure, Robert could start his life with Elizaveta. But she was not Linda. And Henry could feel Robert's lust for his daughter was very much alive.

At the shop, he examined the various guns available. Robert did not have experience with firearms. Activities like hunting or firing at the shooting range were off-limits to him during his childhood days. His father never showed interest in these activities either. So, Robert did not have an adult role model to teach him. As he looked at the various 9 mm, a store clerk came up to Robert and asked him questions about his use of firearms. Based on Robert's answers, the clerk showed a 9 mm that fit Robert's profile. The gun shop even had a mini shooting range in the back so Robert could get a feel for the 9mm he had chosen. After firing a couple of magazines, Robert was happy with his weapon of choice.

A week later, Robert drove in front of Henry's house. He reached into the glove compartment and found the semi-automatic 9mm. Immediately, Robert received a pain in his arm.

Henry communicated with him telepathically. *"You don't need it. Just want to talk. Besides, the gun won't help you."*

Out of frustration, Robert slammed the compartment door without the gun. He exited his car and walked toward the front door.

"It's open."

Following Henry's command, Robert entered the house. But he saw no one.

He heard Henry in his mind. *"I am in the den."*

Robert noticed a portrait of Linda hanging on the wall in the dining room. He continued until he finally entered the den. He saw that Henry was alone, with his back toward him, sitting in his usual recliner. Henry spoke, "So, we finally meet." Henry pressed a button on the armrest, and his recliner slowly turned. Henry and Robert finally faced each other.

"I don't blame you for wanting to kill me. But before your anger overtakes you. Remember this. I could have killed you anytime. So, sit!"

Robert momentarily thought and decided to sit in Muriel's chair, placed some twenty feet in front of Henry.

"You haven't been successful."

"I was merely probing."

Robert smirked. "So, how am I doing?"

Henry changed the subject. "I understand your interest in Linda. Many men share the same desires. But what I can't grasp is her feelings for you. And only you. From what I gathered, she seems to think you both have something in common."

"Ask her?" Robert smirked.

Henry chuckled. "You have many shortcomings. And now you have your Ukrainian girlfriend. Yet you still decided to see Linda, knowing the risk."

"You said she wants to see me. That she has feelings for me. And yes, as you read my thoughts, I do find Linda very desirable. Besides, my so-called Ukrainian girlfriend is in her country now. And I don't know when she's coming back. But of course, you already know this, too." Shrugs. "But I also want to know more about your telepathy. Or should I say your ESP? Since you can do so much more than just read people's thoughts." Paused. "How did you get these strange abilities? And who else knows?"

"My strange abilities, as you call them, are something for me to know. And that is all you need to know. Only those I trust know what they know. And you are not one of them."

"But the things you…"

"It's beyond your comprehension." Henry uncrossed his legs. "I know you want to plug into the network. But it will never happen. It would be best if you had gone back to where you came from instead of trying to find your way in this world. Thinking you'll be so smart."

Robert became upset. "You see people as nothing more than pieces on a board game. To you. Life is cheap. It's too bad you became an Evil Wave Master."

"I don't know how you were able to discover the existence of the Wave Masters. But it doesn't matter. You have no proof." Grinned. "You will always be a mental midget."

Robert's face turned to anger.

"You think I would allow Linda to have a sexual relationship with you? I would never allow her to even touch you. Cochise."

Robert raised his voice. "She's not her. Is she?"

"I can hear your folks calling you back to the reservation. You should go there now."

Robert proceeded to stand and approach Henry. "You-son-of-bitch…" But before he could utter another word, Henry gave Robert a high dose of his wave. Robert stopped as he bowed in pain. Robert managed to get back to his seat.

"Enough of the pleasantries. Now. Let me entertain you." Henry intensified the pain as Robert grabbed his head, yelling in agony. Henry returned Robert's suffering with a smile. With his hands still on his head, Robert took a quick burst of breaths. He decided to lower his head and close his eyes. His breathing became slower and deeper.

Inside Robert's brain, Henry's wave was already latched onto Robert's neurotransmitters and traveled to various parts of the brain. The wave branched out into the frontal lobe area. It began to apply pressure to an artery. The artery wall began to bulge. Robert generated electrical energy, and the electrical impulses from his neurons traveled up from the axons to meet the point in the brain where Henry's wave was applying pressure to the artery. Henry communicated telepathically, *"Now we shall see."* Henry's wave then attacked other arteries. But Robert created other electrical impulses to meet Henry's wave. Like magic, Robert severely weakened Henry's wave.

Robert opened his eyes and looked at Henry with confidence. Henry was not deterred. Dark gray clouds appeared outside the window. They faded the room, giving it a monochrome appearance. Another wave with greater frequency protruded from Henry's head and continued to enter Robert's skull. Henry increased the frequency of the wave. Robert pulled back on the chair. His hands grabbed the armrest. He closed his eyes again.

Back inside Robert's brain, his electrical energy kept Henry from damaging any of his arteries, and his electrical energy again pushed Henry's wave out of his arteries.

Fresh sunlight appeared, bringing back color into the room. Henry was stunned at Robert's abilities.

Robert opened his eyes and looked at Henry in a daze. Everything around Robert appeared blurry.

"Impressive," Henry said.

Robert's vision returned. Robert then saw an image of his old grandfather sitting across from him, examining Robert's palm at 10 years old. The image quickly faded.

"Yes... Your grandfather. I should have known. This would explain your mother." A wicked smile from Henry. "And now it passed on to you."

Robert looked confused at Henry's words.

"Now it's time to leave."

"So, you're finished with me?"

"Don't tempt me, boy! Your electrical impulses are weakening."

Robert managed to stand. He touched his nose and saw blood.

"You're lucky you're still alive. But if you want to joust again... "

"I know I am no Wave Master. To you, I am nothing more than a worthless fool. A dreamer." He ran his finger over his nose again as more blood spilled. "But one day, you will meet you'll deserve fate."

Henry smiled, "I'll save it for the obituary."

Henry's smile turned to a mischievous grin as Robert managed to hobble back to his car.

Robert entered his vehicle and reached for some tissues on the side door holder. He placed them underneath his nostrils to stop the bleeding, and then he drove away.

Meanwhile, Muriel entered the den holding their cat, Gigi. Henry and Muriel communicated mentally.

"You should have killed him?"

Henry stroked his chin, surprised by the turn of events. *"Yes... But no one ever told him. No one ever showed him. Not even his grandfather."*

"What do you mean?"

Henry shook his head. *"Cochise doesn't have the foggiest idea what he has. What he is capable of."* He turned and sternly looked at Muriel.

Muriel now understood what Henry was referring to, as her eyes widened. *"Are you sure?"*

He then stared into space as he slowly nodded his head.

It was 2023; twenty-three years later, and Robert was now forty-six years old. He entered a high-rise Plaza building in New York City (NYC), wearing casual clothes. He walked to the office directory on the wall. He looked for an associate editor named "DAVID HARTMAN – KEYSTONE PUBLICATION." He located him on the 105th Floor". He smiled and walked over to an empty elevator. Robert made his selection, and the elevator slowly began to climb up. The next song in the elevator started to play. It was a jazz fusion-type song that began with a slow tempo. As the music started, Robert stared at the light above. He slowly closed his eyes, and his mind went into vivid dreams.

The dreams started with Robert inside Henry's brain. Robert saw an electrical impulse in one of Henry's neurons travel from the top of the dendrites as it received signals from another neuron. The signal went into the axon of the neuron. An action potential took place, which caused the signal to go faster through the axon in the microtubules and shoot out from the axon terminals. The mental energy then traveled to another connecting neuron. Robert saw an electrical signal go past him inside a neuron as it carried visual data to Henry's visual cortex.

Robert now saw millions of neurons branching, like many branches in many trees. The various neurons communicate with each other through axons as electrical impulses send messages back and forth. Like a vast fiber-optics network that lit up, data was transferred to various parts of his brain. Robert now observed more and more action potentials taking place in the brain, as the electromagnetic fields were highly active, creating negative and positive charges.

Robert closely observed an electrical impulse that pushed the neurotransmitter molecules that connect to the neuron by a synapse. Robert observed the growth of new neurons in Henry's brain as sprouting axons and dendrites formed new synapses during the synaptogenesis process, thereby strengthening Henry's existing neurons and increasing the complexity of his vast neuronal network.

Now, inside the visual cortex, Robert witnessed many streaming visuals being produced from the many electrical impulses streaming data—both the left and right of the visual cortex signal to each other. In one visual, he saw a child playing with her mother. In another visual, he observed a worship service in a local mosque. In another visual, he observed a worship service in a synagogue. And still another visual of a worship service at a church.

He now saw another streaming visual, where he witnessed a couple kiss passionately as they began to make love. In another visual, Robert observed a surgeon perform open-heart surgery. In the following visual, a man slapped a woman several times in a bit of rage in their living room.

Robert briefly moaned in the elevator at the violent image as he continued dreaming with his eyes closed shut.

Back inside Henry's brain, he was in his visual cortex and observed a streaming vision of a basketball game in full swing. Another image shows the President laughing with Hollywood celebrities in the Oval Office. All around, more and more images stream into the visual cortex as Henry's brain mentally observed many images simultaneously.

Robert now experienced a series of quick flashbacks. One image showed a serious look from psychic John Daricek as he spoke to the young, twenty-something Robert, sitting across from him. Another image was of

Wayne, Jim, and Sara at Wayne's desk, laughing hysterically as Robert entered the office. Another image was of Parapsychologist Brad Lance, sitting behind his desk, puffing on his pipe. Finally, a photo of Linda as he remembered her as a young woman on a picture hanging on a wall at the Honeys' house.

A dream now took Robert, in his early twenties, to Central Park in the Big Apple (NYC). He was dressed in a casual suit. He heard popping sounds as fireworks lit up the night sky in bright colors. The fantastic light show was reflected on the glass skyline in Manhattan.

A young Robert, still dressed in his casual suit, walked on a beautiful day in the park. He saw various people enjoying themselves. A dog romped in a pond as the animal tried to retrieve a freebie tossed by its owner. A couple enjoying a picnic with their two children. A young man playing his acoustic guitar to the delight of several onlookers. Many couples hold hands as they walk down the greenery avenues. Robert walked among the various people, but no one made eye contact with him. He smiled at a boy as the cute little lad approached him. But the boy did not smile back as his mother called out. Robert attempted to pat a dog who strode alone. However, the dog did not respond to his touch and wandered off. Robert decided to turn. He now observed a middle-aged woman reading a magazine article on a lonely park bench. He decided to talk to her and ask her what time it was. "Excuse me. But do you have the time?" But she did not look at him or respond to his request as she continued to read her magazine. He tapped her arm. But again, she did not respond. A man walked past Robert on the sidewalk with a beam on his face. Robert decided to follow him and tap him on the shoulder. But the gentleman did not respond as he continued on his merry way. Robert now looked confused as he cast his lonely eyes at the sea of beautiful people at the park on a lovely day. For it all seemed he did not exist.

Robert was still wearing his casual suit as a dream took him to a busy nightclub with intoxicated people everywhere. Robert turned and eyed two young women sitting at a bar with drinks in their hands. It appeared they had eyes for Robert. He waved at them to his delight. They responded as they stood with drinks in their hands and approached him. Robert responded with a grin. However, the two ladies walked past Robert into the arms of two men behind him. Robert turned as a cocktail hostess approached him with a tray of drinks. Robert waved for a drink. But she walked past him without a glance. A very lonely Robert had a gloomy look on his face as he decided to walk away.

Now, another dream carried young Robert to Times Square in NYC. He walked on the sidewalk in daylight with his casual suit. However, people noticed him this time, as he received icy cold stares. This was because Robert now existed in the physical world and the Brain Wave Network. Robert continued walking, and a young mother with her two children noticed him approaching. She pulled her two children away. "Don't touch my children, you pervert!" Her remarks took Robert aback as he gazed at her in disbelief. Several young men approached Robert. They pushed him aside as they continued walking past him. Robert continued to walk down the busy street as several vehicles drove by. Every driver and passenger looked at him with anger.

Robert approached a busy intersection. He saw the pedestrian light turn green. Strangely, no one crossed the street. Robert decided to cross the street anyway. Unexpectedly, he turned and saw a car approaching him from the other direction. But Robert continued to walk. The car sped up, and Robert dove to save his life. He landed by a curve on the other side, as the car barely missed him. He stood up and was visibly upset at the reckless driver. He noticed a tall police officer with sunrays standing just a few feet away as he issued a parking citation. Robert approached the officer and demanded that he pursue the hit-and-run driver. "That guy almost killed me. He ran a red light, for Christ's sake!"

The officer just looked at Robert and spat in his direction. The ball of spit landed on Robert's shoes. Robert looked down and saw the officer's saliva hanging onto his shoes like threads from a spider's web. Robert looked at the officer in disbelief. But the cop gave Robert a big grin as he continued to look down at Robert from his bright sunrays.

Another dream took him to Grand Central Station in NYC. He was in the vast lobby and observed the busy schedule of various trains departing the city. He looked up frantically. He pleaded for help. "Please get me out of here!" To his surprise, people gathered around him from all walks of life. They all stared at him with anger. "What have I done to you people?" Robert said in disbelief.

A stranger replied with icy cold stares, "You should not have written the manuscript, Robert Yellowstone."

Another stranger answered, pointing his fingers at Robert. "You brought the curse upon yourself."

Robert was shocked by their comments.

The young Robert drove down an empty highway interstate as a dream had him driving to an unknown destination at night. He wore his usual attire. He appeared afraid. In the passenger seat was his untitled manuscript. He ran his hand over his hair. Unexpectedly, two vehicles approached Robert at a high rate of speed. The first vehicle came close enough to butt its back bumper. The driver was a white, middle-aged male, while the passenger was a young black male. The driver hit the back bumper again even harder. The impact jerked Robert back and forth.

The black male leaned his head out the open window and yelled. "We are going to kill you, Robert Yellowstone! You should never have written that manuscript."

"Ya. Queer bait." Yelled the driver.

The second vehicle approached from the other side. The driver in the car was a young white female, accompanied by an older white male in the back seat on the passenger side. She honked her horn at Robert as the passenger rolled down his window and began dangling a rope with a noose. "We are going to hang you, Yellowstone! You can't even walk like a man." The female driver honked again. Robert pressed down hard on the accelerator. The two vehicles followed Robert in hot pursuit.

Robert made a quick left turn on a side country road. Both vehicles did the same. Robert saw them from his rear-view mirror. He made another quick turn on still another road. Robert saw another road ahead and quickly took the right instead of the left route. He turned and saw them take the left route. He stopped his car and quickly turned around. He drove hard and was quickly back on the highway.

Robert noticed the vehicles were gone. He rolled down his driver's window and took a deep breath. Without warning, Robert heard the blades of a helicopter hovering overhead. He looked out from his driver's window and saw an attack military helicopter with 7.62 mm machine guns aimed right at him. "Oh, Shit! Now a helicopter! An attack military helicopter!" Robert's foot pressed down hard on the accelerator. He saw a small tunnel just a short distance away. It is just wide enough for a vehicle to go through. His car went full throttle. The helicopter gained distance. Robert's vehicle was almost at the tunnel entrance when the military gunner let out a burst of ammo at his car. The bullets managed to hit the back side of his vehicle as Robert made it inside the quarter-mile tunnel and continued to go full speed.

He reached the other side of the tunnel and made a quick right turn. His vehicle headed to the forests surrounding the tunnel. The trees were spread out far enough for Robert to drive between the tall trees. He looked above and saw the deadly helicopter. The gunner blasted ammo at Robert's vehicle. However, the gunner could not get a clear shot at him. Robert looked straight ahead, saw a cliff's edge, and drove right for it. He reached over for his manuscript and opened his door. He leaped from the car, holding his manuscript for dear life. His vehicle plunged several hundred feet to the valley floor below and ignited in flames. The helicopter quickly saw the aftermath and circled the crashed, burned vehicle like a hungry vulture. The steel bird then flew away. Robert was behind a tree as he held onto his manuscript. He appeared bruised, and his suit was torn in several places. Robert's face was gloomy and despondent as he stared into the distance.

The concluding dream took him to midday. His clothes were in disarray, and he was bruised. He sat on the docks, staring out at the East River. Robert then gazed at the Statue of Liberty.

All alone, Robert walked to the foot of the statue, holding his manuscript like a newborn baby. He decided to go inside the lonely statue. Robert went up the long flight of stairs to the top of her crown. Unexpectedly, Robert felt sharp pains in his lower back and his legs. He struggled to climb, but he knew the pains were coming from Henry Honey.

"You will not stop me!"

Robert heard Henry's voice in his head. *"I am going to destroy you for communicating with my Linda! She should not have trusted you. You cannot be trusted!"*

Robert buckled over as the pain became more intense. He decided to tuck the manuscript inside the front of his pants. He grabbed the rails and continued up the stairs. Again, Henry struck Robert with pain. Robert stumbled and almost fell. For a moment, he cried in pain. He placed his hands on his head. He felt relaxed and began to climb the stairs again. But the pains hit him again as he moaned. Henry responded with laughter. Robert decided to close his eyes and kneel.

Inside Robert's brain, Henry's wave had latched onto Robert's neurotransmitters as it traveled to various parts of the brain. The wave branched into the frontal lobe area and applied pressure to an artery. Robert generated electrical energy, and the electrical impulses from his neurons traveled up the axons. They met and weakened Henry's wave, which was applying pressure to the artery.

He took a series of slow, deep breaths. He opened his eyes. He stood and raced up the stairs.

"The Wave Binding Technique!" Henry exclaimed.

Robert reached the top of the crown and saw the harbor ahead as Henry continued to taunt. *"You have no friends. And nobody wants you. They will never believe your story because you will never sell it. You will be labeled a schizophrenic. I will make sure of that!"*

Several beautiful rainbows in bright colors appeared from the horizon in Upper New York Bay. But these were not ordinary rainbows, as they propelled right past Robert like laser beams.

Henry was shocked. *"What!"*

A smile came over Robert as he reached for the manuscript tucked in front of his pants. He raised it above his head and out of one of the statue's crown windows. Robert laughed at Henry. The dream came to an end.

Another song played over the airwaves in the elevator with the elevator door open. Robert still stood with his eyes closed. An older woman in her seventies noticed Robert but decided to enter. She saw that Robert was in a trance. She moved toward him and tapped him on the shoulder.

"Mister. Are you alright?"

Robert slowly opened his eyes and looked at her, startled. "Where am I?"

"You are on the hundred and fifth floor of the Plaza building."

Robert took a deep breath. "How long have I been here?"

"I can't say. Are you sure you'll be alright?"

Robert nodded as he slowly smiled. "I am now."

Later in the day, Robert was in David Hartman's conference office. They were both sitting across from each other on a conference glass table. David was in his mid-50s. He was the associate editor of Keystone Publications. He was wearing a tasteful suit. He reached over to turn off the digital recorder on the conference table as they concluded their development session regarding the manuscript. Near the recorder were his computer tablet, imported bottles of spring water, the manuscript, and an open, unmarked 9" x 12" envelope containing documents that supported Robert's story. Robert took a drink.

David turned to Robert. "Just like that, huh?"

"Yup. The mental blitzkrieg ended after the encounter."

"The pains and unfamiliar thoughts?"

Robert nodded.

"Then you became a CPA. You married. And then you received an interesting obituary clipping from Linda, which mentioned that Henry passed away some time later. Is that correct?"

"It's in the package."

David reached for the oversized package and pulled out the clipping. He read the obituary.

*"Henry Honey passed away on March 15, 2020.
He enjoyed a long and distinguished career at
Jones Oil and Maverick Oil. He was born and
raised in Oklahoma. He was a good friend,
helping those in need. Cremation services
will be held the following day."*

David turned the article over. The word "Linda" was written on it. David studied the article momentarily and placed the clipping back in the package. "Why wait so long to write the manuscript?"

"I was afraid to write if he was still alive. He could come after me or my family. I needed proof… Linda contacted me after he died and gave me what I needed. The COVID crisis also made it difficult for me to travel the last couple of years." Paused as he took another drink. He shuffled. "She deeply regretted his behavior towards me."

"You and Linda never...'

He shook his head. "No…I was still married. And she didn't give me her contact information."

"When this goes public, many people will ask many questions. Including the Government."

"I know."

"Why did you not wear a wire during the encounter?"

"He was monitoring me."

"Yet you brought the gun?"

"Yeah….I know. But it didn't cross my mind at the time. My adrenaline got all worked up about killing him. Or at least use it in self-defense. Besides… He would have known if I was carrying a wire."

"This Wave Binding Technique. Why couldn't you read other people's thoughts with it?"

"The technique has nothing to do with mind reading. It's just a way of preventing him from applying pressure on the arteries. Reading people's thoughts is on a whole different level."

"But the technique saved your life. And to master this technique, you need to generate energy somewhere in your brain to make it work."

"Reading thoughts involves changes in the consciousness affecting the neocortex. At least, that is what I believe. And I don't know how to do that."

"You just haven't tried."

"Look…Maybe one day, I might be able to pick up other people's thoughts. It's just not on my to-do list."

David reached for his computer tablet on the table. He took out a stylus and wrote something on the tablet.

Robert took a drink and placed the empty bottle on the table. "I felt he was holding back."

"Pardon me?

"The technique was important. But if he wanted to kill me when we met, he would have. I just can't figure out why."

"Linda?"

"Or something else."

"Well…we will never know. Will we?"

Robert was lost for words as he shook his head.

"John Daricek?"

Robert took a deep breath. "I don't know about him." Paused. "He might have."

"Sorry about your wife's recent passing. Her name was Elizaveta. Correct?"

Robert sported a sad look, "Yeah."

"Cancer?"

"Yeah."

"And no kids?"

"She couldn't have any."

"And she knew nothing of your ordeal with Henry?

Robert shook his head, "Nope."

David wrote something on his tablet.

"What about Muriel?

"Linda never mentioned her." Robert reached for another bottle of water. "But I've been having these strange feelings again."

"But, the man's..." David gestured to the obituary.

Robert took a drink. "I know. It's just my paranoid self." He scratched his head." I had these strange dreams coming up here. I was inside his head. Seeing all of the mental activity. It was as if I were on this mental highway… Data… Or should I say images flowing around. Like…Ah…Vehicles zipping through various loops. And people wanted to kill me for writing the manuscript. And then, when I thought all was lost. I was saved in the end. It even surprised Henry."

"He communicated with you?"

Robert nodded.

"What did he say?"

"That I have no friends. That no one will believe my story. Because it will never sell."

David chuckled. "So, you're telling me Henry will rise from the dead and haul the publication?"

Robert shrugged. "I guess… I don't know." Paused. "He was trying to murder me. Although I don't think that was his intent. It was more of throwing fear in me for writing the story and making sure it won't see the light of day."

David became defiant as he pointed his finger, "I guarantee you, it will be published." David again wrote on his tablet. He studied Robert for a moment. "Your mental bouts made you a hero."

"I couldn't stop him."

"He tried to break you. But instead, you survived. Even found love. And now you have discovered this Brain Wave Network all around us." David reached for his water. He drank. "Off the record, if you had to summarize your experiences with Henry, what would you consider the most valuable lesson?"

Robert momentarily ran his hand over his head as he paused. "Heroism exists not only in the physical sense but also inside our heads. In the ability to face unpleasant thoughts every day. Knowing someone is reading them and can place these same thoughts inside our minds for their pleasure... It can't be described… Excuse me." He took another drink of water. "So now I know a hero can come in different forms. And I hope … this ordeal is behind me for good. That Henry is no more."

David smiled. "Maybe there's more than one Wave Master out there?"

Robert shrugged his shoulders. "Maybe."

Later, Robert and David were in the lobby of the publishing office. They shook hands. "We'll keep in touch, Robert."

Robert responded with a nod. He turned to leave but looked back at David. "Is there a restaurant around here?"

"The floor below us. And tell the cashier to bill me."

"Thanks." Robert left.

Robert went to the restaurant but noticed a hair salon next door. He decided to enter. He met a hair stylist at the front desk. She informed him he would have to wait at least an hour before anyone could cut his hair since he did not have an appointment. Robert thought about it for a moment and decided to stay. He looked through the various magazines on a nearby rack, selected the one that piqued his interest, and sat.

Meanwhile, alone in the office, David sat in his conference room and glanced at the 9" x 12" envelope contents. He found a black-and-white photo of Henry in his 60s. "So, this was the Evil Wave Master?" David studied it momentarily and placed the image with the rest of the contents back in the envelope. He laid the envelope at the edge of the table.

David's secretary, Sonja, in her 40s, walked in. "Mr. Hartman. Mr. Trottier is waiting."

David's hand brushed the envelope as he stood. The envelope tumbled to the floor next to a wastebasket as he walked to the doorway, following Sonja. He turned toward the envelope on the floor. "Can you grab that off the floor and give it to Penny in Editorial?"

"Sure, Mr. Hartman."

David was about to exit.

"Your wife left you a gift."

"Really? Where?"

Without giving it another thought, they left the office, leaving the envelope and all of Linda's supplied contents on the floor.

A short time later, a janitor entered David's office. No one was in. With a large trash can on wheels, he meandered over to the waste basket. He saw the envelope with all the contents on the floor and assumed it was unimportant. So, he threw it in with the rest of the trash. He pushed the can as he whistled out of the office.

The janitor entered the building's back parking lot and pushed the large can over to empty it in the dumpster. A trash disposal truck entered and drove up to the dumpster. The truck's retrieval arms lifted the dumpster. The truck unloaded the contents into the hopper. The oversized envelope with the evidence tumbled into the hopper with the rest of the trash. The janitor and driver waved at each other. The truck left.

Another hour went by, and the office hours were almost over. Sonja was about to call it a day. But as always, she made her rounds to see if anyone was still in the office before locking up. She made her way to David's office. His door was closed. She knocked, but there was no reply. She decided to walk in. David was slumped behind his desk. Sonja hurried to him. She nudged him. "David! David!" No reply. She checked his pulse. No beat. She screamed. "He's dead!"

Meanwhile, Robert sat at a table in the Plaza building restaurant after his haircut. He had already finished his dinner as a song played over the sound system. He was drinking a beer and checking his latest news reports on his smartphone. He decided to retrieve a digital photo from his phone. It's a photo of Elizaveta and him hugging each other several months before she passed. His eyes reveal tears. Robert placed the phone gently on the table. He looked across the window as the yellowish sun began to settle. Another song began to play over the airwaves. The song was about someone watching you. Robert became tense. It's as if someone were watching him. He scanned the restaurant but saw nothing of interest. His mind became lost in thought.

Brain Wave

A brain wave is an electrochemical phenomenon that can produce wave energy within the brain. Psychics such as a Telekinesis, a Telepathic, and a Wave Master can transmit this energy outside the skull. The wave energy can then travel as it latches onto the energy fields using electromagnetism, allowing the brain wave to produce PSI events such as telekinesis and telepathy. For all others, a brain wave would only communicate with other neurotransmitters within the brain.

Brain Wave Network

Brain Wave Network (BWN) is a concept that explains some of the synchronicity events that occur in everyday lives. The BWN is also the leading cause of other activities worldwide. In a BWN, everyone is connected with everyone else through wave energy. This is possible because of the energy in the air. All brain waves are interconnected through an electromagnetic force called electromagnetism. Electromagnetism is the force that causes interaction between electrically charged particles; the areas in which this happens are called electromagnetic fields. The force of electromagnetism is manifested in electric and magnetic fields; both are different aspects of electromagnetism and, hence, are intrinsically related. Thus, changes in an electric field generate a magnetic field; conversely, changes in a magnetic field generate an electric field. This effect is known as electromagnetic induction and forms the basis of operation for electrical generators, induction motors, and transformers. Mathematically speaking, magnetic fields and electric fields, when combined, create a single, unified electromagnetic field.

This field predicts the existence of electromagnetic waves that travel through space.

If a person's brain waves can somehow link to many different individual brain waves simultaneously, then this energy flow would create a BWN, utilizing the principle of electromagnetism. This individual can extend this network and access other human brain waves. By creating a BWN, the individual can implement cause-and-effect scenarios for different individuals. Hence, a synchronicity effect is created in which an unrelated event of one individual connects with another event, forming a meaningful experience together. Therefore, the events of two total strangers connect.

A person with complete access to the network would be a Wave Master, and it would be the Wave Master who would have the ability to create this kind of network. The entity should not be mistaken for a Telepathic. In contrast, a Telepathic can monitor or pick up another person's thoughts. However, the Telepathic, also known as a Wave Maker, would not have complete access to the BWN or create one. This psychic access to the network is weak at best. A Telepathic is usually found in such venues in Las Vegas or on talk or radio shows. Governmental agencies can also employ them.

Other supernatural entities could also join or create a BWN to assess the various brains with which to communicate and influence. Who would these supernational entities be? Aliens from another world and spiritual beings come to mind.

The BWN works similarly to a computer network where computers share data through a server. Like a server, the Wave Master will receive and flow brain data from other individuals in the BWN. The waves from the Wave Master make this connection possible, similar to wireless signals on the Internet. The Wave Master will also serve as a router, deciding who will share the data, such as a Single Channel or Wave Rider. A BWN can have as many individuals as a Wave Master can monitor simultaneously.

In this simplified illustration, a Wave Master receives and transmits data from six individuals below. Only the Single Channel is allowed to receive data from other individuals. In this scenario, the Single Channel can receive data generated from the NWR. All this is possible because of the Wave Master.

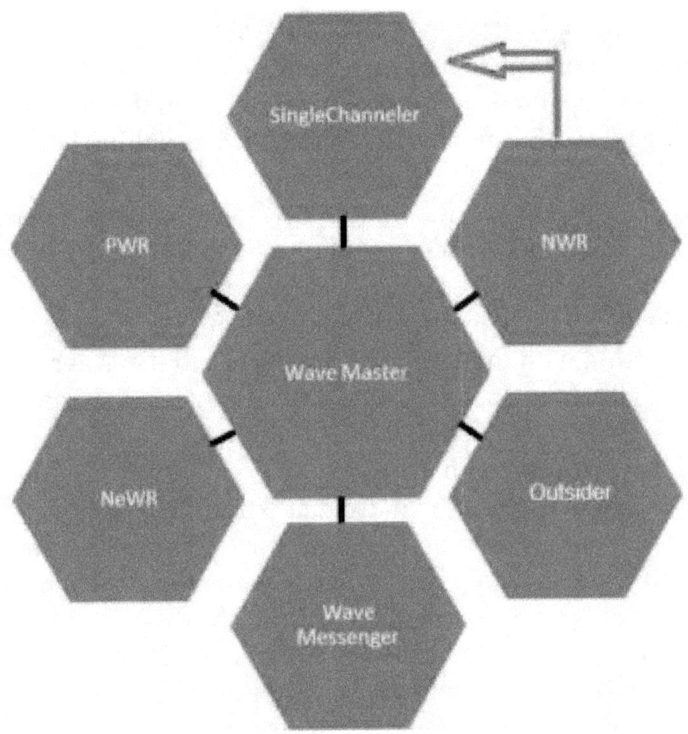

Thus, the BWN can affect people in ways that create either positive or negative results. These are everyday events that can impact personal and professional lives. Since there can be more than one Wave Master, having more than one BWN is possible. Each Wave Master or other supernational entity creates and expands its network. It is also possible for these networks to intersect with one another.

Breathing Techniques

This technique could provide aid against a Wave Master, such as an Evil one, who might want to disrupt the physiology of a person by causing negative effects such as organ pains and excessively sleepiness. Studies has shown effective breathing techniques reduces stress by activating the parasympathetic system. Which can calm the body in fighting stress hormones. Rapid or quick breathing techniques creating forceful inhales and exhales could confuse and disrupts the Wave Master's wave as in entered the person's head. As a result, the wave is less effective in achieving pains, stokes, aneurysms, and excessive drowsiness. The breathing techniques could be used in conjunction with the Hand Technique or aid the Wave Binding Techniques.

Clairvoyant (Fortune Tellers)
The ability to foresee the individual's future by studying objects/photos belonging to the person. Clairvoyants are sometimes referred to as Fortune Tellers. Some Clairvoyants have claimed to have the ability to communicate with the deceased relatives of individuals. However, there has been widespread mistrust of Clairvoyants, who claim they can communicate with the deceased.

Dedicated Wave Connection
A Dedicated Wave Connection (DWC) is a unique mental (energy) bond between two or more individuals' brain activities caused by the Wave Master. The DWC is an essential component of a BWN. Through the BWN, a Wave Master will be interested in specific individuals. It is this interest that creates a DWC. For example, if a Wave Master were obsessed with the brain activity of an individual negatively, this person would generate a Negative Wave Reaction (NWR). Likewise, if the Wave Master were equally obsessed with the brain activity of

another individual in a positive way, this person would be considered a Positive Wave Reaction (PWR). If these two opposite reactions cross paths, a special bond will develop, in which they will be exclusively interconnected to each other through the Wave Master's strong interest in both of them. Therefore, the action of one will ultimately affect the action of the other, such as negative and positive charges. At times, the Wave Master will place images on each of their brains to heighten the DWC.

Here is an example of how the DWC could work in a BWN. A Wave Master was obsessed with a guy named Jack, but in a very negative way. That is to say, the Wave Master loathed Jack. Several factors may contribute to this negative reaction. Maybe it's Jack's sexual orientation. His race or religious beliefs. His political views or simply his physical appearance. It depends on the Wave Master's state of mind. Now there is Jill. The Wave Master is equally obsessed with her, but in a very positive way. That is to say, Jill can do no wrong in the eyes of this Wave Master. She can make mistakes from time to time. But this is acceptable. Because in the eyes of the Wave Master, she is as perfect as they come. Now, Jack and Jill do not know each other. They could be living many miles away from each other. Suddenly, Jack and Jill's paths cross as they work together in the same department. Since Jill represents the PWR and Jack the NWR, there is a strong likelihood that Jill will become Jack's supervisor. The Wave Master would prefer it this way because of the different reactions Jack and Jill produce in the BWN as positive and negative charges. The Wave Master probably orchestrated them to work together to create the DWC. If Jack keeps his nose clean and does not upset Jill, then Jack might keep his job.

Let's say Jack no longer works for Jill and has moved on, never crossing paths with Jill again. However, the Wave Master is still monitoring both of them. Because their path has crossed, the DWC has been established. Because of this, Jack's or Jill's actions will influence the Wave Master's behavior towards them.

For example, let's say Jack is a Christian while Jill is Muslim. Jack is sitting in a local bar conversing with two close friends, Fred and Joe, while Jill is a thousand miles away with her fiancée. Jack states to Fred and Joe that he would never marry a Muslin. And both Fred and Joe agree that they would never marry a Muslin either. The Wave Master will now attack Jack for that remark. Therefore, when Jack reports to work the following morning, the Wave Master will attempt to have Jack fired. What was the motive? The answer was obvious. When Jack and Jill began to work together, a DWC was established between them. Of course, neither of them was aware of the Wave Master or the BWN. But it does not matter. Just like an electrical charge created an electrical current, Jack and Jill made a DWC in the BWN caused by energy from the Wave Master. Therefore, in future episodes, if Jack does anything the Wave Master views as offensive to Jill, the Wave Master will mentally attack Jack because of the DWC that was created.

Notice that the Wave Master did not attack Fred or Joe. Only Jack. Because the DWC was between Jack and Jill, Fred and Joe would be called a Neutral Wave Reaction (NeWR). A NeWR develops when the Wave Master is not obsessed with an individual, like with Fred or Joe's brain activity. They generally do not have any charge reaction in the network regarding positive or negative reactions from a Wave Master and thus can be seen as neutral charges.

The Wave Master would not be concerned with Fred or Joe's daily routines unless Fred or Joe decides to do something outlandish, like formulate plans to destroy the Golden Gate Bridge. Fred and Joe are part of the BWN, just like Jack and Jill. But for some reason, the Wave Master did not have a particular interest in them, as with Jack and Jill. This is why Fred and Joe are only NeWRs. In the scheme of things, most brain activities in the entire BWN are NeWRs.

Extra Sensory Perception (ESP)

Extrasensory Perception, better known as ESP, is the ability to perceive information independently of and beyond the five senses of seeing, hearing, smelling, touching, and tasting. Mainstream parapsychology identifies three primary branches of ESP: Clairvoyance, Telepathy, and Precognition. Wave Masters do perform telepathic tasks. But on a higher level. They also possess other abilities not found in the traditional primary branches. Therefore, Wave Mastery, the noun reference to Wave Master, would be a new primary branch. As a result, the four primary branches of ESP would be: Clairvoyance, Telepathy, Precognition, and Wave Mastery.

Guilt/Fear flight

It creates a state of mind in which the person believes they can commit every thought that enters their mind, no matter the circumstance. Thus, all thoughts must be taken seriously. Thought and not action determine the person's true personality. The action was simply a by-product of the thought. Therefore, the underlying principle was thought and not the action, reflected the individual's true self. A Wave Master can create such a flight through ESP, injecting unwanted thoughts in the victim's head and using pain (usually in the inner ears) as the stimulus to develop such a flight. Thus, causing the victim to have a thought disorder.

Hand Technique

A Wave Master can cause sleepiness by jamming neurotransmitters firing in the brain. Placing hands on the head in the correct location or moving them around can create a jamming effect. This is very useful when driving or studying for an exam. Therefore, the sleepiness will stop or weaken. The Hand Technique is possible because the human nervous system uses electricity to send signals through the body. Elements like sodium, potassium, calcium, and magnesium have a specific electrical charge that makes this possible. Human cells generate electricity with these charged elements, called ions. Therefore, placing hands on the head can cause electromagnetic interference (EMI) in brain waves entering the skull.

This technique could also lessen a Wave Master's ability to send negative thoughts. However, applying this technique in a public forum, such as a social gathering, will make the person appear awkward or strange. So, negative thoughts are usually ignored unless the person is experiencing guilt/fear flight. Hand techniques could help prevent aneurysms. However, the Wave Binding Technique is the preferred method for such attacks.

Interconnectivity

Interconnectivity is the physical reality of atoms that can link together through some form of energy, allowing for the flow of energy, information, or material. It can also refer to the state of being connected or linked together. The Brain Wave Network is a subset of this interconnectivity.

Inner Circle

The Inner Circle are individuals aware of the BWN established by the Wave Master. They hold favor with the Wave Master and are usually Single-Channelers. This is not the same as an Outsider, who is also aware of the BWN but does not hold favor with the Wave Master.

Multi-Channeler

A Multi-Channeler is a psychic who can monitor more than one individual. That is to say, the psychic can read or pick up multiple thoughts from different brain patterns simultaneously, a typical ability of a Wave Master.

Negative Wave Reaction

Negative Wave Reaction (NWR) is a human brain activity that the Wave Master is obsessed with and firmly disfavors. That is to say, the NWR usually does wrong in the eyes of a Wave Master. The NWR is the complete opposite of the PWR. Because in the eyes of the Wave Master, the NWR is a complete loser. The NWR's physical characteristics, religious and sexual preferences, and behavior are just some of the factors that could contribute to this very negative attitude. Ultimately, the Wave Master will attempt to terminate the NWR. However, because the Wave Master has a high interest in the NWR, the Wave Master would rather punish the NWR constantly rather than terminate the

NWR quickly in the BWN unless the NWR's actions become out of control.

When a Wave Master determines an individual is an NWR, the individual begins to experience tragic events in their lives—a sudden loss of a job and difficulty in finding another one. Acquaintances, friends, coworkers, and even relatives begin to distance themselves from them. Random negative thoughts start to appear in their minds, and it becomes increasingly complex to establish a meaningful relationship with someone they might be interested in. Anger, depression, and suicidal thoughts have now become their companion.

Neutral Wave Reaction

Neutral Wave Reaction (NeWR) is a human brain activity that the Wave Master is not obsessed with and therefore shows an indifference to their daily human brain activity. Nothing in particular in their characteristics interests a Wave Master. As a result, they will not create a DWC in the Brain Wave Network. But that would be something the Wave Master might or might not want to do. Therefore, if a Wave Master dislikes a NeWR's negative brain activity, the reaction will probably be to ignore it. However, the Wave Master could terminate the NeWR depending on the severity of the negative brain activity. However, because the NeWRs are indifferent in the eyes of a Wave Master, they are not micro-managed like Negative and Positive Wave Reactions in the BWN. Therefore, NeWRs can usually continue their daily routines with hardly any interference from a Wave Master. Unless the Wave Master has reasons to do otherwise.

However, if an NWR makes contact with a NeWR, the Wave Master will award the NeWR with financial gains and other luxuries if the Wave Master knows this would irritate the NWR because of some jealousy that might develop between the NWR and the NeWR. In other words, the NeWR is not receiving financial rewards because they have some special gift, intelligence, or talent. It is simply because the Wave Master wants to upset the NWR. Once the NWR breaks off its relationship with the NeWR, any ill-gotten gains the NeWR received from the Wave Master will soon evaporate.

This would also work similarly if an Outsider also formed a relationship with a NeWR. The difference here is that the Outsider knows the success of the NeWR is coming from the Wave Master to upset the Outsider. This makes it all the sweeter for the Wave Master to continue with the ill-gotten gains until the Outsider no longer communicates with the NeWR.

The difference between the PWR and the NWR involving the NeWR is that the NeWR will not be utilized to create some form of jealousy with the PWR, as with the NWR. If, however, the NeWR upsets the PWR for any reason, the Wave Master will punish the NeWR.

The Wave Master will also attack an NWR for criticizing a NeWR for any reason. This is because of the negative attitude the Wave Master has toward the NWR.

Outsider
An Outsider is an individual who knows a Wave Master and the BWN. However, the Outsider is not a Single-

Channeler. Also, the Wave Master does not favor or like this individual. Therefore, the Outsider is also not a Wave Messenger. The Wave Master views the Outsider as a loose cannon and a possible threat to the BWN. Not because the Outsider is a Wave Master, since he or she is not. It is because the Outsider was not intended to have this knowledge. An Outsider is extremely rare and poses a problem for the Wave Master. This is because the Wave Master does not trust the Outsider. Therefore, the Wave Master could also view the Outsider as an NWR.

Positive Wave Reaction

Positive Wave Reaction (PWR) is a type of human brain activity that the Wave Master is particularly interested in and strongly favors. That is to say, the PWR can do no wrong in the eyes of a Wave Master. The PWR can make mistakes from time to time. But this is acceptable. Because in the eyes of the Wave Master, the PWR is as perfect as they come. The PWR's physical characteristics, religious and sexual preferences, and behaviors are just some of the factors that could contribute to this very positive attitude. However, the PWR lacks knowledge of the BWN and has no interactions with the Wave Master.

When a Wave Master determines an individual is a PWR, the individual begins to experience positive events in their lives. If they have a job, better opportunities will likely await them through a promotion, or they will find a more desirable career. They become popular with their acquaintances and coworkers. And soon they will want to become the PWR best friends. Coworkers and even relatives will come to the PWR for advice and guidance. And if the PWR has not found that special someone in their lives. They do not have to wait long, for one will appear just around the corner. Happiness is their constant companion.

Precognition

The ability to see or otherwise become directly aware of unfolding events. The event(s) can be defined, and the person does not have to be personally connected to the event(s). Usually, precognitions come in the form of dreams, where visions are created. This ability is rare and not commonly found.

Premonition

The ability to sense or feel that something is about to happen, which is usually unpleasant. This experience can happen at any given time. The person with the suspicion is somehow personally connected with this uneasy feeling. It all depends on which events these unpleasant experiences can be detected before they occur. This is a common phenomenon that many people have experienced.

Psychic Abduction

Psychic Abduction is a forced relationship between a powerful psychic and an abductee. In this relationship, the abductee experiences paranormal events against their wishes, which causes the individuals to undergo negative psychological changes. The encounter involves an entity, specifically a psychic with powerful ESP, who communicates and conducts mental experiments with the abductee for either self-gratification or to refine their ESP skills. The psychic and the abductee are aware of each other. However, the abductee cannot break away from this relationship after the psychic has mentally kidnapped the individual's mind. The abductee has nowhere to turn, and the psychic is aware that no one will believe or accept their twisted psychic relationship.

The relationship between a Wave Master and an Outsider can be considered a form of psychic abduction. A Wave Master may not have initially intended to have this relationship with the individual. But once the Outsider knows the Wave Master, the Wave Master might not want to end the relationship, and could continue with it even after the Outsider wishes it to end. Therefore, the Outsider ends up becoming the abductee of the Wave Master, who is now performing mental experiments and mind games on the Outsider. The Outsider feels like he or she is being mentally held against their will, as they are forced to stay in this relationship and have no way out. An Evil Wave Master would be a psychic who would enjoy and participate in these kinds of relationships.

Single-Channeler (Wave Rider)
A Single-Channeler is someone whose brain wave piggybacks on the brain wave of a Wave Master. He or she is essentially riding on a wave created by the Wave Master. This will enable the Single-Channeler to receive and even send mental messages to an individual in the BWN via the Wave Master. Thus, a Single-Channeler's ability is similar to that of a Telepathic. However, the Single-Channeler can only monitor another person through a Wave Master, while the Telepathic can receive thoughts from someone else without assistance from another source (human). The Single-Channeler, sometimes called a Wave Rider, will work with the Wave Master to achieve some goal or objective that the Wave Master desires.

Switching

Switching is the ability to receive someone's mental image and switch to another image in their brain. A Wave Master sometimes does this to confuse that individual's sense of mental direction and desires. Usually, when an NWR has a positive thought, a Wave Master, usually an Evil one, can switch it to a negative one. The switching done frequently by an Evil Wave Master can create a mental and behavioral problem, such as the guilt/fear flight.

Synchronicity

Synchronicity is the experience of two or more events that are causally unrelated occurring together in a meaningful manner. To count as synchronicity, the events should be unlikely to occur together by chance. Swiss psychologist Carl Gustav Jung first described the concept of synchronicity in the 1920s. The concept does not question or compete with the notion of causality. Instead, it maintains that just as events may be grouped by cause, they may also be grouped by their meaning. Since meaning is a complex mental construction subject to conscious and subconscious influences, not every correlation in the grouping of events by meaning needs an explanation in terms of cause and effect. Many people view life as a series of unrelated events. However, in synchronicity, these incidents are coincidences that are connected, which lay on top of everything that is part of a cosmic unconsciousness.

Several or more factors, like the BWN, can cause synchronic events. Dr. Jung did not address direct causes of synchronicity using empirical studies based on scientific data.

Telepathy Wave Rate (TWR)
The Telepathy Wave Rate is the current brain wave activity multiplied by brain energy from other brain regions. The greater the energy, the greater the wave. In a simplified example, if the brain is in a gamma activity state, the brain energy produced in the brain will be applied to the gamma state to determine the wave rate. Brain energy is the amount of electricity a person can produce in the brain. In a simplified example, a Wave Master is producing brain activity in the part of their brain labeled A. The individual also produces brain activity in another part of his brain labeled B. However, the individual also produces activity in another part of their brain, labeled G. The individual then can combine the activities of A and B, which amplifies more energy and applies it to activity G. This, in turn, will determine the telepathy wave rate of activity G.

Total Conscious Awareness in Telepathy
Total Conscious Awareness, in telepathy, involves the consciousness level of an individual who has become aware of a specific entity communicating and occupying his or her mind. The entity could be a Wave Maker (Telepathic) or a Wave Master. This entity was in the individual's conscious levels. However, awareness was not achieved until the individual became aware of the entity in their mind.

Wave Binding Technique
It is the ability to generate energy in the brain in the form of waves and apply it in the area of the brain where an aneurysm is beginning to develop. Therefore, when the artery starts to swell or bulge because of a wave coming

from a Wave Master, the energy created from the individual will be channeled to meet the Wave Master's wave and jam it before the aneurysm can fully develop. The technique can also be used if a Wave Master is attempting to cause sleepiness by jamming neurotransmitters firing in the brain. However, the Hand Technique is a more straightforward method to use if a Wave Master is causing the sleepiness.

Wave Maker (Telepathic)

A Wave Maker is a person who can create a wave without assistance from another human source, electronic, or mechanical apparatus. The wave is composed of mental energy generated in the brain, which is transmitted through electric fields in space. However, the Wave Maker such as a Telepathic can only monitor one person or other living entity at a time. And the Wave Maker does require sleep. The Wave Maker might be able to manipulate or disrupt electric equipment. However, this ability is only minimal at best. The Wave Maker does not have complete access to the BWN, as the Wave Master does. Therefore, the Wave Maker's ability to control wave energy flows is not at the same level as the Wave Master's would be. A Wave Maker is usually a Telepathic, a Scanner or has other forms of psychic ability, demonstrating success in their limited field of ESP.

Wave Master

A Wave Master is a person or other human-like alien who can create a wave without assistance from another human source, electronic, or mechanical apparatus. The wave is composed of mental energy produced in the brain, which is transmitted through electric fields in space. The wave can connect to other brain waves, thus having Multi-Channeler abilities. This ability enables the establishment of a BWN, linking various brain activities together. Under this scenario, various human brains can communicate mentally to each other with the aid of the Wave Master.

Like a Telepathic psychic, a Wave Master can read or insert thoughts or images into other individuals' minds. However, the Wave Master can also access an individual's nervous system and the blood vessels in the human body. Because the blood and nervous systems branch and travel together, it is easy for a Wave Master to manipulate or tamper with such physiological systems. Thus, this causes various pains, such as back, neck, and inner ear inflammation. Also, more severe actions, such as heart attacks, aneurysms, and strokes, are within the parameters of a Wave Master. A Wave Master can also jam neurotransmitters firing in the brain, thus causing sleepiness. Because of the Wave Masters' abilities, they could attempt to manipulate or control living entities, such as animals and humans. Because of the brain wave activities, the Wave Master does not require sleep.

Wave Masters can also tamper with and shut down devices and equipment that is depend on electricity as their source of power. This would include batteries of various shapes and sizes, as well as aircraft and automotive electronic components, computer networks, and light fixtures. Brain waves are a form of electrical activity, and Wave Masters' powerful brain waves can be attracted to the electrical currents from these devices, potentially disrupting or jamming them.

A Wave Master can be good or bad (evil). It depends on the personality of the Wave Master and what the Wave Master is seeking. A Wave Master can use their abilities to do good or apply their ESP to wreak havoc. It depends on what the Wave Master's motives are. In some situations, the Wave Master will do a good deed; in other scenarios, that same Wave Master will perform horrible acts. A Wave Master will usually know that a violent event is about to unfold in the BWN, such as an active shooter, bank heist, or terrorist attack, and choose to stop it or let it unfold.

Wave Mastery

Wave Mastery is the noun term referring to the ability to perform tasks beyond the level of a telepathic individual in the area of telepathy. This also means employing brain waves to perform functions not found in other conventional ESP areas, such as manipulating or disrupting electrical energy or fields in living organisms and mechanical devices. In contrast, Wave Master would be the adjective term for Wave Mastery, describing the tasks an individual or human-like alien would perform to achieve Wave Mastery.

Wave Messenger

A Wave Messenger is an individual a Wave Master favors and likes. This could be based on the person's physical features, name, sexual gender, political affiliation, or some or all of the above. For example, a person could have physical features or a first or last name that the Wave Master favors. The Wave Master can use a Wave Messenger to accomplish goals or objectives. For example, a Wave Messenger can be part of a corporate network to achieve favorable objectives for the Wave Master. To accomplish this, the Wave Master will promote the Wave Messenger in organizations through the BWN. As a result, the Wave Messenger will establish agendas through involvement in corporate executive committees to achieve the objectives of the Wave Master. However, a Wave Messenger does not know the Wave Master's ESP or the BWN as a Single-Channeler would. The Wave Messenger is similar to the PWR. However, the Wave Messenger will personally know or interact with the Wave Master, while the PWR will not.

ABOUT THE AUTHOR

Mark Ingle

I am married with three children. Contracting duties currently take up most of my working time.

The idea for "The Wave Master" came about after reading a paper by Dr. Jung. However, I wanted to take it further and create a paradigm in which Dr. Jung's synchronicity theory could be explained using ESP.

In synchronicity, two unrelated events intersect with each other, causing a meaningful coincidence or what synchronicity calls an acausal connecting principle. These acausal connections prove we are all somehow interconnected. The problem is that science cannot explain how it happens. There are countless theories on this subject, but they are just theories.

Through research, I explain how and why these connections could occur by exploring ESP, mainly telepathy, and its principles. However, people who create these connections must have strong PSI abilities, such as a Wave Master.

I have written several projects in different genres, such as "Where My Heart Leads Me". I plan to write a sequel to "The Wave Master."...